NO
MISTAKING
DEATH

NO MISTAKING DEATH

A Marian Warner Mystery

SHELLEY COSTA

LEVEL
BEST BOOKS

First published by Level Best Books 2023

Author Photo Credit: Rebecca Bloomfield Photography

First edition

ISBN: 978-1-68512-391-8

Cover art by Level Best Designs

This book was professionally typeset on Reedsy.
Find out more at reedsy.com

For Marnie
Artist, archivist, reader, listener, plotter, friend

Chapter One

On his way over to do a quick repair on a windowsill at the Mission House in Carthage, Ohio, Steve Grey figured the Scotch he'd added to the Swiss Miss in his thermos was at least two shots shy. He pulled the MCG Construction truck over to the crumbling curb on Plum Street and grabbed his toolbox. *Side window, closest to the front,* Jack Girard had told him when he handed him the keys. *Bad gutters, rotten windowsills.* And for a fast moment, the two men had looked at each other like maybe what they were talking about had nothing to do with the Mission House.

The sill was one of those little side jobs Girard paid some of them out of pocket, union scale, to do on his pet projects in a town where anyone who gave a damn had his finger stuffed in a hole in a dike somewhere. The gutters had been replaced last week, before the snow hit, but the repairs to the side window closest to the front had to wait until today. Just in case he had to get inside, Girard had given him the keys.

Snow melt that had poured over the clogged gutters had refrozen in a thick line down around the window. Over the years, the windowsill had eroded like a beach. Steve pushed down firmly with both gloved hands. Too much play. He pulled off his glove and stroked his fingers across the sill that looked powdery from snow and rot. Spongy as hell.

As a piece the size of a dagger came away in his hand, Steve saw what he thought was a tarp heaped on the floor inside. He scraped at the grime on the windowpane. Some old guy sleeping it off. "Hey!" He tapped on the window. "Hey!" The heap was about as responsive as last night's date. Steve stepped back.

There was a No Trespassing sign that went on to tell what would happen to violators, although from the looks of the guy inside, it already had. Was he even alive? Hard to say. No point in going inside. He rubbed at what was left of the grime. The natural thing—the Carthage thing—face it, Grey, the fucking Midwestern thing—was to act like he could raise the dead. He should go clomping inside and shake the guy, yelling encouragements like, "Come on, man!"

He peered hard at the heap.

Dead, or just not trying?

In his own life, Steve Grey had been both.

He looked away. He could just do the job he was sent to do, and leave. Then he swiped his black wool cap from his head and ran his gloved hand over his bald scalp. Would anybody believe he'd repaired the windowsill and not seen the guy inside? Had he really fallen quite that far?

He could see it now in the local paper. GREY DISCOVERS BODY. Jesus Hopping Christ, anyway. INTOXICATED CARPENTER FIRED. SPIKED COCOA GREY'S UNDOING. Going in, staying out. Either way, he'd make the paper. Cramming into his mouth two sticks of Doublemint and a coconut Lifesaver he was too pissed to take out of the foil, Steve Grey headed for the front door to do the Midwestern thing that would mean less trouble in the long run.

Ignoring the sign about what would happen to violators, Steve Grey stood motionless on the front step of the Mission House, then unlocked first the padlock and then the door itself. No turning back. He stepped inside, his boots sloppy on the plank flooring. "Hey, man!" No movement. Worn-out old green coat, a sole on one scuffed black shoe bent back from the leather. With a sigh, Steve set a hand on the guy's shoulder and turned him over.

The air smelled of cold rot and old pee. This guy, thought Steve Grey, this guy is dee damned dead. As the body flopped toward him, the ghastly face came a foot away from Steve's own. In that moment, a sudden white blindness struck him, and the cry got stuck in his throat.

Chapter Two

arthage 12.

C Marian Warner idled at a light just past the sign welcoming her to West Epps: *The American Dream Starts Here* and looked around. Next to her was a low sprawling place with a sagging roof that sold SADDLES ENGLISH WESTERN FINEST HAND TOOLED LEATHER. The shop looked closed, and the intersection was deserted. Across the street, snow blew across the front yard of the First West Epps Pentecostal Church, and a tattered banner snapped in the wind. *Visit Our Now Is the Time Gospel Tent, Wade County Fairgrounds, July 5-19.*

As the light changed, a Chevy Silverado with wheels higher than the top of her old blue Volvo roared past, and the Ohio cowboy behind the wheel twisted his wrist at her. Brown cornfields and roadside stands closed for the season stretched ahead of her, and at the third hand-painted sign for Goat Milk Fudge, she pushed the Volvo to sixty.

What made her leave her cabin on the Delaware River and drive seven hours to Carthage, Ohio, was her friend Charlie Levitan, who had been making the rounds for years as an editor in the Gannett markets that were small or undesirable. Two years ago, the folks at HQ sent him to Carthage to "turn around" the *Toiler*, then seemed to forget to check on how it was going.

When Marian's half-sister Joan Fleck assigned her to look into some "decrepit old Catholic cabin out in the boondocks of Ohio," Marian took it on when she realized the decrepit old cabin was located in the same town as Charlie. Joan was Director of the Artifacts Authentication Agency, housed

3

in a dusty two-room office just below Union Square in Manhattan, where the Department of Commerce stored some old metal desks and Joan Fleck. The agency pretty much investigated the provenance of imported artifacts and issued a DOC seal of approval—or not.

But Joan turfed herself anything else she liked, and when the National Park Service wanted to offload the thorny applications of sites seeking National Historic Landmark status Joan snatched them up and sent the investigative work Marian's way. "Gewgaws and gimcracks make the Parks people nervous," was all she offered Marian by way of explanation.

It was, Marian told herself, a living. Straight out of college—Christ, was it really fifteen years ago?—she had got her PI license for personal reasons. Even then, she knew better than to expect glamour—besides, she didn't have the wardrobe for it—but she thought she'd at least be able to pay the bills. Cheating spouses, insurance scams, elsewhere birth parents, too-good-to-be-true fiancés, these where what she thought she'd be tackling, and occasionally, she did. "You're a moralist," bleated Joan in the early days, scanning Marian up and down like she should go a size smaller in the off-the-rack dress. "Moralists do murder."

"I'm not sure that's what you—"

Joan gave her a cautionary finger. "You know what I mean."

So Marian kept working for her half-sister, who very much liked having a private detective on the payroll, and kept an eye open for other opportunities that came her way. "You give us éclat," penned Joan in the agency Christmas card featuring a photo montage of imported bric-a-brac Joan had tackled over calendar year 2021 with the printed sentiment, *May the old stuff you find be the joys of your youth.* But when Marian wouldn't commit full-time to the agency, Joan turned right around and said, "You've got a part-time kind of mentality, darling."

So much for éclat.

When Marian called Charlie to tell him about the decrepit old Catholic cabin that was stalled in the landmark designation process, he exhaled, "Ah. You mean the first Jesuit mission house in what became Ohio."

"Apparently, its application is a little thin."

"Maybe so," he came back, "but the local furnace on the matter of the Mission House melts diamond and bone."

"That would explain the size of the file. Outraged letters, for and against."

Why was this nomination so heated? It's already been three years since someone named Alice Lowther, head of the county historical society, submitted the nomination of this little one-room, possibly three-hundred-year-old mission house. On the very outside, Joan told her, the whole process from nomination to approval could take up to five years. Park Service was twisting its sweaty camp towel in chagrin because it can't allocate all sorts of human resources "for freaking ever," as the staff member assigned to the case complained.

"How long have you got?" said Charlie.

"What Joan calls a solid week—"

"So, less—"

Marian laughed. He knew Joan. "Then it's report time." Her voice slowed as she added, "Sooner, of course—"

"Is better."

Charlie pushed her, "We haven't seen each other since last summer, which is too damn long." After two years, she had still never seen him in his new town.

Charlie's marriage to Traci with an "I," a Russian major with crooked teeth, had lasted close to nine years. It was one of those college romances that most people manage to turn in like a dorm key when they graduate, but not Charlie. When they finally got married at the end of graduate school, it was because Traci thought she was pregnant, and Charlie couldn't tolerate the suspense. A month later it became clear she wasn't, but by then they had a joint checking account and a lease.

Traci with an "I" chalked it up to poor diet and too much basketball, and found she had better luck with the pregnancy thing after she devoted herself to bean curd. Nine months later she delivered a baby, squatting on the delivery room floor, and announced she was getting her teeth straightened. Two years later, the day the braces came off, she told him she was moving to Vancouver with her friend Rita to explore their own—and each other's—inner selves and open a macrobiotics bookstore.

Charlie got custody of Hannah.

Marian had found him early in high school, back in their New Jersey days, when they scorned proms and ruled the school newspaper like a couple of Hearsts. They read aloud by candlelight from Galway Kinnell about letting our scars fall in love and overlooked each other's bad skin and bad haircuts. Sometimes he'd say, *You know I adore you,* but she'd duck any way she could, and he'd act like he was joking, and they'd get through the embarrassment of any real feeling.

Chapter Three

Marian stood looking at the red brick *Toiler* building over the roof of her parked car.

"It's a replica of Independence Hall, only without the steeple," Charlie had told her over the phone. Grabbing her backpack, she locked up and picked her way over the icy sidewalk to the center of town, where the rope that had hoisted the flag in front of the Wade County Court House was smacking hollowly against the flagpole. Suits that could be suits anywhere clutched slim briefcases against camel-hair coats and crossed against the light, disappearing into the bank and the courthouse.

Across the street, at the Carthage Chamber of Commerce, twinkle lights were still snaking brightly around the front window a month after Christmas. Marian took in a yarn shop, a tearoom, and a Christian bookstore, feeling all around her the hard bright cold of northern winters that pings the skin and hangs unmoving in the air. Charlie must have to go a long way from Carthage, Ohio, to get a Reuben sandwich worth the chew.

On the second floor of the *Toiler* building was a city room clogged with cubicles and computers, lighted by a dusty winter sun and rows of fluorescent fixtures. None of the half-a-dozen people gave her a look. At the back, a woman with a block of bad beauty parlor hair had a retro radio set to a country station playing a song drowned out by Hawaiian steel guitar.

Closest to Marian sat an older guy with stringy hair under a Cincinnati Reds baseball cap, listening to phone abuse of some sort, and then cut in, "Well, you can go ahead and do what you want, but it's just a goddamn restaurant review, Arnold, and yes, I do know the difference between a cockroach and a water bug." With that, he sent his phone skidding across his desk.

Charlie's office was at the far end of this room where time stood still, and Marian spotted him through the glass half-wall, leaning against his desk. Her heart lifted. It struck her how she liked Charlie best in the middle distance, where she could appreciate how appealing he was without actually having to do anything about it. Tall, the kind of concave that made shirts hang loose over his chest, the seal-black hair, the small wire-rims he had to use for reading—all as lovely and reliable as gravity. But the middle distance was the place she had found when they were fifteen, and she couldn't step out of it. As places go, it was safe and troubling all at the same time.

Charlie saw her, and his arms went up. "Marian!" he yelled. Everybody turned, a little alarmed. For a newsroom, they were the last to notice somebody new. Even the watering can hovered for a brief moment. Charlie bounded out of his office, covering the space between them in two seconds. Then he grabbed her in a hug that kept tightening down in about five different places. Like he was inventorying her body parts.

"Hi, honey," she said with a laugh. She noticed his hair was longer, and he was growing a beard. She wasn't sure how she felt about it. And if she came down opposed, she'd have to be careful how she told him. Her opinion always mattered unreasonably to him.

Charlie squeezed her all over again. "How was the trip?"

"Long." She gave a little shrug, enjoying the familiar feel of her arms around his shoulders. So broad and square and balanced, like the Chinese character for man.

"Listen," he said, stepping back, "I've got a body for you—"

"So I see." She decided she liked the hint of new beard.

"—and for once, I don't mean mine. Come on in." He swung her arm like they were kids on a playground. That far back they didn't go, but it was almost as though they had somehow known each other as kids. Before all the spiking desires and missed opportunities.

Tugging at her coat, just to give herself a shot at fashionable, Marian followed him into his office, where a young, pretty blond wearing Frye boots and a long skirt shifted in her chair. She was a beautiful woman, with her hair pulled back in that chic, loose style that just wants to get out of the way of the flawless skin and lips that looked like they didn't need any defense against winter.

"Marian Warner, Bella Murphy," Charlie waved an arm in their general direction, and Marian shook her hand. Long, work-roughened fingers. Hooking his foot around a chair, he pulled it over for Marian and then slid into his own. "Marian's here on a job for the Parks Service," he eyed Bella, "looking into why there's a battle over landmark status for the Mission House"—he turned to Marian—"and Bella trains field dogs." After a second, he added, wide-eyed, "and sees that nothing happens to our local landmarks."

"Or in them." Bella shot him a grim look. Marian dimly recognized her name from a couple of the letters in the case file. Lots of careful prose in support of the nomination, minimal outrage.

"Okay, so this one got by you," Charlie said to her, then turned to Marian. "A man was found dead yesterday morning in the Mission House."

Marian sat back. "The place I'm checking out?" Maybe there was more going on in Carthage than the squirrelly business of landmark preservation. She felt the case file expanding already. When Charlie nodded, she went on. "Any I.D.?" With any luck, it would be one of the outraged letter writers. No, with any luck, it wouldn't be. Although Joan would be ever so happy to hear Marian had tripped over a corpse. She reached for an expensively framed photograph Charlie had taken last summer at her cabin, where Hannah, who was now twelve, was holding up a nice bass. Marian stood smiling behind her, one arm hooked loosely around the girl's neck.

"His name was J.C. Houston, and so far, it isn't ringing any bells."

Not with Marian, either. But she'd check later.

"Which is why," Bella piped up, leaning forward, "You need to put someone on it, Charlie—"

"I can't spare a reporter—and I use the term loosely—to do the kind of digging you want." Then: "You know that."

When she started to argue, he held up a hand to stop her. "Listen," he said with some energy, making a sweeping gesture in Marian's direction, "hire

Marian. She's a licensed PI."

Bella turned to her. "Are you interested?" She re-crossed her legs and gave Marian the arch and friendly look of a '40s movie star, the sort of natural grace only a whole lot of practice can achieve.

Marian looked at both of them, then opened her hands wide. Just how much time did she want to spend in this town? "Maybe," she said, with the kind of equivocating Charlie had come to expect from her, "but I'm not sure you need the services of a PI. An hour on Google should do it."

Bella rubbed her chapped fingers. "Already done. There's nothing. At least," she smiled, "nothing we can use to handle things out on the street."

"What do you mean?"

"Oh," Charlie said with a mighty sigh, his eyes on the ceiling, "there's a local developer who wants to tear down the Mission House, so—"

Marian had read his letters, but for now, she would keep that information to herself.

Bella turned to Marian. "—we've been trying to make the case that the Mission House is a national treasure." With that, she pushed back some artful blond strays. The unmistakable woody scent of Balenciaga drifted toward Marian.

"And your job gets tougher when a corpse turns up."

"Right now, all we're looking at is just more bad publicity."

"I understand."

Bella went on. "Before we can prepare a response, we need to know what we've got." It sounded like a line she had used before. Then she added: "We need to know *who* we've got."

"In other words, spin."

The woman looked apologetic. "Spin," she said with a sigh, "and we need it fast."

Marian swung toward Charlie. "So what have we got?"

"Does that mean you'll do it?" Bella nearly clapped her hands.

Nice to bring such easy joy to somebody. "I guess I'm hired."

Charlie pulled over a pen and piece of paper and started to flip through an old Rolodex. Jerking his head toward Marian, he flashed Bella a quick smile. "You'll find her reasonable."

Why should that bother her? "I always thought I was the high-priced spread."

Charlie went on scribbling names and numbers, "She'll eat some expenses, and she'll get you more than you can possibly use, but first—" he threw down the pen, got up, and came around to the front of the desk, "—you've got to interest her."

Marian shook her head. "It's going to have to be pro bono."

"Why?"

"I'm already on the payroll of the DOC on this job. There can't be a whiff of conflict of interest."

With a nod, Charlie slowly held out the list to Marian.

Bill Cain, Jack Girard, Alice Lowther. The Historical Society director, who nominated the Mission House.

"J.C. Houston's driver's license shows a Cleveland address," Charlie said as he leaned against his desk with his arms folded, still looking at Marian with the kind of fond sorrow she had seen for the last few years. Whenever she saw that look, it was like trying to breathe in a place where a sudden fireball had sucked out all the air.

While Charlie described what else the cops found in the dead man's wallet—*Golden Buckeye card, ATM card, UAW card*—Marian moved around the office. There were Chagall prints on the wall, dense bleeding blues and smiling figures swirling in a dream with goats, and a couple of framed photo enlargements. One she had seen before, a Lower East Side shot of Levitan Dry Goods from 1932 with Julius Levitan pointing at the sign.

Next to it was a high-contrast black-and-white photo of a light motorboat, tipped with the weight of its one occupant, tied to a small, warped dock, everything bruised with the beauty of the summer sun. The woman—Marian—was sleeping on her back across the middle seat of the boat, her head on an old canvas creel, her thin top in a twist that pulled down over a breast. Her lips were parted against her curled hand. She looked all of four and all of thirty-six, in her barefoot and knock-kneed sleep. At the bottom of the photograph was a penciled line, *Sounds of the Real World.*

It was the first Marian knew about the picture. He must have taken it the week last July when he and Hannah came to see her. Hardly anyone knew her better than Charlie. Hardly anyone else tried to. She pictured him standing silent by the boat, waiting, just waiting, for it all to come together—every angle of her body, every needle of light, every breath he couldn't even capture—before pressing the button. She had always counted on his damn relentless patience.

"—plus sixty-three bucks and a Mega Millions card."

"Old?" Marian leaned next to Charlie. "Young?"

"Older guy, no marks of a struggle—"

"Natural causes?"

"That's how it looks," Bella put in.

"Which is a real shame," Charlie said, scratching his cheek. "Considering I've used up all my weekly rumors about Hyundai coming to Carthage, I could use a good headline."

"What about the autopsy?"

"The coroner's working on him right now," he said. "And if he says the deceased croaked of his own free will, we can believe him."

Marian nodded, twisting around a cheap acrylic frame so she could see the photo—a snapshot of Charlie and a redhead who looked merry and broke. Three of her fingertips were just visible at Charlie's waist. "Car?" Marian asked, suddenly restless.

"Not that they can find."

"Greyhound?"

"They're checking."

"Who found the body?"

"Steve Grey, who works for Jack Girard." Charlie looked at his watch. "Girard can fill you in on the recent trouble."

Bella stood, stretching her long arms into an alpaca sweater that looked like all she needed in twenty-degree weather. "So can Bill Cain, the developer who wants to tear down the Mission House." Marian watched her flip her hair out from under the hooded collar and settle her square shoulders.

"Green pants, canned speech, you know the type." Charlie smiled at them both. "Naturally, you'll talk to Alice Lowther, head of the historical society."

Bella gave Marian an arch look. "She can tell you where every board was milled."

"Is Girard cozy with Cain?"

Bella shook her head. "Most of Jack's work comes from government contracts, so no, he doesn't work with Bill Cain. Besides," she said quietly, "Jack's a preservationist." Marian noted she made the word *preservationist* sound like viscount or vegan.

"Last year, when he couldn't get a restraining order to protect an old grain elevator, he stood in front of the wrecking ball."

"Cain's crew?"

Charlie nodded. "I went, along with half my staff and most of the town. Same players, different fight." He crossed his arms. "It's all Southern-fried chicken, if you ask me."

"This is Ohio."

Charlie narrowed his eyes at her. "In my experience, Marian, the South has very little to do with geography," he said. "Give us a week."

Chapter Four

They agreed to meet the next day, and Marian watched her new employer, the tall, golden Bella Murphy, walk through the city room. Even the guy in the Cincinnati Reds cap turned and looked like he couldn't recall the difference between a cockroach and a water bug, after all. Marian looked at Charlie. "What's a woman like that doing in Carthage?"

"It's her home," he shrugged, putting his feet up on his desk.

"People leave home."

"Face it, honey," he smiled at her, "there's just something about this town Bella likes."

She crossed her arms. "Is it you?"

The scent of Balenciaga remained.

"Actually, no. It's Jack Girard. Even if I were available," he smiled, "for Bella, it would still be Jack Girard."

She couldn't help blinking at him. "You're not available?"

His answer was slow, but he looked her right in the eye. "No." Marian picked up the acrylic frame and turned the picture to Charlie. He didn't even have to look. "Her name's Derry Wilson."

Marian didn't have to look, either. "Pretty."

"I was going to tell you at dinner."

Thinking, she guessed, they'd both need the shelter of the wine.

"Local?"

"Local."

"So it's a convenience thing?" Close meant uncomplicated, like swinging

14

by a 7-Eleven for a loaf of bread on the way home from work. Over the years, she had even had some conveniences herself.

"Well, no," he said slowly, "not really." When he widened his eyes at her, she felt herself lift off the ground clothed in excruciating white, dreaming in a curling blue path where colliding with a goat seemed the sweetest thing imaginable. "What's the matter?" he said.

"I'm just tired, Charlie." The lie was easy. "It was a long drive."

All of life was just a long damn drive.

Marian looked at Charlie, who was rolling a pencil between his fingers, watching her. The office walls, the Week-At-A-Glance, the Inbox—and his life—were full without her, and somewhere close by was a redhead whose fingertips were comfortable on his waist. What she remembered was Charlie leaning up on his elbow on the grass behind school. *You know I adore you.* The offer apparently expired at midnight; only she never knew which one.

"It's me, Marian. You can't slide with me. So what's wrong?"

She could tell him the truth, but for the life of her, she didn't know what it was.

As she slung her backpack over her shoulder, she felt the Chief's Special inside thud against her kidneys. If it weren't for the fact that she kept the gun unloaded, she had visions of blowing her damn fool tail from here to kingdom come—an airy place where halftime bottomless dicks could add their personal perspectives to the Big Bang theory. When she looked him in the eye and smiled, "Nothing, really," she sounded like she meant it. "I'll be ready at seven."

"Marian," Charlie shouted into the phone that late afternoon in January during their second year at Rutgers. She heard furniture hitting the walls. "Are you busy? Do you want to see assholes in funny hats?" Then to someone nearby, he yelled, "Not my office, you don't," and the line went dead. Shaking, she grabbed a ride across town to the men's student union, where demonstrators were protesting the surge of U.S. troops in Iraq.

She found Charlie upstairs in his newspaper office, where his overturned desk had been pushed up against a front window. Three scruffy guys in what must have been their parents' old Che berets were pulling out his file drawers and hurling papers out the broken window. "Go on, I got a newspaper to run, go sing or make signs or something." In the center of his trashed office, Charlie suddenly saw her. "Was I right, or what?"

She made a grab for his arm. "Let's get out of here."

"What are you talking about?"

A couple of the protesters were eyeing Charlie and Marian like any second they'd be joining the papers fluttering two stories to the ground. "This is dangerous, Charlie."

"You're afraid of these guys?" He opened his arms wide. "This is FIAT, Marian. Free Iraq from American Terrorism. First, they ransack, then they go out for felafel. These guys aren't dangerous. Come on, tell her."

One of them looked up, his long fingers scanning the pages of a file marked ROTC. "I guess we'll find out," he said. He wore Army fatigues, the short jacket open over a faded green t-shirt. His black hair was combed back from his forehead, and there was a colorless quality to his skin she found remarkable. He held out a hand to her. "Norberto Sartre."

Charlie hurled a book at him, shouting that only a serious idiot would have a nom de guerre like Norberto Sartre. It was the only time in what became their shared lives with Marian that Charlie and Norberto Sartre, whose teachers knew him as Paul Seeks, were face to face.

Paul closed and replaced the book, and in the quietness of his action, Marian felt a moment of heart-stopping desire. Two days later, he came to her dorm, and they sat together feeding the ducks at Passion Puddle. He had some time—any day now, the FIAT gang was going to appeal their suspension from the university. An unspeakable violation of their civil rights, he said, gazing across the water.

Marian had never known anyone like him.

He was raised by his grandparents in Atlantic City, he told her, in a pink bungalow with a plastic flamingo in the front yard. One day their difficult daughter turned up pregnant and gave them the baby to raise. The twelve diapers she changed before handing over the infant made her realize she wanted a life of the mind. This decision was followed by a good deal of disowning on everybody's part—including, in time, the baby's. The grandfather was a Teamster. The grandmother belonged *to ILGWU.*

By the time Marian met Paul, there was a radical edginess to him that she knew had something to do with identifying himself with abandoned people everywhere, and Charlie knew had something to do with needing to get laid. The first time she and Paul made love, it was in someone else's bed; she never knew whose, which made the whole experience urgent and reckless—like any minute, the feds would break down the door and take him away. Charlie saw Paul as a temporary affliction, and Paul saw Charlie as a permanent one.

They kept a calculated distance.

Paul spoke with increasing disaffection about the movement—FIAT is too timid, he would tell her, too easily placated by demonstrations—and what on these occasions Marian mistook for his convictions was really something different, the color and contours of doom. When Paul disappeared, she knew he had gone underground.

Chapter Five

Marian drove two blocks down Mission Street to the address Charlie had given her for the Mission House. The day was collapsing the way days do on winter afternoons in northern places, before dusk, when the sky comes closer, and the ground thickens. As she pulled a quick U-turn to snag a parking space, she saw a red Toyota pickup squeal to a stop at the corner, and two men get out quickly, slamming the doors.

They were shouting, heading across the frozen grass. Marian got out of the car. Set back from the sidewalk by about fifty feet was an old, weather-beaten gray building on a raised stone foundation. Unless she missed her guess, the Mission House. It had the self-conscious look of all historic buildings, alone and out of fashion and set apart on its little plot of land.

"—the fuck you think you're doing?" One of the men from the red pickup headed for the middle of the yard, where two men in dress coats were pounding five-foot wooden stakes into the ground.

"Dugan, don't come over here," one of the dress coats waved a hammer, "don't come over here, Dugan."

Marian scanned the street. It was just a matter of time before someone threw a punch and someone else called the cops. She pulled out her phone and got Bella Murphy on the third ring, telling her to get her friend Girard over to the Mission House right away. "Otherwise, people are going to jail, and spinning corpses will seem like the least of your PR problems."

She hung up.

"What have you got there? What are you doing? I asked you a question."

"None of your damn—"

The younger man from the red Toyota reached for a large roll of plastic on the ground, but one of the dress coats got to it first as the other one pushed the kid away. The man they called Dugan grabbed the roll. "Hey!" The scuffle started.

The younger man was trying to unroll the sign. "Future Home of—"

"Like hell!" roared Dugan.

"Destruction of property," the other two started to taunt the charges, "trespassing—"

Dugan thrust out his chest. "This is public property."

"Not for long, you stupid—"

"—Future Home of Great Seal Power & Light," the younger man blared, getting to the end of the roll with one of the dress coats hooking him around the neck. As Dugan jumped on them, pummeling the back of the dress coat, Marian watched the fourth man wrench one of the stakes out of the ground and swing it hard against Dugan, who cried out and fell to the ground. Then the one standing flung aside the stake and kicked him in the groin. The younger man elbowed himself free and turned on the other man. Both of them were staggering as the young man's wobbly fist connected with the other guy's nose.

Marian loped over the snow with a quick look around—still no cops, but plenty of trouble—scooping up a fallen ski cap on the way. She pressed it into the young man's hand and grabbed his arm. He looked very young. "Take your hat and go back—"

"—the fuck are *you*?" slurred the guy in the dress coat, glaring at her as he pressed a wad of snow against his bloody nose.

Marian ignored him and gave the young kid a gentle push. "Go back to the truck if you plan on eating your next meal at home."

The young man was blinking at her, gave her a strange look, and lurched over to Dugan—like he'd already been through too many winters, and all of them were arctic. Dugan had rolled onto his stomach on the crusty snow, moaning, as the dress coat who had whacked him looked like he had swallowed his lips they were so tightly compressed as he hammered the

19

stake back into the ground. The younger man was tottering, winded, over his buddy when Marian saw it happen.

Suddenly Dugan lashed an arm out, hooked the dress coat by the ankles, and pulled him clear off his feet. The hammer went flying just as Marian saw an old Army jeep tear up the side street and jam to a stop. A man in a dark leather jacket came striding over the snow, his eyes taking in everything on the way. "Rodie," he clamped an arm on the young man's shoulder, "get in the truck. Now."

Rodie pulled his cap down over his ears. "Jack," he flailed at the others, "they were going to —"

Girard gave him a quick look. "Tell me later." He jerked his head toward the curb.

Marian picked up the hammer, which had landed near the steps to the Mission House.

"Girard!" The dress coat with the nosebleed pulled himself up straight. "Who the—"

"Wait your turn, Rocker." He bent over Dugan. "Can you walk?"

The man sat up slowly. "It's not my walking I'm worried about," he said, wincing.

"Get in the truck with Rodie and go straight to the trailer, where we'll talk. I'm out of whiskey, so pick some up on the way." Dugan ran the back of his hand hard across his nose. "Sorry, Jack," he said gruffly, nodding to Marian as he lumbered over to the red Toyota.

"As for you, Rocker—" Girard grabbed the wooden stakes, hitting them together, "—and you, Rice—" A door slammed weakly behind them, and Marian watched the pickup take off up the street. He stood looking them over. "You're dressing better these days."

"We're in management now." The one on the ground was holding on to the other, who was bracing him as he tried to stand up.

"So I see." Jack Girard picked up the Future Home of Great Seal Power & Light sign lying in a heap in the snow.

The one staggering to his feet sneered. "Not like the trash you got working for you."

"Well, I could promote them," Girard suggested as he brushed off the sign and started to roll it up. "I could buy them nice coats the way Bill Cain did for you."

"Yeah, but then they'd just be trash in nice coats." The two guys now in management roared.

Girard smiled. "Then maybe they'd go to work for Bill Cain." He smacked the rolled-up sign against the wooden stakes under his arm. "I'll just be keeping these."

"That's our sign."

"Very premature, boys."

"What about the stakes?"

"It's a cold day, and I could use the firewood."

"Mr. Cain isn't going to like this."

Girard looked at them skeptically. "Sure he is. You're in management; you should know that. Now get going."

"We don't take orders from you."

Everything about Jack Girard had come to a stop. "Sure you do."

After another few moments of indecision, the dress coats slapped snow off their butts, adjusted their gloves, and headed for the street. Marian presented Jack Girard, the man who stands in front of wrecking balls, with the hammer. She put him in his mid-forties. Just under six feet, the kind of average build that goes well with uniforms and outdoor work. His hair was short and thick, his eyes dark. When he looked at her, something rippled in his expression, and then he closed down. "Thanks for the call." They shook hands. "Bella got me at the bank up the street."

"So you know she's asked me to look into the recent death?" Marian jerked her head toward the Mission House.

He nodded. "She told me."

"I'd like to talk to you about this place."

Girard shifted the signs. "About the body?" he said, then shook the signs with a slight smile. "Or the war?"

She looked up at the stringy clouds in the wintry sky. "Officially, I'm in the employ of the DOC, who's running out of patience and personnel in the stalled nomination process. So whatever you can tell me about the war might be helpful." Marian stamped her feet against the deepening cold.

"You must have the file."

"I do."

"So you've got my letters."

She nodded. Then: "It's going to take more than the letters to explain—" she opened her gloved hands, "the letters."

Jack Girard seemed to come to a decision. "How's tomorrow morning at work?"

"Nine?"

He nodded. "I'll be playing catch-up with some paperwork."

"Where?"

"Just north of town, highway eight," he said, hunching his shoulders against the cold. The leather in his jacket was cracked in several places. "MCG Construction." Girard started toward the jeep. The ground was higher, the sky came closer, and the air itself was bursting with the prickly blue of winter afternoons.

Marian watched him go. "What happened to the grain elevator?" she called after him.

He slowed for a second. "I bought it," he said and kept on walking.

Chapter Six

Steve Grey sat in the dark exactly three feet from his 42" HDTV. His grandmother had read something very persuasive once about how sitting too close to a television set leads to rays pulverizing your brain. When he asked what kind of rays, she took a moment to answer, "Gamma rays," at which she whistled like a UFO coming in for a landing and asked him to help push back the orange velveteen couch.

Personally, he had thought it was all crap, but he loved this woman who meant everything to him, and helped her push the couch back three feet. She decided to put him just inside a ray risk-free zone, and he had been setting his furniture that way ever since, long after the death of his hard-working grandparents. At least the truckload of grief he had ended up depositing on their doorstep didn't last long. Six years afterwards, both were dead. So he heard.

For Steve Grey, sitting in the dark as his thumb clicked through euphoric commercials for Levitra and Lyrica, there was a strange remoteness to death. He thought of those old pink pads receptionists use for messages: While-U-Were-Out. That was his life, as it turned out. He was out. Always out. So there was a sense of unreality about it. Not for him those deathbed declarations of love and regret and best fishing holes. People simply disappeared. On his lap, in the pale light from Lester Holt on the Nightly News whipping up audience interest in some old timer in Georgia making a difference in the lives of abandoned alligators, Steve Grey set down his fork in what he was pretty sure was a Salisbury steak dinner.

Of all the people who had shucked their lives—death helped—or what passed for death—he never expected to see that one face again. Not here, in Carthage, Ohio. Had Steve not wandered far enough all those years ago? For there he was, dead on the cold, dusty floor of the Mission House. Floppy hair, purple lips, the face of the man Steve had only seen maybe three times in his life.

The man who had waited for him out of sight of Gran's house and given him a one-hundred-dollar bill—for college, although college was ten years off. The man who had given him a book on how to build a deck, because a boy needs a trade, he had said when for some reason, he had re-thought the whole college thing but didn't ask for the C note back. The man who showed up again, around the time Steve was restless in high school, passed him a CD of the early Woody Guthrie.

Steve knew, despite the gifts, that there was no way he would let the guy know anything that mattered about himself, that the guy with the cadaverous cheeks and unruly hair and baseball jacket was his father. The same way he knew it all over again when just yesterday, he had rolled the body over. He should have been a stranger, a bum, a cipher. He really should have been. And maybe, in some ways, he was all those things. But in that strange moment in the Mission House, where Steve had been sent simply to do a repair, he saw that time had run out for this guy and that there would be no more C notes, not for anybody.

And Steve would never be able to tell the dead man how the songs had led him in the direction of his own fate. And his father—he would never be able to take that name to the cops—would never be able to tell his kid how he had seen a great no-hitter in the last game of the regular season, and maybe they could go together sometime. Steve crumbled the roll in his TV dinner tray. The cops were most definitely on their own in the matter of his father's death. Oh, yes. Because he realized the old man had been locked in and left to die.

The Wade County Historical Society was a white brick, black shuttered Georgian-style building behind a black wrought-iron fence with the kind of spikes Vlad the Impaler would like. Inside, Marian found Alice Lowther alone, winding the grandfather clock in the center hall. No one was stopping by to see the documents and trinkets locked in glass cases or the campaign flags framed on the walls. And no one was stopping by to see the mannequins in antebellum costumes. The air was oily with furniture polish.

Lowther closed up the clock and lifted her chin at Marian. "I can see you now," she said and led the way into the south parlor. Her left shoulder was hitched up in a frozen shrug, and her forearms rowed as she walked in a way some demented aunt must have told little Alice was graceful fifty years ago. She was wearing a pale blue knit dress buttoned up to her throat. Pushing back a hank of gray hair, Lowther sat down at a kneehole desk. A copy of the *Toiler* had been folded open at the story about the body in the Mission House, next to an update on high winds in South Dakota.

Marian sat across from her. "My name's Marian Warner, and I've been sent by the National Park Service to investigate the nomination of the Mission House for Historic Landmark status. You nominated the building—"

"Yes, yes—" Lowther clawed at her hair. "Three years ago." It was accusatory.

Marian considered her. Was it possible she didn't know? "The process has been stalled by the public outcry."

"Outcry?" She shook her head, not comprehending. "Outcry over what?"

"The committee's file on the Mission House in Carthage, Ohio, contains fifty-three letters either passionately for or passionately against the nomination." Lowther sat blinking at her. "Including, of course, your own letters and required documents."

"Let me see them."

"I can't."

"Well," she went on, shifting in her chair, "who wrote them? Can you tell me that?"

"No more than generally. Developers, preservationists, utilities shareholders, town council members, three members of your state legislature, land conservancy folks, schoolchildren—"

Now Lowther was aghast. "Schoolchildren!"

"Elementary school kids are for it. High schoolers are against it."

Alice Lowther collapsed against the back of her chair. "I had no idea." She shot Marian a helpless look. "Why did I have no idea?"

Marian had no answer. "The process can take up to five years, but the committee can't even begin their work, really, until there's some resolution of this—battle over the Mission House."

Lowther was barely audible. "And if there's no resolution?"

Marian glanced at how wet and worn her snow boots were looking. "I believe they'll ask you to withdraw your nomination—"

"Withdraw."

"—until times change, tempers improve—"

Alice slammed her hands on her desk and started to stand. "You don't understand. If the Mission House isn't protected, then that awful man will reduce it to smashed boards and shattered glass within twenty-four hours."

"Bill Cain?" asked Marian, taking a chance on just what awful man Lowther meant. While the head of the Wade County Historical Society stood braced against her kneehole desk, brooding in silence, Marian wondered whether Bill Cain was just running out the clock on the problem of the Mission House. Flood the Park Service with enough dissenting letters until finally, in exasperation, the landmark committee gets Alice Lowther to withdraw. Was that man just that underhanded and wily? Marian would have to find out.

Suddenly, Alice Lowther dropped her hands at her sides. "Have you seen the Mission House?"

"Only the outside."

"It's very beautiful," she said with a strange kind of insistence. Then she shrugged and rearranged some papers. "I've never understood why it hasn't drawn more tourists."

Marian folded her arms. "Now that it's had a corpse, it might be more of an attraction."

The other woman gave her a thin smile. "Not quite what we're looking for."

"So Bella Murphy says, too. She's asked me to look into it. Any ideas?"

"Ideas?"

"As to his identity?"

Lowther tapped the *Toiler*. "The paper says his name is J.C. Houston."

"That's just his name."

"My circle of friends doesn't include vagrants."

"So," said Marian, trying to sound neutral, "if you don't know him, he's a vagrant?"

"In this town, yes." Alice Lowther pulled two books from a lower desk drawer. "But I can help you with background on the Mission House. Whatever you bring back to the National Historic Landmark Committee might buy us a little time." She held up a blue hardcover. "There's Elam Temple, who claims the Mission House is sixty years younger than everybody thinks, so it couldn't have been built by the Jesuit Claude de Chardin." She shoved it across the desk, then held up a gray trade paperback. "And there's Peter Shaughnessy, who says that Jesuit missions simply didn't exist in what became Ohio." She gazed up at Marian in a provocative way. "It's a popular opinion."

"Ah, but not yours."

She actually beckoned Marian with her forefinger. "Come with me."

In the north parlor, Lowther tugged aside a heavy drape to let in some winter light. A small wood and glass display case held a single document, a letter in French dated January 1763. "In this letter to the territorial governor," said Lowther in an oratorical way, "Chardin states his intention to establish a mission between Whitetail Creek and Bear Run. He includes a rough sketch."

"And —?" Marian had seen a copy of this Chardin letter in the file.

Alice Lowther opened her hands wide. "And where it sits near the center of town, the Mission House is two miles from Whitetail Creek and a mile and a half from Bear Run," she said smugly.

Marian's eyes took in the books lining the wall. Mostly local and Ohio historical references, she noticed, and genealogies. *Stark, Hughes, Payson*—nearly two dozen histories on Wade County families. "But all the letter proves is Chardin's intention."

Lowther frowned. "As Peter Shaughnessy pointed out to me years ago

27

when I sent him a photocopy." She pulled a white lace handkerchief out of her cuff and cleaned a smudge on the glass display case. "Which was when I realized," she sniffed, "that scholarship has very little to do with the free exchange of ideas." Lowther stroked away a nonexistent film of dust from the wood. "For years," she said softly, "no one doubted the authenticity of the Mission House. Now that it's on a piece of prime real estate, it's a fake." She looked at Marian. "It's meant to make us all feel better about tearing it down."

A new thought. "Maybe Mr. Girard will buy it first."

"Jack Girard's resources are not limitless," she said impatiently. "He can't go around buying up little squares of Carthage like they're Boardwalk and Park Place."

"Why can't the two of you work together?"

"Sometimes we do, although we're both people who prefer to work alone." Lowther eyed her. "If you want information on group efforts, you'll have to ask Bella Murphy, Jack Girard's—" she raised her pencil-thin eyebrows, "friend." Her mouth thinned out. "She heads up a group she calls Save Our Sites," she said. "More like See Our Shenanigans, if you ask me."

In the south parlor, the sun had shifted and paled. Alice Lowther walked into a narrow panel of brightness. Out of a Louis Vuitton tote, she pulled a yellow plastic bag from a local shoe store and wrapped up the two books. "The Mission House is one of the oldest buildings in the state, but nothing will keep it from becoming the site of the new electric company." Lowther looked down at the floor, shaking her head. "So much for the lessons of history."

Marian zipped up her down jacket, then smiled. "It's not smashed boards and shattered glass yet."

"What will it take?" Then she sneered. "More letters from elementary school kids?"

Marian let it pass. "Something—" she narrowed her eyes, "—something that truly authenticates the Mission House." Then she shrugged and pulled on her double-knit gloves. Before her eyes, Alice Lowther's face took on a sadness the likes of which Marian had never seen. "It matters to you," she said.

The director of the Wade County Historical Society nearly spat. "Of course, it matters to me."

"The building, I mean."

Lowther stepped back. "Less the building, I'd say, than the history." At that, she looked past Marian's shoulder. "It's the only thing in life that—" she searched for the word, then her pale eyes widened when she came up with the right one, "accrues." But even that held no hope, and finally, she added quietly, "The only thing at all."

"You know," said Marian suddenly, "you're not responsible for what happens to the Mission House."

The woman blinked slowly, her face nearly metallic with control. "So you say."

Chapter Seven

Only Charlie Levitan would suggest swinging by the morgue to pick up the autopsy report "and have a look" on the way to dinner. How soon could she be ready? "Look, Charlie," Marian said into her phone, "I'm cold and tired. All I want is a bath."

"Say in an hour."

"What's the hurry?"

"Deadline."

"You make the deadlines."

"Doesn't mean I don't respect them," he said illogically. "Besides," he added, "Carney's got hold of some union guy in Cleveland. Houston had some sort of burial policy. They're having him boxed and shipped tomorrow."

Then, tomorrow she'd look around the Mission House and keep working her way down the list of contacts Charlie had given her. She filled the clawfoot tub at the B&B she'd found online, adding three times the RDA of Mr. Bubble. At the mom-and-pop drug store in town, the choice was between escapist powders, foaming therapies, and Mr. Bubble. No contest. The idiot bubble face was the only one showing the right spirit. Marian pulled her hair into a quick topknot and eased herself into the hot water.

That week in July was the closest she and Charlie had ever come to going to bed together. Partly it was the solitude of the place, partly the bright lassitude of the days. There was a high sexiness to the most forgettable things. Except for Hannah, who insisted on playing Speed Scrabble every night, they were alone. Between them fell a body awareness that was riveting.

Charlie was straddling a lounge chair on the screened-in porch. "So," he said slowly, folding a map. "What's going on here?"

Marian lifted a hand. "What if it's lousy?"

"What if it's great?"

"Charlie, it wouldn't be great."

"How do you know that?"

"Because it would have been great for a hell of a lot of years already."

"Not necessarily."

With the smell of hot grass all around them, buzzing with katydids, she watched him slowly crease a map. "Sex isn't what our relationship is about," she said.

"All the more reason to go to bed."

Her cheeks burned. Here was Charlie—Charlie—saying exactly the right thing. If he got up, got out of the chair, she was a goner. That much she knew. And she couldn't tell him. It was the first thing ever she couldn't tell Charlie. And if he got up and came over to her, right here on her front porch, she would feel her life slip away into rumble and steam. It would be like finding out suddenly she was really a bus driver in St. Louis or a sheep farmer in New Zealand. She felt her ribs creak with the effort of catching her breath. "Charlie," she said, "I would lose you."

He started to move. "I'm not going anywhere."

She shook her head. "What I mean is, you'd lose me. I just don't stick around very long with men. I lose heart or something."

His blue eyes were narrow. "And it wouldn't make a difference that it's me?"

"That's something I don't want to find out." Sometimes—she realized as she tried to read his face—the truth is the wrong answer.

He bit his lower lip and eased himself up. "Yeah, well, I think I'll go find Hannah and see if she wants to go out in the boat." There was something about the way the screen door slapped behind him that made her crazy.

"Charlie!" she yelled. He was halfway across the yard and still walking. "See what I mean! We can't even talk about sex without getting screwed up." She raved at the screen door, kicking and slamming it half a dozen times, then crawled into bed at one o'clock in the afternoon and stared at the aspen tree outside her open window. In the slight breeze the heart-shaped leaves clicked at her in something like comfort, or regret.

After a long soak she chose her gray flannel slacks and blue lambswool pullover and quickly brushed her hair. When Charlie arrived at the Briars, the noise level tripled. The Hausers, the lookalike owners, gushed, and right there on the spot gave Marian after-hours kitchen privileges. It was the first time in twenty years that knowing Charlie Levitan had some kind of payoff that didn't involve either scorn, disciplinary action, or bail. She could swear she felt tectonic plates shifting underfoot.

Helping her into her down vest ("Is this all you have?") Charlie managed to kiss her cheek, tell Cy Hauser something about throwing rock salt on the front path, and argue with Barb Hauser about whether chicken divan is the Tuesday night special at The Gleaner, the only Yelp three-star restaurant in all of Carthage. When he satisfied himself that Marian had her key and her lipstick, they picked their way down the front walk. Inside the Buick she and Hannah managed a long hug over the front seat.

Charlie's daughter was a twelve-year old who shopped at Goodwill for the t-shirts and jeans she wore to school every day. These got paired up at random, leading to such memorable combinations as Gucci jeans topped with a mustard-color t-shirt depicting a steer and the words MISTER BRISKET THE MEATMOBILE. She had Charlie's blue eyes and Traci's long lank hair, but her smile was all her own. Tonight, she was wearing a fedora a little too tired to pull off hardboiled, and aquamarine wool gloves with eyelash yarn cuffs and only two moth-eaten holes. More Goodwill, Marian figured. Then the two of them hugged all over again.

The old county hospital was a brick, two-story building located in a residential part of town "outside," Charlie noted, "the historic district." It had been built early in the forties and abandoned in the seventies, when a modern facility went up just off the highway north of town. It was sleek and white with smoke-tinted glass and a parking lot as big as a football field.

Over the years, health-related services had moved into the old hospital, including Planned Parenthood, drug and alcohol counseling, and "Quick," the Carthage and Wade County Clinic—and, in the basement, was the odd pairing of vending machines and the morgue. Hannah waited for them by the cheese curls, tugging at all the knobs to see if she could coax out a snack. Or possibly even some change. The kid would do fine during the broke times in college. Vending machine crawls had kept Marian in pizza slices.

Inside an overlighted room the size of a small OR, a man in his early fifties dressed in scrubs and an open tweed duster sat with his feet up at a desk, paging through an old issue of *Good Housekeeping.* His hair was thick and white, and a stylish pair of half-glasses had slid to the tip of his angular nose. Next to him on the shiny tiled floor was a plush red dog bed with CONSTANCE stitched in white. The occupant was a tricolor springer spaniel who lifted her head inquisitively as Marian and Charlie entered. Marian and Constance exchanged arch looks, and the dog's docked tail thumped softly against the red plush.

On the autopsy table, the body of J.C. Houston was covered with a white cotton sheet.

"Hi, Doc," Charlie looked around. "Been waiting long?"

"Nah." Jim Carney shook hands with Marian and folded his glasses. "Gives me a chance to catch up on my reading about Meghan Markle and award-winning chocolate tortes." He rolled his eyes, tossing the magazine into a Bengals trash can.

"What have you got?"

"Here," he said. "Take a look."

As he pulled back the sheet, Charlie and Marian moved around the table to get a better view of the remains. The remains most definitely—remain. *We're right,* she thought, *to put off death as long as we can.* It's so utterly unlike anything that goes before. What had been a man was now a cadaver, looking like some new petroleum byproduct.

The man's thin gray hair was even wispier across his chest than on his head, and his lips and one eyelid were slightly parted, making his final expression kind of lewd and winking. The halves of his body had been roughly pulled back together with black, even stitches. Marian took a look, but all she could feel was the collapse of years, back to when Paul Seeks last figured in her life. Somehow there seemed to be more humanity left in whatever bloody fragments of flesh Paul had been reduced to than here, in this whole object

33

that had been someone named J.C. Houston.

The ammonia in the air stung her cheeks.

Carney snipped two spidery black threads with a pair of small scissors. "Time of death," he said, flicking away the trimmed threads, "roughly ten o'clock evening before last." He rolled a stool over and sat at the head of the table, where he considered the dead man's face. "I can't tell you diddly about this man's life, but I can tell you a thing or two about his death."

"Heart?"

Jim Carney shook his head. "That was my first guess until I got inside. No," he lifted a dead hand, scanning the fingernails. "Gross didn't show much of anything. Liver, bowel, kidneys normal. Had his last meal about one o'clock. Heart a bit enlarged, nothing worrisome. But when I put a slice of lung under the microscope, I hit pay dirt. Radically enlarged alveoli, scarring, muscle spasms. Mr. Houston, here," Carney replaced the dead man's hand, patting it twice, "wheezed to death."

"Asthma?"

Carney nodded. "Given the condition of his lungs, I'd say he's had it most of his life."

"So, what you're telling us," said Charlie, studying the ceiling, "is that this guy found his way to Carthage, illegally entered the Mission House—"

Carney pointed a finger at him. "Ah, we don't know that."

"All right, all right, entered the Mission House and keeled over with a fatal attack of asthma."

The coroner nodded. "That's about the size of it," he said, his eyes twinkling.

"Shit," Charlie plunged his hands into his pockets. "You didn't overlook some purple thumbprints on his windpipe?"

"No," said Carney, "and his head wasn't stuffed in a Hefty bag."

Marian clapped an arm around Charlie. "You've still got a story," she told him. "You just don't have a murder."

"Oh, I wouldn't say that," said Carney, rolling the report into a cylinder. "This man was a lifelong asthmatic. What I'd like to know is—" he turned to Charlie, "where's his inhaler?" The doctor stuffed the report into Charlie's breast pocket. "Down the rabbit hole," he said with a laugh.

Chapter Eight

"Jim Carney's just being provocative," Charlie complained to her at The Gleaner as the hostess, whose hair was gelled into immobility, guided them past Ye Salad Barre. "I remember the last time I saw my father's cousin Zev, who died of emphysema. He was sitting up in his hospital bed chain-smoking Camels."

"Thumbing his nose at death."

"You got it," Charlie said. "So the absence of an inhaler doesn't mean a whole hell of a lot."

"Maybe not."

"I'll have a cheeseburger and French fries," Hannah announced, killing any suspense on the topic. She hurried on ahead to their seats, one in a line of booths with high-backed benches overhung by low swag lamps. The hostess waited with a fixed smile, clutching menus to her chest.

Charlie slid in next to Marian.

The waitress, slim and energetic in black pants and a white shirt, tilted her chin in a way family members had been telling her was adorable from the age of five. Her name pin said KIM, and she had a wash of freckles over smooth white cheeks. As they ordered, she annotated everything as they went along, nixing the fish, approving the ribeyes, and pushing the tomato basil soup. After she departed with a final adorable chin tilt, Marian put her arm around Charlie's shoulders.

When their drinks came, Charlie pushed Marian's cabernet closer to her and raised his beer. "*L'chayim,*" he said, clinking Hannah's Dr. Pepper and Marian's wine glass, though she hardly raised it. It had just struck her that

Charlie's hair was nearly blue-black, and it made her think of "Black Swans," a cross-hand piano piece. His hair was very nearly blue-black, and she had never noticed. Jesus.

Hannah twirled a fry. "Is Derry singing tonight?" She looked at Marian. "Dad's friend."

The redhead. Marian thought suddenly of Alice Lowther, describing Bella as Jack Girard's friend. Friendly town, Carthage.

Charlie shook his head. "Not until tomorrow night."

"Can we go for hot chocolate tonight anyway?"

"Deal."

Marian picked at her meal. Assaulted by tenderizer and charcoal, the ribeye had crossed the line into some other food group. She was content, finally, just to wedge herself into the corner of the booth and listen to Charlie. "So, fill me in."

The Mission House, he declared as he speared a parslied potato and waved it at her, had been minding its own business for almost three hundred years. Then, about three years ago, so he's been told, Bill Cain started a "downtown renewal" project. Up to that point, he'd been applying himself outside the town, turning cornfields into shopping malls.

Nobody much minded. Starbucks, Petco, Chipotle, and Party City meant jobs for locals. But then Cain started to nose around the old buildings downtown, hopping like a crow from one carcass to another. Too much space being "underutilized," as his pet expression goes.

Look at the Meers Hotel.

Look at the grain elevator on the riverbank.

Look at the Mission House.

"He calls them eyesores," Hannah put in, looking up at them from under the soft brim of her fedora.

"Are they?"

Charlie rested his arms on the table. "Depends on your taste. Personally, I don't think so. Places like that give the town its character. Their only sin, in Bill Cain's eyes," Charlie said, "is their vacancy."

Marian set down her napkin. "I can understand wanting to put them to use."

"So can I," said Charlie, "but restoration isn't part of Bill's vision. Tear 'em down, start from scratch, put up a newer, bigger Global Insurance Company, preferably in yellow brick straight out of the fifties."

"And local companies go for this?"

He nodded slowly. "The realtors, the insurance agents, the local utilities gang—the ones with cash and ego, they're the ones who go for it."

Marian drew her legs up under her. "Okay, I know what happened to the grain elevator, but what's the Meers Hotel?"

Charlie took the check from Kim. "The Meers Hotel was the first to go. Bill Cain got it through before anyone realized what was happening. It was a little hotel, been around since the First World War when it housed doughboys for a while. After that, a string of owners took it through their nightmare visions of vaudeville, speakeasy, casino, massage parlor. And when all the visions ran out, vacancy."

Charlie folded his receipt. "The kind of vacancy," he went on, "Bill Cain fills. He razed the Meers Hotel for Eagle Mutual Life Insurance." He handed Hannah her parka. "When Cain went after the grain elevator, people like Jack Girard and Bella and some others got the wind up. Then Cain started on the Mission House. To listen to Cain, it's sitting on the perfect site for Great Seal Power & Light. And since it's public land, he's been sweetening town council with just about every legal means at his disposal—only, believe me, because Girard's on him like a rash." Outside, Charlie took her arm and Hannah's and nodded to the right.

"Why?"

He frowned. "Ions in the air. Phases of the moon," he shook his head. "Who knows?" Halfway down the block, they crossed the street. "Actually, I think Cain's pattern has made people finally sit up and take notice. Jack Girard's tack has been to publicize the struggle. Get some statewide interest in the Mission House, he figures, and maybe some lawmakers more powerful than Bill Cain will throw public money at it. He sees to it that AP and Reuters get any *Toiler* stories on the Mission House."

"Girard's got half a dozen letters in the landmark committee's file."

Charlie nodded. "Whatever helps."

They came to a doorway in the block of buildings just up from the shadows where the Mission House stood. Overhead, creaking in the wind, was a wooden shingle with a crudely carved figure of a naked man lashed to a wild horse. *Mazeppa's Ride, 1865.* Hannah, shivering, ducked by them and went inside.

"It cuts both ways, though," Charlie said.

"What do you mean?"

He blew into his gloved hands, light snow falling like stars on his shoulders. "Oh," he said, "there've been incidents. Like what you saw this afternoon. Nuisance calls. Slashed tires, broken windows, graffiti. Both sides, back and forth, Girard's men, Cain's men—"

"Rocker, and Dugan—"

"They all begin to look alike. Last week there was a brawl at Gringos, a roadhouse just outside of town. One of Cain's men took a knife in the hand."

Marian watched a snowflake melt on his lapel. "Are Cain and Girard behind the incidents?"

Charlie shrugged, then said, "My guess is no. Jack Girard fired the guy the next day."

"Only to rehire him next month, I suppose?" She tucked her chin as far into the warmth of her coat as she could.

Charlie snorted. "If he does, he'll have to post bond first."

"Then what's behind it?"

"What's behind anything?" Charlie said, looking over Marian's shoulder. "Fear. Turf. Saving face. Lines in the sand."

"Sex."

He laughed. "Sex?"

"Yeah, you remember sex."

He squinted at a yellow Honda going by. "All the time."

"Well?" She was laughing.

He considered. "Damned if sex is the one thing I don't see at work here."

She raised an eyebrow. "Not enough of a concept for you?"

"Quit flirting with me, Marian," he said quietly. "It never goes anywhere."

He was right, she realized, walking stiffly into Mazeppa's Ride. Only she thought he'd have the good grace not to point it out.

Chapter Nine

"Coffee?"

"Sure. Thanks." What with the two cups she'd had earlier with Barb Hauser and the one Jack Girard was pouring for her, Marian figured she could burn up the highway back into town, without ever getting into her car. Inside the trailer, Girard stood next to a two-burner hot plate on a narrow counter. Her eyes took him in. Old jeans, old blue flannel shirt, the cuffs rolled back over white thermal underwear.

The percolator looked like it had been battered by a goat. "No Keurig, huh?"

He paused. "You like that stuff?"

"No." A little too defensive.

"Cream?"

"Sure." Against the far wall was a low metal bed that looked like an oversized single, covered by a green Army blanket. Two office chairs were pulled up to a small metal desk he must have bought for five bucks at a fire sale. Some floor cushions, stacked. A Turkish rug. A closet that was probably a john. Footlocker. An electric space heater that was red and humming. An overturned orange crate. It was a desktop kind of life, strewn with ledgers, books, a laptop, and loose papers with a rock for a paperweight. On the wall next to Marian was a framed Edward Hopper print she had always liked.

"Here." He handed her a cup of coffee in a hand-painted Spode China teacup, tulip-shaped with gold leaf.

"This is beautiful," she said.

"One of my mother's." He sat down in the other chair and leaned back.

"Saucers all broke a long time ago." His gaze was steady. "So how can I help you?" he said. "What do you want to know?"

Marian blew across the top of her coffee. "Do you live here?"

"Yes."

"I thought you lived—in town." Did she? Did it matter?

He sipped his coffee from a plain brown mug. "Some nights I spend in town. But this is where I live." He sat up. "What does this have to do with the Mission House?"

He was right. "Nothing," she said. "I'm just friendly."

"I'm not." He gave her a frank look.

She narrowed her eyes at him. "You agreed to talk to me."

"That's business."

She held up her cup. "You made me a cup of coffee. Is that business?"

"No, that's not business," he said, killing a smile. "But it's just a cup of coffee."

Not a man with a whole lot of roads to the interior. "I spoke to Alice Lowther about the Mission House. She has no doubts about its authenticity."

He shrugged. "No doubts—and no proof."

"What about the letter from Chardin?"

"Alice's Grail. Apparently, it's not good enough."

She studied the tulip-shaped cup. "You sound like you don't care."

"Force of habit." Jack Girard set his coffee down on the desk and slowly pushed it away with a fingertip.

"So," she said, trying to get the picture, "for the Mission House to be preserved, it has to have landmark status —"

"Pretty much, and that would help. So would some ongoing grant money."

"No doubt. But what you need is proof —" she liked the taste of the word so much that she said it again, "—proof of eighteenth-century building materials, or architectural design, or artifacts, or —" Her voice slowed.

"Or what?"

"Or—I'm just guessing here—proof that your Mission House is historically significant—"

"Go on."

And here it was. "To the nation."

He let out a small groan.

Marian downshifted. "Tell me about the body they found."

"Tell me about Levitan," he countered. "How do you know him?"

"We're old friends." She felt unsettled. And maybe it had nothing to do with losing control of the interview.

"College?"

She nodded. "And high school."

"Sweethearts?"

Enough. Marian held up her cup. "Ah, but it's just a cup of coffee," she said, "remember?" *Sweethearts.* Quaint. No, downright Paleolithic. Wrap it up with Spode China teacups and Edward Hopper and white thermal underwear. Interesting package. Like Bella, Marian thought, I'd train dogs and take my chances with the local beauty shops, too. "The body in the Mission House," she practically blared at him, trying to get back on track.

Girard clasped his hands behind his neck. "Name?"

"J.C. Houston."

"Houston." He slowly shook his head. "We've got Hestons in town. And Hugheses. But no Houstons. Suit?"

"Suit?"

Girard made a slow gesture. "Was he wearing a suit?"

She smiled. "Not when I saw him."

"You saw him?"

"At the morgue." She watched his reaction.

Girard rocked softly. "So are you licensed?"

"I am."

"Got a weapon?"

"Yes."

"With you?"

She tried very hard not to blink. "Do I need it?"

A slight pause. "Not at the present time."

"Why all the questions?" she said impatiently.

Girard stroked two fingers across his mouth. "Just curious."

"Not friendly, just curious. Well," she said, "it's a start."

"To what?"

Human feeling, she wanted to say. Instead, she sipped. "My guess is J.C. Houston came to town on personal business."

"So —" he narrowed his eyes, "nothing to do with the nomination process?"

"Right now, I don't know."

Girard inhaled. "Somebody in Carthage must know him."

"And isn't admitting it."

"Maybe Mr. Houston was an embarrassment."

She went along. "Or a threat."

"Or," Girard spread his hands, "a secret."

"You mean a sweetheart?" Christ, she was beginning to talk like him. "Lovers?"

"Why not?"

"In which case," Marian said, remembering the man laid out on the table, "we're back to embarrassment and threat."

Jack Girard pushed back his chair. "Look for somebody affected by those things, and you'll find out what brought Houston to town."

She cocked her head. "I'll start with you."

"Me?" He tossed Marian her vest. "I don't embarrass," he said, pulling on his leather jacket. "And when I was shipped stateside after a bad ten days at Haditha Dam in Iraq, I stopped feeling threatened. I was twenty-four. And that was a long time ago." He turned off the space heater, its coils paling. "Let's walk."

"You had a commission?"

"Major, by the time I was discharged. Army Rangers."

Outside the trailer was the sort of winter daylight that never quite cast shadows. Marian took a good look around. Considering it was a place of business, it was oddly private. "Then what? You came back here?"

He glanced at her. "I worked out west for a while."

"Engineering?"

"And construction, mostly. Not to mention a marriage that lasted five years before we figured out we didn't like each other very much."

"When did you come back to Carthage?"

"Two years ago," he said, stuffing his hands in his pockets.

"Why?"

He started to walk away from her. "Family matters," he called back. "Are you coming?" It was an alpine landscape, with snow-covered mountains of four different grades of gravel, from fine to coarse.

On her way down to the trailer that morning, Marian had passed a swinging metal gate standing wide open, MCG CONSTRUCTION posted alongside. Driving through the woods down a wide, unpaved road, she came to a clearing where earth-moving equipment was stored. She had pulled over for a cement mixer and dump truck passing her in the other direction, the drivers' hands flapping at her. There the trees thickened, and the road continued downward, opening into a snowy plateau where she found a silver Airstream trailer and the Army jeep, which looked about as old as his percolator.

Marian came to a stop beside Jack Girard. She started turning slowly in place, seeing as much as she could. The path at the left led into the trees, and the one on the right went directly down to the gravel pit. The far side of the pit was a rocky slope that dropped off vertically into the water, now covered with an icy veneer. All along the left side of the gravel pit, the rock eased off into a steep hillside. Behind them were mountains of gravel. Everywhere she looked, the proportions were unsettling. The rockface was so tall, the mountains of gravel so vast.

Only the trailer was small. A small silver sanctuary, with a humming heater.

She turned to Girard. "Who has keys to the Mission House?"

"I do. Bella does." He thought. "Alice Lowther, Bill Cain, the local law. Then, I suppose, there's no telling how many duplicates have been made from each of those."

"Did you?"

"Make a duplicate? Only the one for Bella. Why?"

"Houston was locked in from the outside."

Girard frowned. "Must be the padlock, then."

"What do you mean?"

"Up until a few weeks ago, there was just the one lock on the Mission House. An ordinary Yale. You'd need a key to get in. But once it's locked, there's no telling whether it had been locked from the outside with the key —"

"Or from the inside, manually?"

He nodded. "A few weeks ago the Police Department installed a padlock."

"Why?"

His eyes narrowed. "They call it a deterrent."

"To what?" She clamped her arms across her chest.

"They didn't say." Girard looked at her. "Levitan fill you in on the conflict?" When she nodded, he picked up a crushed pop can, shaking off the snow. "Police felt they needed to indicate an awareness, that's my guess."

"So twenty bucks at the hardware store and they restore public faith in law and order."

He gave her a wry look. "That's about it."

"Who has keys to the padlock?"

"All the same people."

Great security. "Keeping the Mission House locked sounds more symbolic than anything else."

"Damage control, I'd say." He looked around as though he was seeing the site for the first time. "Limit the current conflict to the key players."

"Including J.C. Houston?"

"Meaning?"

"The man died in the Mission House. Maybe that qualifies him as a key player. What do you think?"

Girard stared at the ground, then slowly shook his head. "I can tell you one thing for sure," he said, with a sigh. "Nobody outside of Carthage gives a damn about the Mission House."

Cool and factual. He believes what he says. Marian gave him a steady look. "Or, if they do, maybe it's for reasons that don't make sense to you."

"Nice try," said Jack Girard. "Like what?"

"I don't know."

"Then National Historic Landmark status sounds like a longshot."

Maybe J.C. Houston had other reasons, different reasons for his interest in the Mission House. Theft? Marian blew into her gloved hands. Theft.

Or.

She stood very still. *Nobody outside of Carthage.*

Maybe J.C. Houston wasn't an outsider.

Finally, she looked at him. "I hear the guy who found his body works for you."

He gave her a slow nod. "Steve Grey." Then: "He has a set of keys, too. He was doing a repair for me. You need to talk to him?" He pulled a phone out of his pocket and started to thumb through his contacts.

She did the same. "I do."

Jack Girard held up the phone. She entered Steve Grey's name and number into her contact list, then added the address. "Got a card?" he asked.

She nodded. "You?" And they made the exchange, then walked over to a narrow, slippery strip that sloped downward into the gravel pit. Marian stepped closer to the water's edge and looked in. Hard to tell, but the drop-off seemed severe. She looked over at Girard. "Good for swimming?"

"If you like it cold."

It was a great vat of water. No current, no waves, no vegetation. Her eyes raised to the tree line, Marian scanned the perimeter. A remarkable place. Like living in a crater. Here life forms could be delicate anomalies, for all anyone would know, the greenery ancient, the sensibilities fresh. Carthage toiled up there somewhere, hundreds of feet overhead. Roads, houses, utility lines, smokestacks, feuds. The mortal coil. The sun, a hard white brilliance, rose above the tree line. Nothing gets to be as painfully stark as the winter sun.

"According to Aristotle," Marian found herself saying, "what's astonishing brings us pleasure." She scuffed at the snow.

"I take it you like it here." Was all he said.

She turned to Jack Girard. Ten bad days at an Iraqi dam. Broken saucers. A failed marriage. A silver trailer in an ice crater. Maybe Cain's wrecking ball was nothing new. "Let's just say I find it astonishing," she said, her eyes slipping away. Why mention that fear is the part of beauty we only see at second glance?

Chapter Ten

"Forty-eight Providence," Bella had told her on the phone that morning. Since it was just a few blocks from the Wade County Library, where Marian had spent the lunch hour skimming Alice Lowther's books, she decided to hoof it. Along the way, she tried calling Steve Grey, who discovered the body in the Mission House. When it went right away to voicemail, she left her name and said she'd like to talk to him about the body, and thanks.

She gave up on Shaughnessy when she realized that his premise that Jesuit missions didn't exist in Ohio was based on Temple's prior claim that the Mission House was built many years after the priest Claude de Chardin died. Wouldn't some time down in the County Records office help resolve this question about the building's age? As Marian stashed Lowther's books in her backpack and then zipped up for the walk to Bella's, she reminded herself she was sent to Carthage to get to the bottom of the letters in the Park Service file on the Mission House, not to add any new research on the problem. No one, least of all Joan, wanted an even fatter file. But maybe Marian could push her assignment to include loosening up the tangle among the players. Something had to shift in the way the fate of the Mission House was viewed.

Turning off Main Street, Marian could tell that the town had been laid out on a grid of streets and alleys back in the horse and wagon days, when the stables that later became garages ran along the backs of the properties. The alley that connected Main Street and Providence was unplowed, so she trudged carefully over the snow packed like mortar between the rough

49

cobblestones. Thick brown vines spread out along the brick walls, and bare bushes, heavy with snow, spilled untrimmed into the lane. An alley in Carthage was a place where people could set out their garbage on collection day and wonder what the hell they were doing with their lives. Marian sniffed. Snow always smelled old to her. The kind of old that outlasts everything fine and sweet.

Providence was a short, narrow street lined with trees so tall and dense their branches looked laced together in the winter sky. Number forty-eight was a two-story stone house with a low-pitched roof on the corner of the alley. Ivy that was practically black from the cold curled around the shuttered windows, and across the front was a porch that was empty except for the drifting snow. Marian's knock set off scrabbling sounds and muffled woofs.

"Marian?"

She leaned close to the door. "Hi, Bella."

"My hands are full of paint," came the voice from inside. "Come on in."

As Marian started to open the door, two Labs wedged their heads in the opening and looked apologetic. "Well, hello," she said, scratching a yellow face and pushing her way inside. The dog had a paint rag dangling like a dead mallard from his mouth. While she stomped snow off her boots, two other Labs came charging downstairs, and Marian patted what she thought was all of them.

Bella appeared, smiling. "Ralph and Alice are the two blacks," she said, "Norton's the yellow, and Trixie's the chocolate. These four have house privileges most of the time. And I rotate the others through, too."

"The others?"

"Out back in the kennel," Bella told her. "Right now, I've got three I'm training for their owners."

Marian crouched next to Trixie, scratching the coarse brown fur. Her dark eyes were modest. "Sweet dog," she said. "Where do the others come from?"

"All over." Bella finished drying her hands, then pushed down the sleeves of her white shirt. Her hair was tied up with a man's handkerchief in a haphazard way that looked wonderful. "Two came up from Kentucky and one from North Carolina. A real hammerhead," she added. When she opened the back door to put the dogs out, the rubber dog flap swung slightly.

"Norton, Trixie," she called, "outside. Ralph, Alice. Come." The dogs bounded out, and as Bella closed the door, Norton's head started back through the flap. "Norton," she shook her head at him, and he ducked back out. "Clown," she said fondly, then turned to Marian. "Come see my dining room. It's finally finished."

The smell of paint was strong, and the furniture stood covered with sheets in the center of the room. The walls were a vivid green. "I've just been touching up the crown moldings," Bella said, hammering down the smeared lid of the paint can. Not asking if Marian liked it. No groveling for compliments, no anxious second thoughts. And, Marian concluded, looking around, she did like it. The room was exquisite with its high ceilings and elegant crown moldings, a French-tiled fireplace set into a central wall shared with the living room. In the winter sunlight, motes of dust floated.

"Jack grew up in this house," Bella added as a mild point of interest, as if the man who invented the butane lighter had lived here. Marian couldn't make sense of it. What was this gorgeous young dog trainer doing here while Jack Girard was living in an old trailer? Bella brushed off some paint specks and set the drop cloth on the sheet-draped furniture. "It was in the Girard family for—" her eyes narrowed, "close to a hundred years."

"How did you—?"

Bella smiled. "It was a gift."

"From Girard?"

"Clayton Girard, Jack's father." Bella looked around. "He was my guardian," she added in a thin, vague way. "Just let me find my sweater, and we'll go."

"So—you lived here with them?"

"Actually, no. I was ten when my father pitched his Cessna into a cornfield in Ontario. He and my mother were taking my brother Ben up to the science museum in Toronto," she said, as if she were describing a perfectly uneventful day. Maybe after a dozen years, what's left are simply the facts. Given enough time, maybe there was nothing too painful to describe. "By then," Bella grabbed a sweater off a chair, "Clayton was living in a new ranch house outside of town. Tan aluminum siding, metal awnings, no front steps," she shuddered. "Elinor—that's Jack's mother—had died, and Jack was long gone, and I really don't think his father cared where he lived. He just couldn't live here."

Bella's voice was muffled as she pulled on the long, alpaca sweater she had worn yesterday at the *Toiler*. "But he couldn't bring himself to sell the place, either. So he rented it. And when I turned twenty-one, he signed it over to me." She clipped what looked like a jailer's key ring to her belt. "About a week later, he had a stroke." Her eyes slipped past Marian as she tugged on her sleeves. "What do you say we walk?"

A stroke. A crumpled plane. The science museum, unseen. And, for that matter, everything else. Saucers broken, cups abandoned. Family, home, guardian—and Jack—gone. What about Bella, left behind by all that death? "Why weren't you with them?"

"I had softball practice that day," she said with a weak smile, "so they found a sitter."

Chapter Eleven

So much for theft.

There was nothing to steal, unless J.C. Houston had some urgent need for a card table and folding chairs, or slick tri-folds on "Carthage Area Attractions." Marian stood with her hands on her hips inside the Mission House, where the mystery had nothing to do with dates or bodies. Or even, for that matter, why its fate as a potential National Historic Landmark was under siege. Oh, no. The mystery was why Alice Lowther had called it "very beautiful." From the looks of the place, Bill Cain might very well be performing a public service.

The building was a weather-beaten gray, one-and-a-half-story New England Colonial, built on a raised stone foundation. The floor upstairs was broken or buckling, and the downstairs front room had water damage and a crumbling hearth. The place had been reroofed, Bella was saying, about thirty-three years ago—the last time for any real attempts at renovation. The roof, the interior staircase, and all the downstairs windows were replaced, and some plasterwork was done, then the money ran out. "Again," Bella smiled.

"And before that?"

"Before that?" Bella shook her head. "There probably isn't anyone in town now who was alive at the time."

It was small.

It was cold.

Most of all, it was unpleasant.

Bella said defensively, "This was the first Jesuit mission in the Northwest

Territories, Marian. Easily nearly three hundred years old. It's important in our national religious history. Sure, it's not a showplace." At that, Marian raised her eyebrows. "But it can be—and it should be—and the grant money from landmark status will make it happen."

Marian felt bad for her and lifted a hand. "Not my decision, Bella. I'm just here to figure out what's stalled the process. Maybe make some suggestions to move it along." Now for the first suggestion… "Can you…postpone the application? Say, until tempers have—"

Bella straightened up. "That'll never happen. If we withdraw the application, Bill Cain wins. It's that simple. All the damn letter writing is a way to buy us some time to—to—"

They looked helplessly at each other.

"Find new information?" said Marian.

Bella let out a breath. "I guess that's what it comes to. New information even Bill Cain can't dispute."

They sat next to each other in heavy silence on the bottom step until, finally, Bella pointed out the electric baseboard heating units that had been installed about ten years back.

Marian's eyes took in the whole empty room, imagining a carpenter named Steve Grey who had looked through the nearest window and discovered what turned out to be J.C. Houston, an auto worker from Cleveland who had come to Carthage to wheeze his last. This much Marian knew, but she felt too defeated to tell Bella. At the center of the room were great whorls of dried mud and wheel marks, left behind by whoever had taken away the body of J.C. Houston. "Bella," Marian said, pushing herself to her feet, "who cleans up around here?"

"Whoever uses the place. There's a broom and dustpan in the closet under the stairs."

Marian took a deep breath. "So, who uses the place?" Who pays good money to enjoy the rot and mildew?

"Well, sometimes I hold S.O.S. meetings here, and every so often, the Garden Club or the League of Women Voters uses it." Bella raised her eyebrows. "The meeting room at the library isn't always available."

"I see." But she didn't. She felt baffled.

"And Alice Lowther insists on opening it up for state occasions."

"State occasions?" She sounded as incredulous as she felt. Inaugurals? Funerals? Embassy balls? What on earth could she mean?

"The Carthage equivalent," Bella smiled. "Memorial Day, the Fourth of July, Veterans' Day," she explained. "Have you met Alice? It was her idea to hold an Open House at Carthage's historic homes on those days, so she puts together a little committee to spruce up the Mission House, and then, a few days before, she runs a nice little box ad in the *Toiler*, announcing Open House at the Mission House. That morning she hangs a grapevine wreath on the front door, sets out some watery lemonade in Dixie cups, and receives the public."

Marian looked at the crumbling hearth and fireplace. "How much public does she receive?"

Bella widened her beautiful green eyes. "Well, she never runs out of lemonade."

Nice little ad, nice little committee. Meaning, Marian suspected, anything but. She watched Bella chip critically at some paint peeling at one of the windows. It must be hard for someone younger and more restless, like Bella, to deal with Alice Lowther's Band-Aid attempts at mustering local interest in the place. Wreaths and Dixie cups weren't going to save the Mission House. Marian's toe scuffed at white ash on the hearth. "Why does she do it?"

"Personally," Bella said, crossing her arms, "I think it's her chance to play Colonial Dame of America." Her eyes narrowed, sparkling. "As head of the Wade County Historical Society, she gives herself permission to prance around in one of the costumes for the better part of a day."

Marian could see it: Alice Lowther in musty taffeta and crinolines, becoming a nineteenth-century coquette in blue satin or brown velvet—if only in her own mind. "Where does she live, Bella?"

"Over on West Fourth Street."

"What's her house like?"

"I don't know. I've never been inside."

Neither, she'd bet, has anyone else. "How long has she been heading up the Historical Society?"

Bella thought about it. "All my life," she said finally. "She came to Carthage around thirty years ago."

"Not a native?"

"No," said Bella, "I think she grew up out east somewhere."

"Any other candidates for the job?"

Bella's eyes narrowed. "There isn't a vacancy."

"Still," Marian persisted.

"Who'd want it?"

"What about you?"

"I have my own group," she said. "And our tastes don't run to lemonade in Dixie cups."

See Our Shenanigans, Lowther had sniffed. "Well, I'm wondering," Marian said, pushing at the sash windows—locked tight—"How much longer can Alice Lowther pull it off?"

"Alice has worked very hard," was all Bella said, and Marian felt outclassed. Still, whatever she told Bella, she knew it would take more than age or failure to dislodge Alice Lowther from the Wade County Historical Society. Scandal, maybe, or even disgrace. *Look for somebody affected by those things,* Girard had said, *and you'll find out what brought Houston to town.*

As Marian snapped some photos of buckling boards, she looked over at Bella, languid and bony, one arm curling gracefully above her on the wall over the fireplace, her long, capable fingers drooping. Like Atalanta, reaching for golden apples. Bella's embarrassments would always be inconsequential. She might acknowledge her own scandals with a sublime shrug, but that would be all.

Chapter Twelve

"What did you expect?" Charlie spread out his hands, which were covered with raw beef and egg yolk. "Monticello?" She watched his strong fingers work over what was billed as a meatloaf like it was the champ's lats.

"Certainly not a shack." She felt seriously out of sorts.

"The fact," he said, grinding away at a celery stick, "folks are knifing each other—not to mention dropping dead—over a place in such disrepair means there's more going on here than outraged letters."

He was right. Marian stared into the glass of cabernet sauvignon they were sharing.

"Fortification, please," Charlie said, and she held the glass to his lips. "Mm," he savored, "a bodacious little wine."

She eyed the raw beef. "You need more pepper."

"Ah." He peppered, slammed the baking pan into the oven, and washed his hands. "So tell me what you got on the Mission House today." He motioned to the living room, grabbing a second wine glass and the bottle of Shiraz as he went. "Besides a firsthand glimpse of decrepitude."

Marian felt herself getting sucked into the oversized white sofa that jumbled all of her limbs together. She arched her back, checking to see whether she was still a vertebrate.

He went on, "Did you get to talk to Jack Girard at all?"

She peered around a mauve vase holding a wilderness of dried flowers. "This morning."

"Was it useful?"

Marian sipped. "We talked about J.C. Houston."

"Did he know him?"

"Says not." She crossed her legs with a wince. "Charlie, I'm pretty far from writing Joan a report. Nothing's straightforward. Is Houston's death tied up with the struggle in the National Historic Landmark process? I can't separate them in my own mind."

"So, don't. Odds are they're linked, anyway. Any hunches?"

She set down her wine glass. "Why does a retired auto worker from Cleveland come to town one night? What's the likelihood he's a preservation hobbyist with some important new information about the Mission House? Not great. Are his purposes honorable or dishonorable?"

"Tough call."

Marian shook her head. "Dishonorable," she said. "No one's come forward to claim him. No one's admitted to being there the night Houston died."

"Maybe no one was. Maybe he was alone."

She raised her glass to him. "Then how did he get in?"

"He had his own key?"

"I don't buy it," she said. "What about the padlock? Jack Girard tells me the padlock is recent." They were silent. "Somebody was there with J.C. Houston, Charlie. And somebody locked him in and left him to die."

"So that's your theory."

"That's my hunch."

His eyes widened. "So, a falling out among thieves. Tell me more." He downed the rest of his wine and pointed the bottom of the bottle at her. "You saw the guy on the slab, Marian. Can you feature him as part of a conspiracy to damage the Mission House?"

She couldn't. Besides, the damage already existed. The crumbling fireplace, the water-stained walls, the gouged plaster. "I considered arson," she said, peering out the dining room window into the dark, where a snowplow was clearing the parking lot behind the row of townhouses.

"Houston came to town to torch it?"

She shrugged. "What do you think?"

"A bold move by Bill Cain, is that how you see it?"

"But it doesn't make sense, Charlie. Cain isn't going to want anything premature to happen to the Mission House. Given his high-handed letters in the file, he'd be the first one the cops would suspect."

"So, you're saying—" he stared at the ceiling, "Girard or Bella was behind it. To discredit Bill Cain."

"Doesn't wash, though, does it? To save the Mission House, they discredit Bill Cain by destroying the Mission House."

"Are you sure Sophocles didn't write this?"

"Ask me again in a week." No, J.C. Houston came to town with his own agenda. But, what brought him? Two doors down from Charlie's townhouse, a back door opened, and an old man dressed for the gulag made his slow way across the parking lot to the dumpster. In one arm, he carried a brown paper bag tightened into a parcel, and in the other, a stack of twined newspapers. There go Charlie's best efforts. "Charlie," it struck her, "has the *Toiler* run anything on the Mission House in the last, say, two or three weeks?"

"Well, there was the body. That was a hit."

She shook her head. "Back it up. Before the body."

What brought J.C. Houston to town?

Why him, why then?

Charlie's fingers dug through his hair. "There was some indirect stuff."

"Like what?"

"A mention in a piece about City Council. Upcoming votes and issues, that sort of thing. Something in a piece on local utilities and their plans for expansion."

"Something heftier. Something just on the Mission House."

He snorted. "Well, Donna Ardizzone did a decent piece on the lack of public funding for local antiquities."

"Do tell." Marian followed him into the kitchen.

"Actually," he groaned, tossing her a head of lettuce, "it was part of a series, and the day the piece on the Mission House appeared, we ran a three-column color shot of a local potter on the front page. She's a great gal, very pleasant, and this shot showed her in her studio surrounded by all her pots and dishes, which—" Charlie brandished a paring knife, "the caption actually called the poor lady's 'primitive bowels.'"

"Oh, no."

"So, what with chewing out the copy editor and the proofreader, I didn't pay much attention to Donna's piece on the Mission House."

"Who was mentioned by name, do you remember?"

"Well, she interviewed Lowther and Cain. Girard too, I think."

Nodding, she pulled out her phone and tapped in the number Jack Girard had given her. He answered on the first ring. "Girard." His voice sounded like she'd taken him away from something.

"Marian Warner," she said. "Listen, did you send any *Toiler* clippings on the Mission House to AP or UPI—or directly to someone at the Cleveland paper? Any time over the last couple of weeks, say."

Silence. Then: "It would have been about three weeks ago, sure. I sent clippings to the AP bureau in Columbus—and a few state reps."

She nodded at Charlie, who popped a smoked oyster into his mouth. "What was the piece?"

Jack Girard inhaled, trying to remember. "Something about the lack of public funding for cultural and historical projects. It was—"

"That's it, thanks. Bye." She disconnected, then rested her forehead against the wall. *Half a glass of cabernet, and I can hardly tie my own shoelaces.*

"So?" With his forearm Charlie swept dunes of sliced vegetables into the salad bowl he held just below the edge of the counter. "Talk to me."

"Where do you keep your old papers, Charlie?"

He looked up. "In the garage. What did Girard say?"

"He sent the piece to the AP." Marian pulled on her vest and fumbled the zipper.

"What's your guess?"

"My guess? One morning about two weeks ago, Houston was sitting in Dunkin' Donuts with the Cleveland daily paper when the piece about Carthage caught his eye. And, depending on what he read there, I'd say he just about dropped his cruller."

She opened the door leading from the kitchen to the unheated garage, which was dead cold. She found the light switch and walked around the side of the Buick, where black metal bins were filled with back issues of the Carthage *Toiler*. Marian started thumbing through them, looking for the happy potter. Charlie stood in the doorway. "And," she said, "unless I miss my guess, J.C. Houston discovered a perfect way of supplementing his Social Security."

"Blackmail?"

She raised her eyebrows at him. "I like it better than arson."

He ran his hand once around his face, then shook his head. "There was nothing incriminating in that piece, Marian. You'll see."

"Not to you. But something. A name, a fact, a face, a quote. For Houston, something clicked." Halfway down the stack, the photo of local potter, Polly Gundersen, smiled up at her. Marian pulled out the issue, flourished it like a winning lottery ticket, then folded it neatly into thirds. Should slip nicely into her backpack. Between the cold garage and a brain suddenly in overdrive, Marian leaped up the step next to Charlie and kissed him squarely on the lips.

He grabbed at her shoulder. "Well, aren't you going to read it?"

"Later's soon enough."

"What self-control."

"Who knows better than you?" With a quick squeeze of his arm, she brushed by him.

"Lucky me."

"I'll get Hannah," she said, stuffing the folded paper into her backpack. *Nobody outside of Carthage gives a damn about the Mission House.* Nobody outside of Carthage. *We've got Hestons and Hugheses, but no Houstons.* She thought about who had seen the corpse. She and Charlie, newcomers to Carthage. Jim Carney, in town maybe fifteen years. Sperry the Police Chief, early forties, from what Charlie says. A rookie cop. A carpenter. Marian chuckled. So simple, really: none of them go back far enough. What she needed to discover was why a man calling himself J.C. Houston left Carthage thirty years ago.

And she knew where to start.

On Hannah's door was a well-worn poster with black lettering on a background wash of sky colors: IF YOU ARE NOT PART OF THE SOLUTION, YOU ARE PART OF THE PROBLEM. Marian knocked. From inside the room came scrabbling sounds, then Hannah opened the door about six inches, biting her lip. *What's she hiding?* A pimply boy? *Fifty Shades of Grey?* "Listen," Marian said, crossing her arms, "I've got some poking around to do tomorrow afternoon and I could use your help after school. Are you game?"

"Is it dangerous?"

"I don't believe so."

"I'll help anyway," she said. "Just a minute." She shut the door, and in a few seconds, Marian heard a soft click, maybe the closet door closing. The strip of light disappeared, and Hannah came out, shutting the door firmly. "Are you and Dad going to hear Derry?"

Marian nodded. "She's good, huh?"

"She's good," she said, taking in Marian's black microfleece pants and oversized sweater with the white t-shirt poking through the deep vee. "You look nice."

"Thanks, honey."

"Only the shirt should be black."

"You think?"

"Dad's got one you can use. I'll get it out for you after dinner," Hannah smiled back at her, running on ahead. "You'll really give Derry a run for her money."

Marian rolled her eyes.

Chapter Thirteen

The definition of difference, Marian thought: Mazeppa's Ride on a Tuesday night with just a few regulars, and Mazeppa's Ride on a Wednesday night, between the weekly darts competition and a late set by Derry Wilson and the Second Shift Band. So named, Charlie told her, because all the musicians have daytime jobs. Apparently, the band had humble, garage origins back in the day, and even with a fair amount of musician turnover, they had finally settled into playing twice a week at Mazeppa's Ride. Their one gig. Despite their local celebrity, one gig was all they wanted.

"Same old story," Charlie said out of the side of his mouth as they pushed their way to the rear, passing the band as they unpacked their instruments. "You can take the band out of the garage, but—" He left it unfinished. Making music was still just a hobby, even after twenty years—what they're doing instead of building ships in bottles or carving decoys. A teacher, an insurance agent, a bailiff, a carpenter, a podiatrist, an auto parts dealer, and Tim Rinehart, the owner of Mazeppa's Ride.

Built in 1865, the saloon had a high ceiling and a cheerful unevenness to the plasterwork and plank flooring that Marian liked. Along the right wall ran the brass and mahogany bar, Civil War memorabilia on the shelves not covered by siphon-topped bottles, and a long, beveled mirror. Small tables with votive candles and unmatched chairs ranged along the left wall, which held a gallery of framed sketches and photographs of Carthage's history.

Marian worked her way around the darts players to look at them. "Cold Spring River Flood 1902" was one. "Intersection Main and Mission Streets

After Flood 1902," "Volunteer Effort During 1902 Flood," "Bethel Tabernacle Church Before and After Fire 1897." What is it about small towns, Marian wondered, that they make entries on their timelines on the occasion of natural disasters? The Flood of Ought Two. The Fire of Ninety-Seven. The Drought of Twenty-Three. The Cholera Epidemic.

Different from a place like New York, where nothing short of complete incineration would make an impression—which was why she gave up the apartment on West 79th Street and moved to the cabin on the Delaware. The complete incineration she'd witnessed had been her own. And Paul's. She stared into the rubble of the Bethel Tabernacle Church, the "After" shot a century ago, until all she saw was an East Village brownstone.

"They're here for Derry," said Charlie, who took her arm and guided her to the back. "Second Shift never pulled this kind of crowd until Derry came back to town a few weeks ago." It was a downtown crowd—people she'd peg as profs from the branch of the state university, artists, managers. The appeal of Derry Wilson didn't seem to extend to the county, where tastes ran more to Carly Pearce and Morgan Wallen. On two crude risers, the Second Shift Band was tuning up with blares and scales.

At the end of the bar were three booths, the equivalent of box seats at Mazeppa's Ride. Two were taken. Sitting alone at the edge of the third, where a small "Reserved" sign kept other comers at bay, was Derry Wilson, adding up a customer's check and scratching absently at her hairline. Because she was thin, all her joints seemed to come together in lovely, angular ways. Over jeans and a plain white top, she wore a cocktail apron, one hip was raised off the bench, and her legs were outstretched down to her Keds. No vanity, no greed. She looked too hardworking to have so few expectations. One of a legion of women in the wrong town, at the wrong time, with all the wrong men.

Until, maybe, now.

"So," Charlie said to Derry before she noticed him, "what do you hear from Bill Bailey?"

Without looking up, Derry shook her head slowly. "That man," she started to smile, "that man has stood me up one time too many. I'm not asking 'round for him anymore." Her pencil rolled off the table as she gave Charlie a quick hug and turned to Marian. It was all the same smile, no less light or warm than the one she had for Charlie. Wiping her hand on her apron, she thrust it out and shook Marian's hand, then waved them both into the booth while she untied her apron and slipped a scribbled check at the next table where an older couple was sitting. "Maud, Donald, you all are staying, aren't you?"

After a few bluff protests that they wouldn't think of leaving and was she doing any Hoagy Carmichael tonight, she said, well, she'd just have to surprise them, which delighted them no end, and then slid in across from Charlie and Marian.

"Two minutes, Derry." A man dressed in old brown cords and a shapeless green polo shirt patted her back as he passed.

"Okay."

"Hey, Charlie," he called back, setting a watery Scotch down on the top of the battered upright piano.

"Tim."

"My boss." Derry smiled at Marian. "One of my bosses."

"How many have you got?"

Derry signaled to another waitress, holding up two fingers. "Last count, three, including my mother." She looked at them. "Why is it the more jobs you have, the broker you are?" And Marian caught that merry look she'd seen in the snapshot on Charlie's desk.

"Three bosses." Charlie was saying. "Who's the third?"

"Bill Cain."

He sounded surprised. "Bill Cain. Since when?"

"Mm, didn't I mention? This past week," Derry told him. "Days."

"Doing what?"

"Filing, phones, coffee." She raised an eyebrow. "Typing, when there's no one else. Only thing he won't trust me with's the books." Derry folded her arms on the table, and her head dropped into her angular shoulders like she was settling in for a good long gab. "So, Marian, tell me," she said, her cheekbones golden in the dim light, "what do you think of Carthage?" She seemed genuinely unaware of the noise around them.

Marian looked at her helplessly.   Whatever she wanted to say was impossible over the shrill whistles and table thumping. "I like it," she gave up, laughing.

Tim Rinehart leaned over Derry. "The sax just went home sick."

"Steve? Is he okay?"

"Came over him suddenly." The big man jerked his head toward the back.

"Oh, I hope he's okay."

Rinehart's face got tight. "So we're a bit screwed for a sax tonight."

She beamed at him. "No worries, Timmy. I can cover."

He briefly set his hand on her head, nodded at Charlie and Marian, and lumbered back to the stage.

Heads were turned toward a large, square wall clock in '50s kitsch. When the minute hand moved across the swanny chest of a former Miss Rheingold—9:30—Rinehart cued his singer with lusty arpeggios.

Derry covered Marian's wrist with her hand. "I'm sorry," she had to yell. "Have breakfast with me tomorrow, seven-thirty, okay? Charlie, tell her where. We can talk then." Then she smoothed her fingertips across her eyebrows and framed her face with her hands. "Well, Levitan, what do you say?"

His face lost expression. It was what Marian called his journalism face, a cross between hanging judge and cooling steel. His eyes were on Derry. "You'll do," he said quietly. Derry pushed up her sleeves and leaped onto the riser. Pulling the mike from its stand, she thanked the clapping crowd twice and sang "Stompin' at the Savoy" as a duet with Tim Rinehart, pushing the song through easy swing and lengthy scat. Bony, plain dressing, no makeup, three-job Derry, with her short auburn hair and coppery voice.

What made it such powerful showmanship was the baldness of it. No set, no costumes, no choreography. During "'Tain't So, Honey, 'Tain't So," an old Jack Teagarden number with a bouncy trombone solo, Derry turned, and Marian expected the song to come at Charlie. Instead, winking, Derry sang to her.

Marian bit the inside of her lip.

Charlie was inscrutable.

Occasionally, while Derry sipped her ice water, the Second Shift Band lumbered into some arthritic Dixieland. The crowd was tolerant, using the time to visit the john and order more drinks. Finally, the music stopped, the crowd hushed, and Derry replaced the mike. She made one small gesture toward Charlie, placed her hands at her sides, and sang an *a cappella* "Star Dust" that was breathtaking. She looked like a twelve-year-old girl, singing hosannas in the church choir. Her gaze was fixed and distant, and each perfect note was a revelation of feeling.

When it was over, there was a stricken silence, followed by the slow confusion of clapping that happens when people know they're in the presence of something special. Tim Rinehart pulled Derry over to the piano to go over some music, pursued by Maud and Donald, and a few others. The drummer stretched. The clarinetist tried a complicated riff, then gave up and went in search of a beer.

Charlie sat back, his fingers drumming the table.

Marian felt like she had been drop-kicked into a zone where she didn't recognize anything.

Time to go.

She had to sleep.

"Charlie, I'm ready to go."

He nodded, and without a word, they slid into their coats. When he went over to Derry, whispered something, and gave her a quick kiss, Marian turned away to pull on her gloves, and for the first time since she had met Charlie Levitan when they were fifteen, she felt like a distant second. He led the way through the slow-moving crowd, which was fine with Marian because she suddenly felt like all her limbs were prosthetics. Charlie was gone. Swept away in the Flood of Ought Two, the Drought of Twenty-Three, and the missed opportunities for love over the past few years. Charlie was gone, and all that was left was for him to tell her once and for all. When was he going to do it? How hard could it be?

Chapter Fourteen

When they got through the crowd blocking their way to the front door, Charlie seemed completely congested with some emotion she couldn't identify, and they collided with a man built like a concrete pylon in a sheepskin jacket. He had bristly gray hair and a face with vertical folds in the tough skin. Under an overhanging brow, his brown eyes were sharp. "Evening, Charlie," he said, reaching for the door. Charlie introduced her briefly to Hank Khartoukian, "the County Sheriff," he added.

Shaking hands with Khartoukian, Marian discovered, was like inserting her hand into a boxing glove. They walked out together into the cold night, and she glanced at the frost on the windowpanes of Mazeppa's Ride. In the draft, a wave of snow rose around their feet. She shuddered. The sheriff settled a bulky fur cap around his ears, nodded at them, and set off up the street. Marian was grateful not to have to make small talk.

Charlie scratched his forehead. "Well," he exhaled, "what do you think?"

She clamped her arms around herself. "Nice place."

His lips thinned out. "I mean Derry."

So this was it, out here in the cold. "Derry," she said. "Derry's wonderful."

He looked past her down the street, squinting at nothing. "You mean her voice."

"Her voice, yes." She squinted in the other direction and tried to fill in the blanks. "And probably the rest of her, too. I only just met her, Charlie." She gave him a quick smile.

"So you don't like her." It was his journalism face. "Is that what you're saying?"

Oh, man. "Charlie, don't put words in my mouth."

"Don't avoid the question."

She felt lost. Couldn't he tell? "What's the question?"

"See?"

Her voice rose. "My God, you're nasty."

"Nasty? You call that nasty?"

"You heard me." This wasn't going well. "All these years, I never saw it."

"All these years, you never saw anything."

She snapped. "I see you're in love with a saloon singer."

They grabbed each other's lapels and pushed themselves up against the window, where Marian found herself a foot away from a darts player, who was watching them from the inside, horrified. "Is that what you think she is, a saloon singer?"

Marian hit a patch of ice and started to slip, pulling Charlie down. He yanked her up under her arms, and she struggled between fighting him and clinging to him. "She's terrific, though why she'll have an asshole like you," she grunted, "is beyond me."

"So you do like her." He got his footing, and they let each other go, panting.

"Right now, Charlie," Marian said, moving out of the way of the two couples who had just come out of Mazeppa's Ride, "right now, I like her a whole hell of a lot better than I like you. Shit," she said with feeling, stepping back, "I never met a man who needs more approval around a woman he takes to bed than you. It's like you're conferring a goddamned knighthood."

He looked stony. "I don't need your approval."

"Then why are you asking for it?"

"I don't need your approval," he yelled. "All right?"

"You don't know what you need."

"At least it isn't you."

Marian heard herself gasp. "Well," she said, "won't that be a refreshing change?"

The trouble with exit lines, she thought, turning away from Charlie, the trouble with exit lines is that then you have to exit. She made it down

Mission Street to the center of town, fueled by something that felt like pride, which was hard to pull off in a headwind on an icy sidewalk. If she didn't know better, she'd swear she'd been knocking back tequilas straight up, and with her luck, she'd get hauled in for being drunk and disorderly without enjoying the benefits of either.

Star Dust, like hell.

Not this galaxy.

A year after their college graduation, Charlie was doing journalism at Columbia and Marian was working days at Macmillan and taking some graduate courses at Hunter College at night. They heard once from the FBI about Paul, wanted in connection with a grenade hurled during a demonstration against the war in Afghanistan at the Lockheed Martin Building in Bethesda—a guard was killed—and twice from Paul himself before the final time. "They tell me you're still running with scissors," Charlie said into the phone when the call came.

"Who?"

"Two gentlemen in nice suits with skinny ties," Charlie told him. "I don't like your friends."

"The gentlemen in nice suits?"

"Them—and the Pashtun for Idiots Club. I don't like any of them. Myself included. I've got premarital problems you wouldn't believe," and he went on to explain how the shy Russian major with crooked teeth proved to have the tenacity of a mongoose. "Face it, Norberto, we're never going to get out of Afghanistan, so why don't you just pack up your fatigues and learn a nice trade?" When Paul said something about the disenfranchised underclass, Charlie handed her the phone. "He's all yours."

She made what she thought was a date.

When Paul didn't show up at the Guggenheim, she walked over to Lexington to catch the train. Halfway down the steps she felt a hand on her arm. It was Paul, wearing a shiny blue Yankees jacket. "Take me home," was all he said. Home those days was the apartment on 36th near First Avenue she was minding for a friend out of town during hay fever season. Once inside he peeled the top three layers of his clothing before he stopped at his jeans. She felt shocked by the scar that made his chest look like a contour map of Canada. "Is it all right?"

She didn't have the heart to tell him she was seeing the ad executive who handled the Lipton soup account. Instead, she had once more the old sovereign Paul feeling—it wasn't love, it wasn't pity—more like an overriding sense of participation in something time limited. "Yes," she said. Sometime later, after they had made love—still in other people's beds—seeing each other only by the city lights and slab of moon through the open drapes, he rolled on top of her. She lay very still, feeling the livid map that no longer resembled skin pressing into her. Crushed against her breastbone was the reality of his life.

"Chemicals," was all he had said about it when she asked. Tightening his forearms against her shoulders, his thumbs smoothed back the hair from her forehead, and he shook his head slowly.

"Paul, what is it?" She wanted him to say something to make her believe he could surface, do some time, and become a cabinetmaker with a mortgage.

"I don't even know," he shuddered, rolling away.

"Charlie says you need a shrink."

He looked at her over his shoulder. "Charlie needs a shrink," he said. "I need—" he snorted softly, "new skin."

Chapter Fifteen

Damn Charlie.

She sobbed once and drew her sleeve across her face. At the corner, a car swung alongside, easing to a stop in a spray of snow. "Need a lift?" Khartoukian swung open the door on the passenger side.

"Sure," Marian said with a weak smile, "thanks." How much of the argument had he heard? She sat hugging herself stiffly, grateful for the noisy heater—although the only thing it really seemed to be warming up were the smells of a half-smoked corona, an empty bag of barbecue chips at her feet, and some lime aftershave. With one sheep-skinned arm draped loosely over the steering wheel, Khartoukian sat looking at her, like he was trying to figure out just how many local ordinances she was breaking.

"One beer," Marian crossed her heart, "I swear."

His chuckle sounded more like a grunt. "I had two."

"Maybe I'd better drive," Marian said, smiling. So was he. Although in that face, she thought, a smile looked more like an interesting geoformation.

"Where to?" He flung a battered briefcase into the back seat.

"The Briars."

"I'd have pegged you for a Days Inn sort of gal." Oh, great. Like the evening wasn't already as sour as yesterday's socks. She looked sidelong at his deadpan face as he shifted into drive and flipped the fan to Hi, producing more noise and even less heat. "You the out-of-town lady friend Charlie mentions?"

Accent on the *out-of-town*. My, her old friend seemed to be enjoying quite a reputation. Very different from freshman year when Charlie decided the only way around his family's veiled questions about his love life was to become a Zen Buddhist, which lasted a term and a half. "Out-of-town's the only thing you got right," she said, looking out of the window as they turned down Main.

On the seat between them were a couple of neckties, a battery-op shaver, and a crumpled bath towel. Marian eyed him. "You live out of your car?"

"Only when I'm entertaining," Khartoukian said, wiping the windshield with his forearm. "Otherwise, I've got a place on the West side."

"Married?"

"Wife's dead six years now," he said. "Two kids, both grown. You?"

Marian shook her head. "None of that."

"What brings you to—"

"'Our fair city'?"

Khartoukian checked the rearview mirror. "Wade County's where I've got a job I don't mind doing. I leave the illusions to others," he said. "What about you?"

"Me?" She closed her eyes. "Mostly, I do investigative work for the Artifacts Authentication Agency out of New York."

"Getting the goods on cheats and scammers?"

"Pretty much."

"So you deal in illusions."

"Come on," she scoffed. "Crime isn't real?"

"Crime's real." He eased the Impala around a corner where the only source of brightness was a row of streetlights. "Reasons aren't."

Marian was quiet.

"And you're here," he went on, "why?"

"You know the Mission House has been nominated for National Historic Landmark status?" she said, leaning back.

"Ah, right."

"The committee wants me to get to the bottom of the animosity."

"Clock ticking?"

"On their patience." Marian went on, "Then Bella Murphy gave me a job."

"Ah," said Khartoukian softly, "now this I didn't know."

Marian turned to look at him. "What do you think about the body?"

He shrugged. "Shame."

"She sized him up. You don't think it's much of a story, do you?"

"Not the way you mean it." He pulled the car easily out of a slight skid.

"So you don't think there's a crime?"

He considered. "Bella Murphy's making it her business."

"No, she's making it mine."

"I see," he said slowly. "You interest me."

"Why? No crime, no story." In just four city blocks, the streetlights were left behind them, and Marian stared down the street where whatever the dark winter night held suddenly seemed sweet.

He pulled the car over to the curb. Inside The Briars was a distant light. "No story."

Damn his equivocations. "You're saying, then, there's a crime."

"One or two."

She was watching his face. "But it's out of your jurisdiction."

"There are some things I uphold," Khartoukian said, finally, reaching across her to open the car door, "besides the law. Be careful getting out."

A moral relativist for a county sheriff. She could see his campaign posters: *Retain Khartoukian. It's the Right Thing to Do. Depending on How You Look at It.* Still, for five blessed minutes in Khartoukian's motel on wheels, she had forgotten Charlie. That alone was worth the price of admission.

Marian slipped upstairs to her room. What with the television on somewhere at the back of the house, the Hausers wouldn't hear her. All she wanted was to float herself into oblivion on the raft she called her bed. Marian picked up a pink note that had been slipped under her door. It was from Barb Hauser. *Marian: din Fri Bella M's 7:30 bring Charlie. Real "party"—inc Girard, us, you 2—maybe coulibiac. B. exc cook, trust me.* Well, Marian thought, at least I've got the dogs to look forward to.

But tomorrow, she'd have to invite Charlie.

She heaved a noisy sigh.

All the effects of Khartoukian were wearing off—the corona, the chips, the citrus aftershave. We return you now to our regular programming: tight diaphragm and heart palpitations. Charlie. There isn't a moment he can ever just let me have without his infernal interference. Not the loss of Paul. Not her own refusal at the cabin. Not Derry's singing that scoops and swaddles. *Well, Levitan, what do you say?*

You'll do.

Make yourself see it, Marian. When they'd said those words before. Be the witness they didn't have. There, in the improbable daylight, at her place. Charlie, with his hands in his pockets, as wide-eyed as a springbok in the Kalahari, and Derry, merrily mourning her electric bill as she pulled her top over her lustrous hair, asking him if he knows where she can get a good secondhand car, cheap. Charlie, bemused. The self-reliant Derry, slipping off her jeans—*ever hear of a jazz great out of St. Louis called Eva LaPierre?* You'd swear she's chatting it up with her pals in the girls' locker room, where naked is just another outfit.

Well, Levitan, she says finally, *what do you say?* And what he wants to say is something about his appendix scar, the Calvinist concept of grace, Hannah's rock collection, and maybe, Marian. Maybe even Marian. But in the age of minimalism, what he says is, *You'll do.* And he never meant it as something small.

Chapter Sixteen

Toast, eggs over easy, hash browns, grapefruit juice, coffee she'd no sooner sip than Cindy Wilson would descend on her with a refill. Only it was about five times the amount of food she normally consumed. "Can I get you some oatmeal?" Derry's mother looked positively pained, like she'd been derelict in some matter of hospitality.

Marian held up a hand. "No, really."

"It's Irish." Apparently, the breakfast equivalent of enriched uranium.

"I couldn't possibly."

"Very nourishing," she said balefully.

"I can't."

The woman was relentless. "A small bowl."

"Fine."

Jubilant, Cindy clattered the coffee pot into place on the warmer and disappeared into the kitchen. Marian turned to Derry, who sat beside her at the counter, her chin in her hand. "It's the only way to get rid of her," Derry laughed.

"I figured."

Cindy Wilson's coffee shop was in the block of old two-story buildings on the part of Main Street near Cold Spring River—a doughnut's throw from what Marian figured was Jack Girard's grain elevator on the riverbank. Arriving at seven-thirty, she discovered the place had been dishing up eggs and hotcakes since six.

Over the sounds of a brisk breakfast trade came the clangs of steam heat. The regulars seemed to be cops and wizened locals in John Deere caps. The shop was light and warm, and on a bleak winter morning, there could be nothing better, even with the faint smells of disinfectant and bacon grease. Derry, in a purple mock turtleneck and navy cords, sat on a counter stool with one leg tucked up underneath her.

Scattered around the shop were the kind of touches that personalize a place and keep it from ever growing beyond a certain point. There was a crucifix on the wall behind the cash register, sprouting spiky palms. There was a framed Irish Prayer—"May the Road Rise Up to Meet You"—nailed to the wall over a booth. At the back was a latch hook wall hanging of a demonic gremlin ("Ma likes crafts," Derry explained. "That one's a boxer pup"). Some bowling trophies took up space on a shelf over the stacked water glasses. There was a framed fiver so old it could have been foreign currency, and a Health Department license.

And photos taped to the corners of the long, scratched mirror over the counter. A school shot of Derry from maybe twenty years ago, wearing a white headband, looking goofy and confident. Derry from thirty years ago, in pigtails, looking goofier and even more confident. A man, smiling into the summer sun, cradling a carp. A dark-haired boy in a Boy Scout uniform. Others. Cindy herself, high-waisted and energetic, half out of every shot, always holding a dish towel.

"I came back to Carthage a month ago," Derry was saying, "after ten years on the road."

"Ten years."

"Singing. Hey, Hal," she slid a small glass pot down the counter. "You look like a man who could use some ketchup." Hal, who sat hunched over a platter of scrambled eggs, was a man near retirement age in jeans and a stiff new Kenworth cap. The right side of his face was pulled down with palsy. He jerked a hand at Derry and said much obliged.

Before bed last night, Marian shuffled again through all the letters in the Parks Service file on the Mission House. Nothing from any Wilson. Still, she had to try. "You got back just in time for the battle over the Mission House."

"The what?"

"Mission House."

"Oh. Right."

"Hot and nasty."

Derry's smile was rueful. "It's nothing to me, Marian, that old place. I've got troubles of my own."

"I understand."

Derry brightened. "But you can ask Tim. He knows everybody, and he's been here since the pigs ate my brother." When Marian looked at her, alarmed, Derry laughed. "Donkey's years."

"Got it. What about your third boss?"

"Bill?" Marian nodded. "Sorry, Marian. I haven't been with him long enough to hear anything worth repeating."

Marian sat back. She'd have to try Tim. Then: "Was it good on the road?" If they talked about road life, maybe she could get through breakfast and then go.

Derry thought it over. "The first five years," she said. "Maybe more. While I still thought I had a career." While she still bought the lame dreams of the other band members. Nights made jumpy with glib promises from vague contacts, the word "demo" spoken so reverently you'd swear it had something to do with drugs, sex, or God. Only the "demo" proved more elusive than any of those other things. Days, starting out, that went from kinetic eating, phoning, and rehearsing stoked by enough adrenalin sufficient to fuel the space program, to days, finally, that felt like long, Saharan stretches unrelieved by change.

She found herself in Amarillo long enough to get a post office box. In Carson City, long enough to move into an efficiency hotel and get to a first-name basis with the produce man at the IGA. In Oxnard long enough to serve as recording secretary for the PTA at Andy's school.

"Andy?" A new name.

"My boy. Who," she raised her voice, "is going to be late for school if he isn't out of here in the next—" she glanced over at the Pepsi-Cola clock, "five seconds."

So Charlie was in love with a single mom. Did Hannah know Andy? Did they talk on Snapchat about cyberbullying? What the hell had happened, Marian wondered, when she wasn't looking? And that, Charlie would point out, was the problem: she never looked. She felt deflated. Not even hearing about the best place for burgers in Oxnard was enough to take her mind off an emptiness that was growing.

From the kitchen came scuffling sounds. "Okay, okay," called the boy, shouldering his way through the kitchen door, Cindy tucking a musical instrument case under his arm. In her other hand was a bowl of Irish oatmeal.

"Zip up," Derry said.

"Ma." At least his long-suffering tone sounded affectionate.

"Zip up. Here." While she closed his coat, he stood tolerantly, flipping back the dark lanky hair from his forehead. Like his mother, the boy had good-natured features, with those frank eyes and curving mouth. A laughing face, but without Derry's bones. Or, if they were her bones, on him, they had more flesh. His would be a lifelong struggle between Domino's Lava Cake and the forces of good.

After she introduced him to Marian, calling him Andy Wilson, Derry patted the boy toward the door. With strict instructions—no trading his sandwich for Cheetos, keep his eyes on his own paper during the spelling test, and come straight home after school—Andy set off to the clatter of sleigh bells mounted on the front door.

"Can I get a ride to work?" Derry asked, swinging a leg over her stool.

Marian sagged. "Sorry," she said. "I walked."

"It's okay. I'll hitch." After Cindy urged the bus, which Derry said didn't go anywhere near Bill Cain's, she condemned to eternal perdition the habit of hitchhiking. Then they argued over whether Derry did, in fact, know everybody in Carthage, as she claimed. And, finally, whether knowing somebody by sight was sufficient proof against rapists, perverts, and—the older woman said darkly—"worse."

To Marian, it had the weary sound of old battles. She drifted, looping her spoon through the steaming oatmeal Cindy had set down. "How old is Andy?"

"He's nine." Derry leaned closer, her bright eyes roving Marian's face. A strange feeling. Sexy without intent.

"Were you married?"

"No, never was." With a bland regret as though she was asked whether she'd ever been Homecoming Queen.

"Andy's father?"

Derry unfolded her hands. "A guy on the road." It was a deliberate answer: this, she was saying, is all you need to know. Nothing more about the relationship, if there was one. Or the occasion, if there wasn't. "When I left Carthage," Derry went on, sharing the oatmeal Marian had pushed between them, "I left for good. People kept telling me I had a big-city kind of talent."

"You do."

Derry laughed, as tolerant as Andy getting his coat zipped. "Well, okay." If you say so. "Only I figured out finally I had just small-town luck." She landed up with Andy. And landed up singing for a bunch of regulars in Oxnard and chairing PTA Bake Sales. Hell, she thought, she could be doing this back in Carthage and sharing expenses with her ma. Be good for all of them. And Andy could have his gran around, not to mention some real friends. The most he'd learn from the band would be how to make beer come out his nose and moan about what a sorry-ass thing life is.

"What's it like being back?"

"A blessing," said Cindy, pulling a pen from her bright blond hair to tally up a customer's check. There were jagged lines of ink on her scalp. "A real blessing."

Derry licked the spoon, front and back. "It's been good. I met Charlie right off, and that was nice. Only, what with working and singing and taking care of Andy, I haven't had any time really for the old-timers. Family friends. School friends."

"Namely?"

"Oh, Toby Mainwaring, Polly Gundersen."

The happy potter. "There must be others."

"There's Jack," Cindy put in.

"Right."

"Girard?" Marian asked. "You went to school together?"

"No, he's older, but our daddies used to work together at MCG."

"The difference being," Cindy laughed, "his daddy owned it."

"Part owned it."

"Even so."

"Still," Derry said, "the Girards were always pretty regular."

"Even Elinor," Cindy said, her eyes distant. "Jack's mother. What a queen," added Cindy, with a nod from Derry. "What a sin."

"A sin?"

The woman stared at a bent spoon as though it held the secrets of the universe. "Dying like that."

Like what?

"Heart." Cindy wrinkled her nose and refilled Marian's cup.

Derry had a thought. "It was Jack who taught me how to drive," she nodded to Marian. "Once when he was home on leave."

Marian pushed away her bowl. Here, she realized, are excellent sources of information: long-time residents, natural watchers, no apparent personal agendas. "What about the Murphys?"

Cindy lowered her head. "Also a fine family." Her blue eyes narrowed like truth and history were an eye chart, and she needed some specs. "Though we never really knew them. Not well. Not to speak to them, you know. They always held themselves—" Here she made an airy gesture, "off."

"Aloof," Marian suggested.

"That's it." She squeezed Marian's arm, pleased. "Aloof."

"I used to babysit Ben and Bella," Derry put in. "Before the accident."

"A real sin, I can tell you that." Apparently, the really great sinners were God, fate, and the forces of the universe.

"And afterwards, that one summer. Before Bella went away to school."

"When was that?" Cindy wondered.

"You were in County Londonderry, Ma, burying Great Gran and yelling at the rest of the family."

"That," she frowned, remembering, "took weeks."

Marian felt mischievous. "And now there's Jack and Bella." Derry had no reaction, but she was a woman who didn't question liaisons. They were a happy commonplace, like coupons in the Wednesday newspaper.

Not Cindy Wilson, who raised a pale hand. "Enough said," she said, her face solemn. And again: "Enough said." Although, it occurred to Marian, on that particular subject, none of them had said a thing.

Chapter Seventeen

Marian took out her phone about fifty feet away from the entrance to the Carthage *Toiler.* What she should do is just go on inside and make peace with Charlie, only this way, she decided, all she had to control was her voice. Yes, this was better, just as long as he couldn't see her out of his office window.

She stepped closer to the building. "Sorry about last night," Marian began.

"Yeah, so am I."

"We should talk."

"Yeah, we should."

"You sound tired." And distant.

Why did it all seem so bland?

"Not tired, really, just—flat," he said. "Did you get home all right?"

Marian smiled. "Khartoukian gave me a lift."

"Oh." A fillip of interest.

"I like him."

"So do I."

On that, at least, they could agree. Her five minutes with Khartoukian was one of those post-argument safeties—something completely unprovocative—for which she was always grateful. She thought of another. "Bella Murphy's having a dinner party Friday night. She's invited us."

"You and me?"

A ping of irritation. "Right. You and me. The two of us."

"Does she think we're a couple?"

"I have no idea." She worked hard to stay neutral.

"Sounds fine."

"Being a couple?"

She could hear him smile. "Going to dinner."

"Less work, huh?" Her voice was quiet.

"You got it."

Marian chuckled. On the whole, she had to agree. Last night, Charlie told her, he went back into Mazeppa's Ride—Derry and the Second Shift Band did another set, a short one—and he drove her home. Must have been late, Marian commented, trying to adjust to this new topic of a love life that didn't include her. Not late enough, Charlie said humorously, his voice pulled out of shape, like he was rubbing his face. Then she mentioned the morning at Cindy's greasy spoon but found all her bright words clattering to the floor of their conversation.

"Good," was all Charlie said in a disconnected sort of way.

After they hung up, Marian tapped in another number. Bella picked up after the fourth ring. In the background was Vivaldi's "Winter," in all its lovely urgency, which Bella turned down. "Charlie and Marian are coming," she told another voice, inquiring. Girard's, Marian thought. Then came distant barking. The voices, the Vivaldi, the throaty dogs, the offers of dinner and—sometime tomorrow—a run with the Labs. Marian accepted it all.

Dominion, was what she thought. Some place, familiar to her somehow, of gentle powers, quite possibly her own. A place she felt herself moving toward with no resistance. *And death shall have no dominion.* What could death have to do with Vivaldi and the promise of something called coulibiac? What could death have to do with a voice dark and quiet like a banished king's? There were fifty-eight hours until Friday evening, and she was unafraid. But for the life of her, Marian thought as she gripped the phone long after she'd hung up; she didn't know why any of it felt important for her to know.

Chapter Eighteen

Marian waited for Bill Cain in the foyer of the Wade Lake Country Club, a sprawling, one-story clubhouse built in the forties. He was late, so she scrutinized the Audubon prints and sucked a few pastel pink mints. Then she signed the guest book illegibly and wandered back to the narrow window, where the stiff lace curtain sported a pattern of ducks. When she paid attention to the faint Muzak piped in overhead, she realized it was a hundred and one strings doing "By the Time I Get to Phoenix" as a waltz. She watched a honey-colored Audi pull into the parking lot and come to a demure stop in a reserved space.

Bill Cain emerged. Green pants and white shoes, Charlie had said. On the golf course, maybe, but not today. Already he was not what she expected, a cross between a tasteless opportunist and a bit of an ass. Charlie had not prepared her, but then, why should that come as a surprise? What Marian saw in Bill Cain was the first sign of affluence since she'd arrived in Carthage two days ago. Long, camel hair coat. Cashmere muffler. Leather driving gloves. Tassel loafers. If he was an opportunistic ass, he was one with an eye for threads. And wheels. Suddenly, as he entered the foyer, Marian felt something shift in her understanding of the struggle over the Mission House. It was less silly—and less gentlemanly.

"Marian." Cain held her hand in both of his. As if bundling her right away into his camp was as much for her own good as his. For in the Cain camp, she could be assured of the psychic equivalents of Jacuzzis and Italian leather. She would be schooled in the righteousness of demolition and yellow brick straight out of the fifties. She would hear of the true pleasures of the Cain flesh: eighteen holes under par, Cincinnati sashimi, weekly massage, and silk monogrammed boxers—this last reserved for his dear wife of thirty-two years, Corliss, for he was a good Presbyterian.

An earnest waiter named Ronald took their coats and suggested something Marian didn't quite hear about halibut. "Ms. Warner would like to see the club first," Cain smiled, "before we sit." Ronald, who appeared to be cursing himself for prematurely suggesting a table and being unable to name whatever substance the halibut was stuffed with, disappeared. "Let me show you the place," Bill Cain said in that reverent voice the wealthy use whenever they mention one of their investments. They were only halfway across the parlor when he mentioned that, since he's been a trustee, the club has been completely refurbished.

At French doors overlooking flagstone terraces leading down to Wade Lake, the largest natural lake in southern Ohio, Cain had his hand lightly on her shoulder, pointing out something on the far shore. His gray hair, side-parted and sprayed, contrasted with his black eyebrows and light brown eyes. She spent a few minutes trying to figure out whether he dyed his eyebrows black or his hair gray, and so as not to make herself crazy, concluded it was natural. He wore tan gabardine pants and an impeccable blue blazer. Suddenly he removed his paisley tie with all the flourish of a strip tease. "Do you mind?"

Ms. Warner would like to see the club first. He had a proprietary way about him that a wooly nitwit of nineteen might find attractive. What Ms. Warner would really like, she wanted to say, is a free lunch and some information. She felt cheered when Ronald showed them to what was apparently Mr. Cain's customary table overlooking the water and pulled out her chair. Half crouching, she gripped the table as Ronald struggled to land her at the table's edge. The result was a lumbering two-step that seemed to last forever. Then, in one of life's more useless gestures, he dropped her heavy green linen napkin in her lap and backed up, happy.

Cain was scrutinizing the wine list like an Allied cryptographer. "Ms. Warner will have the Riesling, Ronald."

"A glass, sir?" Ronald murmured. Marian almost lost it. No, Ronald, a

86

bottle. A case. A truckload.

"Yes, a glass." Like it was a perfectly reasonable question. And, for himself, "the usual." When Ronald departed with a jaunty step, like he was really pretty good at this dang job, Marian and Cain looked at each other. She decided to lead with the battle over the Mission House, saving J.C. Houston for later.

"So, I'm assigned by the National Park Service to look into the hostilities over the nomination of the Mission House for landmark status. With half a dozen letters from you yourself—"

"For starters." He smiled complacently.

"—I thought we could have a discussion."

At that moment, "the usual" came, a martini, which Cain stirred slowly with an impaled cocktail onion. "I don't oppose landmark preservation," he said, sipping and savoring, in words she could tell he'd used before. What he advocates—he moved the martini around in his mouth like mouthwash—is finer discrimination in what we consider landmarks in the first place. "An old hotel, say," he offered, "little better than a rundown bordello."

"The Meers Hotel."

He raised his eyebrows. "The Meers Hotel." A tip of the head. "Correct." She was at risk of becoming his favorite pupil. "A landmark?" He made a face. "Hardly. The place wasn't up to code when it was built. And it didn't improve with age. Buildings," he added, "never do. How's the Riesling?"

"Nice."

"No, Marian, nothing of any consequence happened in the Meers Hotel to make it worth saving. General Pershing didn't sleep in it. Thomas Jefferson didn't die in it. Harriet Tubman didn't hide in it. No treaties or articles of confederation were signed in it. Nothing," said Cain with finality. "So, please," he smiled, "let's not call it a landmark."

He had said all the same things in two or three of his letters. "What about the Mission House? Nearly three hundred years old, the only Jesuit—"

He was shaking his head like a bobblehead doll on the dashboard of a Caddy low-rider. "Pure speculation," he said. "There's no proof." It was an argument, she could tell, that bored him.

"What if there were?"

"Proof? Of what?"

She put on Charlie's journalism face. "That the Mission House was built by Claude de Chardin in 1765, making it—" here she struggled to recall what Alice Lowther had told her, "one of the oldest buildings in the state, and the only historic Jesuit mission in the Northwest Territory."

Cain inhaled, then tipped his head dismissingly. "Then it might be worth moving."

She blinked, surprised. "Moving?"

"To a new site, board by board. A real nuisance, mind you. But it could be moved, out of the downtown area, to a place where the land isn't so valuable."

She said slowly, "But the history didn't happen in the new place. How can you separate the building from the land?"

Cain smacked his lips. "Who've you been talking to, dear? Alice? Sounds like Alice." He motioned to Ronald for the menu.

She kept her voice level. "That would be like taking the Alamo. . . and moving it to—Brooklyn."

"I really don't see the problem."

A sense of place, she wanted to say, but it would have been at the expense of Charlie's journalism face. She stared into her pale wine. What's history but the place where truth and character collide? And sometimes there are buildings and sky and purple gentian, besides, where the many things of life are gathered in a setting. More beautiful than she could say. Not all things need to be useful. Across from her, Bill Cain was ordering—for them both, as usual—the halibut, which Ronald declared was stuffed with stuffing. "Maybe," Marian said, "the Meers Hotel was just beautiful." She looked at her host.

"Beautiful." He shrugged without altering the line of his blazer. "So's the Eagle Mutual Life Insurance Company that I put up on the site. Forget landmark preservation, Marian. Let's talk about landmark creation. That's how I view what it is I do for this town. Venerable," he said, shifting in his chair, "doesn't have to mean old. Let's not worship at the altar of decrepitude."

That, too, found its way into his letters opposing the nomination. Another phrase, she guessed, from what Charlie had warned her was Bill Cain's canned speech.

"I happen to find new construction very beautiful, mainly because it's designed with contemporary use in mind. Handicap access. Elevator banks. Climate control." Cain was piling up nouns. "Open concept office design. Everything for the American worker."

"And consumer."

"Nothing wrong with that."

She stared into her Riesling. She hated Riesling.

"Except a failure of spirit." Careful, Marian.

"How so?"

"Comfort and—" she reached, "nourishment aren't always the same thing."

"I disagree," he said with no bad feeling.

Marian lifted her shoulders. "Maybe a place like the Meers Hotel was beautiful because it endured."

He rolled the cocktail onion around inside his mouth. "The space was being underutilized."

"Maybe we find some comfort in looking at what endures."

"Now you sound like Jack Girard." Minimal scorn. This, too, he bore from long habit. "The Mission House, the grain elevator. Man's so tied up in the past he can't let go of a damn thing, even when he flies in the face of progress."

The battle cry of the moneymaker. "Progress?"

"I make money. That's what I do. I buy land and sell up. I put together deals." He raised his glass to her. "I prosper."

"I see. You mean your own progress," she smiled.

"Partly."

"Jack Girard flies in the face of your own personal progress."

Cain was unprovoked. "And, if you ask me," he said distantly, "his own." The salads arrived on clear glass plates. Ronald bent in front of Marian, holding the peppermill like it was some kind of tiki. When she nodded, he twisted pepper over her plate. Cain declined. "Like his father before him.

Which is why," Cain prodded his greens, "I sold my interest in MCG, finally."

"MCG?" she asked innocently.

"Murphy-Cain-Girard," he chewed. "Construction. John Murphy and Clayton Girard. I was the junior. Then John died, and Clayton and I tried to hang on, but it was no good. For me, mostly." With that, he fingered his way through the breadbasket. "Prisons and highways and official outhouses started to wear a little thin."

"Bella Murphy's asked me to look into what happened at the Mission House two days ago."

"Ah, the scuffle. Rocker and Rice are good lads, just overzealous."

"No, the dead man."

"Yes," he got a faraway look, rotating his glass, "that was inconvenient."

Marian nearly laughed. "For him as well."

"Not so much for me, mind you. Mysterious death? Just one more reason to bring the old eyesore down."

Just how badly did Bill Cain want that?

"Any ideas?"

"About—?"

She spread her hands. "Why? Who?"

"Some bum, a free crash pad." Bill Cain tucked into the fingerling potatoes next to the ghastly white halibut.

Marian set down her fork. "The dead man was locked in."

"Nonsense. The windows at the back are always unlocked." He made a swashbuckling move with his knife. "School kids have been crawling into the godforsaken place for years."

"Are you saying J.C. Houston locked himself in?"

"I'm saying I couldn't give a good goddamn. In two months, we'll be breaking ground there for Great Seal Power & Light. You're wasting your time. So's Girard. Although if John Murphy's little girl is writing you a check—"

"She isn't."

"—I can understand you need to run up the meter." He eyed her conspiratorially. "Although you may want to look up the term conflict of interest."

"My work for Bella is pro bono."

Unmoved, Cain shot her a skeptical look, then held up his empty glass at Ronald, who got the reproach pretty quickly and disappeared. "John Murphy was always throwing money at lost causes, too. Not a sterling quality in a business partner. Part of the reason I eventually sold out."

"To Clayton." Marian was trying to piece it together.

"Jack."

"After Clayton died."

"Died? Who said he died?"

Isn't that what Bella said? "He had a stroke—"

"That's right, and he's been in a nursing home for a couple of years. Out of the county somewhere," Cain said. "As good as dead, from what I hear." No, Cain explained, he sold out to Jack roughly eight years ago. Clayton couldn't meet his price but wanted the company to stay in the family, and Jack was agreeable. He came across with the money more to oblige his father than anything else. Why, he wasn't even in Carthage then, having set himself up way the hell out in Colorado. He had no interest in having a hand in the daily management of the company, so Clayton went along in charge. Cain got out, Clayton got more security, and Jack made a decent investment. Everyone came away happy.

"Then Clayton had a stroke."

Cain nodded. "The son came back, naturally. He had my fifty percent already. Then about a year and a half ago, he went into court and had his father declared incompetent."

"So the company—"

"Is his."

Marian sat back. What she wanted to know was why. Consider the possibility, Marian, that Jack Girard came home, fell in love, and needed a job—and, along the way, became the sole source of discomfort in the life of Bill Cain. "Why didn't he sell it outright," she said, "considering he had a life out west somewhere?" Cain was twirling his fork, attentive. "And hadn't shown any interest in MCG up to that point?"

"You'd have to ask him," Cain said abruptly. *Family matters,* Jack Girard had told her. Were these the family matters he meant? "Maybe he's attached to the old man," Cain mused.

"Could he have found a buyer?"

"For MCG?" Cain asked. "I'd have bought it."

"You?" Marian speared whatever hadn't been peppered. "You didn't want half of it eight years ago."

"You're right." He pointed a cherry tomato at her. "I didn't."

"So why would you want both halves of the company two years ago? Or, for that matter," here she took a chance, "now?"

"Eight years ago, I didn't know what I know now."

"Which is?"

"That I'd be willing to pay a lot of money to get rid of the son of a bitch," he said with a tight smile, motioning to Ronald to clear for dessert. Over decaf and a rubbery flan, Marian asked Bill Cain about the last restoration of the Mission House. He was a perfect source: a lifer in Carthage, old enough to recall the event, sharp enough to pull up some names for her.

Names over thirty years old. Mags Oldham did the roofing—this he recalled because he and Oldham had been classmates—Seamus Wilson the carpentry—Wilson went on to work for years for MCG, during the glory days—and Connie Hughes the masonry. Hughes…. At that moment, Marian felt like leaping around the Wade Lake Country Club. Instead, she asked Bill Cain how she could get in touch with those workers.

"Dead," he said, jiggling his coffee cup, "all dead or gone." She felt deflated. When she went on to ask him who had hired the workers, paid out disbursements, that sort of thing, Cain looked around the club dining room, empty now except for Ronald setting fresh places. "It must have been the Wade County Historical Society," he said finally, blotting his lips carefully on his napkin. "There's no one else."

Marian noticed his fingernails were buffed, filed, and polished. She had a strong prejudice against men who paid more attention to personal grooming than she did. Bill Cain, she could tell, was a product lovingly tended every night. Eyeshade. Hair net. Bidet. All after the obligatory fifteen-minute exercise in "marital relations" with Corliss, getting through it with thoughts of Derry Wilson or Ronald or his next dividend. It bore, in Marian's imagination, a strong resemblance to a dead man's float. And was an act with much less *frisson* for Bill Cain than the possibility of putting the screws to Jack Girard.

Chapter Nineteen

Oh, no, don't tell me, did I go and forget your books back at The Briars? What a cluck. Standing in the entrance foyer of the Wade County Historical Society, Marian promised to be back soon and watched Alice Lowther disappear with a full wastepaper basket. When the other woman was out of sight, she deftly lifted the key ring from Lowther's Louis Vuitton tote. As long as Alice Lowther didn't suddenly have to lock up, all would be well.

Back inside the Volvo, Marian flipped through the keys on the Ohio State Buckeyes ring. Safe deposit box keys, padlock key, and a key that looked a lot like the one Bella had used to open up the front door at the Mission House. Since she couldn't picture needing to make any clandestine visits to the place, Marian let it go. Then she hoofed it to Alpha Lock Service, three doors up from The Gleaner, where she handed the owner two Keil keys with a smile. Surely one of them had to open the Wade County Historical Society, just in case she needed to take the investigation up a notch, and the other Lowther's house on West Fourth Street.

Marian drove over to Hopewell Middle School, where she idled, waiting for Hannah. Keys-While-U-Wait. Life should be just that simple. Tired of replaying the fight with Charlie, she picked up the issue of the *Toiler* she'd taken from his garage the night before and skimmed the Ardizzone piece. It mentioned the difficulty of funding further excavation of the local prehistoric Indian mounds. It mentioned the difficulty of funding a proposed renovation of the old canal bed or a restoration of the cache of Charles Brockden Brown first editions found water damaged in a barn sold at sheriff's auction.

On the Mission House, the piece mentioned its nomination for Historic Landmark status, and included a few quotes, two by Alice Lowther. In the first, she offered Chardin's letter of intent as the single most persuasive evidence authenticating the Mission House. In the second, she upbraided Carthage as the kind of community that supports a local demolition derby as a "sporting event" while failing to support a nearly three-hundred-year-old historic landmark like the Mission House. From Girard, they got a Churchill quote that must have furrowed a lot of brows at Cindy's coffee shop that morning. And from Bella, as head of S.O.S., came grand, slippery words like "fiscal challenge" and "historic obligation" that left readers with a sense that they got the point when, in fact, they couldn't tell you what the bejeezus it was.

In a related piece on an inside page was a small feature story on Alice Lowther, who was one of only two Ohio recipients of the prestigious Nelson Markworth Award for Lifetime Commitment to Local History. The award recognized Lowther's "unstinting efforts" to publicize the historic attractions of Carthage and Wade County, coordinate interstate exhibitions of historic artifacts, and support landmark preservation.

Marian was impressed. Next to the piece was a three-quarter shot of Alice herself, her face twisted in a close-lipped smile. She stood alongside the display case containing the Chardin document, and in her eyes, Marian saw a peculiar vanity that was hard to define. How could the woman be so successful in all these other instances, and yet so clueless about how to win public support for the one project that may mean the most to her—namely, getting the Mission House named a National Historic Landmark? What explains it? Why the Mission House? And why the ineptitude? Marian sat back, watching Hannah approach. Most likely, Lowther was just out of her element, intimidated by the federal agency part of things.

Hannah flung open the car door, dragged down by a Lululemon backpack loaded with binders and textbooks. "Hi."

"Hi. Just throw it all in the back."

Hannah got in and registered about a minute's worth of halfhearted complaints. She was never talking to someone named Scott again, although she wouldn't say why. They canceled the class talent show she was working on, although she wouldn't say who. And Waggedorn, the science teacher, has revealed some diabolical new torment, although she wouldn't say what. When Marian asked her what she meant, Hannah merely looked out the window and muttered something about floppy frogs, the assistant principal, and an unpunished foul during basketball. Suddenly cheerful, she turned to Marian. "So what's the plan?"

"You're the decoy."

"The decoy." Her eyes widened.

"It's your job to keep the head of the Historical Society busy."

Hannah sniffed. "Old Alice?"

"Right," Marian said. "Old Alice." Dreading the day when some twelve-year-old somewhere might refer to her as Old Marian, like it was part of the name. "The plan itself is simple. Wherever I am, you're not. And take her with you."

Hannah nodded. "I like it," she said. "How much time do you need?"

The child had the heart of a commando. "A solid ten. Unbeheld by human eye. Can you do it?"

"Take fifteen."

Marian laughed. "Here," she pushed the *Toiler* at her, tapping the piece on the award. "Maybe you can use this." Her lips thinned out into a line of concentration, Hannah picked up the paper and started to read. In front of The Gleaner, Marian pulled the Volvo to the curb and grabbed her phone. "One call to make first," Hannah grunted.

Marian dug out the business card Bill Cain had given her just two hours ago and dialed the number of the Carthage Development Corporation. Cain got on the line after what might have been the briefest hold in the history of telecommunications. "Marian." He managed to sound occupied and intimate all at once. What a trick.

"Bill." She got right to the point. "Oldham, Wilson and Hughes."

"What about them?"

"Oldham did the roofing, right?"

"And Wilson the carpentry. Exterior stuff. There was a lot of dry rot on the lintel and some of the casements."

"Exterior." She felt predatory.

"Right. Oldham and Wilson did the exterior work."

"And Connie Hughes—"

With good Christian patience. "The interior."

"Bill, you said they're all dead. Dead and gone."

"No, dear, I said they're all dead *or* gone," he corrected her. "You misheard me."

"I see." Marian found herself smiling at melting clods of dirty snow.

Cain described how he went to the funerals of Oldham and Wilson. Very sad. Mags Oldham broke his neck in a fall on a job, and Seamus Wilson had kidney cancer. About Connie Hughes, who knows? He left town not long after the restoration. Just—went. Nobody noticed until masonry jobs started backing up, and a few of them finally put together that it wasn't that there were more jobs, there were fewer masons. "It's been so long, he's probably dead, too," Cain finished. "Just like the rest."

"Thanks, Bill, bye," Marian hung up, her gloved hand steady on the receiver. She watched Carthaginians cross against the light and four-by-fours rumble by in every direction. Unless she was mistaken, in all of Carthage, Ohio, only Marian knew the identity of the man found dead in the Mission House. You, sweetheart, she reminded herself, smiling, as she got back into the car, and the killer. The man calling himself J.C. Houston was really Connie Hughes, one of the three men who made repairs to the Mission House thirty years ago. But it still didn't explain what brought him to town to die—or who had helped him on his way.

The real reason she worked more part-time jobs than Derry Wilson was to give herself room for these occasional investigations that didn't involve portraits of cracked sidewalks. It was what she had instead of facials.

Or, for that matter, sex.

Chapter Twenty

Back inside the Wade County Historical Society, Marian and Hannah discovered Brownie Troop 1463. True serendipity, Marian thought, catching Hannah's eye. There were a dozen restless nine-year-olds who, between them, had a complete regulation uniform. One girl had the beanie, but a Catholic school plaid jumper. A few girls had brown sashes over neon crop tops and stretch pants. Another one was wearing the Brownie twill pants under a butt-length pink sweatshirt with trashy silver beadwork.

They were all crowding Alice Lowther, who was attempting to answer such historical questions as the location of the john and whether she colored her hair. The troop leader, a petite brunette who looked like she should be reffing girl's field hockey, boomed various commands aimed at crowd control.

When Lowther saw her, Marian held up the two books, mouthing thanks and nodding toward the kneehole desk in the other room. The other woman smiled wanly. Hannah leaned into Marian. "Take as long as you like," she whispered, sidling over to the Brownies, who looked prepared to trample Alice Lowther if she delayed another minute. Backing up the narrow stairs, Lowther was valiantly trying to tell the Brownies about "our fine collection of antebellum costumes." Finally, she turned and hurried. Once the trampling was safely overhead, Marian dropped the Buckeyes key ring into Lowther's tote and set the books on her desk. Then she slipped quietly through the four downstairs rooms of the Wade County Historical Society.

No files anywhere.

The rear rooms contained a photo exhibit of the excavation of local prehistoric Indian mounds, a permanent collection of Civil War memorabilia, and oil portraits of early governors. Mounted vertically on a narrow wall beside a lace-paneled window were three framed sketches in sepia ink with fine detail. "The Chardin Series," said the acrylic plaque, "From the Sketchbook of Claude de Chardin S.J., 1769." The first sketch showed the Jesuit in a fireside conversation with a Shawnee. The middle sketch was a pensive portrait. The last was a pastoral scene of Chardin, whose arm was curled around an open volume, surrounded by acolytes. There was a timeless, placeless quality about the sketches that gave them a wash of the universal.

In the north parlor, Marian scanned the bookshelves. There were regional, state, and local histories. Histories of trade, industry, and agriculture. Cultural histories. Family histories. Is there any real need for this stuff? Does Cindy Wilson or Tim Rinehart pop over to have a look at Brewster's study on Silt Formation Along Wade County Natural Waterways in 1910?

Hughes, the spine said in dusky gold. Marian pulled it.

Hughes: Settlers of Wade County, Ohio. Marian flipped to the front, where the copyright was 1985. Perfect. Recent enough to include living generations. Marian thumbed through the usual descriptions of early settlement, Indian hostilities, church foundings, war service, famous elbows rubbed, and various freak falls and tractor manglings —all written with a reverence usually reserved for Tudors.

In the index, no Connie. Nothing even close. No Conrad, Conroy or Constable. She felt momentarily stymied. Overhead, sudden creaking signaled major Brownie movement. And then she saw it: Jesse. Better yet, Jesse Connor Hughes—Connie?—and an entry number denoting his location on the Hughes family tree. She found the entry not far from the index itself. He turned up as the second of three children of Harvie Weldon Hughes and Vita Louise Stout Hughes. Older brother Arthur died in Vietnam; younger sister Clella "d.y.," died young. About Jesse, there were three lines: ii. Jesse Connor, b. 31 Aug 1953; m. 11 June 1993 Alice Lowther.

J.C. Houston.

Jesse Connor Hughes.

Slipping the book back into place, Marian dashed to the south parlor—at the top of the staircase loomed many pairs of Brownie legs—and scribbled the Jesse Connor Hughes information on a post-it note from Lowther's desk. She jammed the note into her vest pocket and bent over the pictorial account of the Flood of Ought Two, just as Troop 1463 clomped downstairs and spread like kudzu throughout the first-floor rooms.

Lowther hurried by.

"How's it going?" Hannah whispered.

Marian nodded. "Any archives upstairs?"

"Archives?"

"Files of any sort."

Her eyes narrowed. "Maybe," she said. "Smallest bedroom, northwest corner." With her index finger, she touched the dial of her wristwatch.

Marian held up five fingers.

"Good. She's just about to give up on our girls in brown," Hannah said, slipping away.

From a series of small wall racks, Marian pulled a slick guide to the costume collection and went upstairs. The largest bedrooms contained maybe a dozen mannequins clothed in authentic dress from Wade County history. Men in toppers and tails and brown velvet day coats and leather breeches. Frontiersmen and local nobs. Ladies compensating for hoops and bustles with satin and lace furbelows in emerald and claret and doe. Straw boaters. High-buttoned shoes. And the dress blue of 1863. Heads forever bent, their smiles were deathless. Which ones, Marian wondered, does Alice Lowther Hughes strip for her own appearances on State Days at the Mission House? Where she sets out watery lemonade in Dixie cups and hangs a grapevine wreath on the front door.

And lets her ex-husband die.

In the smallest bedroom, lighted by thin vermilion slats from the setting sun, Marian looked around. It was partly a workroom, housing a Singer sewing machine and open crates of remnants. An easel, the sort for mounting presentations, held large sheets of blank poster board. There were two stools at a long worktable, strewn with the trappings of sewing, drafting, and minor carpentry. And, near the door, was an old oak filing cabinet. She tugged at the top drawer, fully expecting it not to budge.

It opened.

Five blasted minutes. Not nearly enough time. From drawer to drawer, Marian scanned the typewritten labels on the folders. Prehistoric Indigenous, Civil War, costumes, wiggy honchos, library. And then there was "Other Projects," which turned out to include community outreach and interstate cultural exchange. Marian's fingers moved the folders along their metal rods.

Toward the back, she found the file on the Mission House, full of clippings, receipts, copies of paid bills, and correspondence from thirty years ago. And one of those slim Compositions books with the marbled cardboard covers she used to use as a girl. It had been set up as a bookkeeping ledger divided into Accounts Receivable and Accounts Payable called "Repairs to the Mission House, August 1995." How Alice Lowther handled bookkeeping ever since was a mystery. Did she move to QuickBooks? But Marian was pretty sure she'd find some answers in the Compositions ledger.

"You'll just have to come back again," she heard Lowther say.

Then, Hannah, sweetly: "But there's still so much to see." The sound of footsteps on the perfect polished wooden staircase was unmistakable. They were coming to find her. She glanced back at the file.

There were the receipts, of course. And the correspondence. Damn. No chance to go through them. And she'd really need to compare the receipts and paid bills against the ledger, the official record of disbursements.

What the hell.

She stuffed the file into her backpack.

Chapter Twenty-One

Since the Hausers were out for the evening—a local amateur theater group called The Downstagers was grappling with a Brecht play—Marian had The Briars to herself. Barb made room in the refrigerator for the few groceries Marian had bought at Kroger's, told her to set the oven ten degrees higher than she really wanted, and asked her to do them all a favor and finish up the cheesecake.

Marian locked the door behind them.

What is it about sheer silence in great spaces that is so unsettling? At home on the Delaware River, she never thought about the quiet. Outside, for the most part, was a desolation, and only in winter was it ever completely silent. But inside her small cabin, silence had nothing whatsoever to do with fear or loneliness. The cabin, with its few pictures and pieces of furniture, was like a sheath around her. Sometimes at night, outside her bedroom window, a herd of deer would thunder past on their way down to the river, and once, a black bear lumbered across her porch, knocking a rattan table into the front door. Marian sipped her sassafras tea and went back to *Middlemarch.*

It didn't pay to have too much imagination in the country, that much she knew, and if she couldn't confine her imagination to paper, then she had no business living in near isolation on the Delaware and no business owning a gun. Her life in the cabin, then, became a kind of precondition to her investigative work. The minute she entrusted her personal safety to anyone else, she would give up investigations, because, without wits, nerve, and an imagination in check, they'd become too dangerous.

Marian spread out her notebook, newspaper, and ledger on the Hausers' dining room table. According to the records in Lowther's old ledger, funds for the repairs on the Mission House, totaling less than four grand, came from three major sources: state and local historical societies and a private foundation in Cleveland. Nominal donations came from the Carthage *Toiler*, County Democrats, County Republicans, Knights of Columbus, and something called the Downtown Renaissance Project. Listed, too, were donations made by individuals—among them, Clayton Girard, who gave one thousand bucks. Nickels and dimes arrived from bake sales and the allowances of elementary school children.

On the debit side, Lowther had recorded the cost of labor and supplies. She had accepted estimates for work from the ones Bill Cain had named, Oldham, Wilson and Hughes. Since there was no record of other bids on the job, Marian concluded the repair work on the Mission House was, even in its day, minor employment in the Wade County scheme of things—minor employment, minor public interest, even then. Lowther had gotten reasonable estimates from men whose work she knew, and apparently, no one kicked that the mason she chose was her husband.

For some reason that probably had something to do with her need to retain some control over the project, Lowther had paid out expenses on the job as they arose. The lion's share, up front before work began, and then every few days as small items cropped up. So for every roofing nail and trowel and quarter-round they needed, the workers had to go through her. Nowhere could Marian find anything that smacked of padding or fiddling. In fact, when debits finally outdistanced credits by a couple hundred dollars, Lowther paid the difference herself.

So where was the flim-flam? What was wanted, here, she gingerly pulled a potato from the oven, popped it on a plate along with salt and a margarine tub, was some skullduggery: something worth blackmailing Lowther for, something worth killing Hughes for. Alice Lowther may be a painstaking bookkeeper, scrupulously honest where money is concerned, but Marian was positive she had fiddled something thirty years ago. Something to do with credentials or possessions. Something she found irresistible.

What Marian needed was another look at the Mission House. Tomorrow, early, before meeting Bella to run the dogs. Tonight, outline the report for Joan, make a pass at fleshing out a bone here and there, then give herself over to Mr. Bubble, a cup of tea, and the latest S.J. Rozan novel, all at once. The easiest, most certifiable feel-good thing she did for herself, guaranteed to hold at bay whatever wrangled her mind—namely, Charlie, investigative tangles, unproductive sexual fantasies, and bank overdrafts.

Chapter Twenty-Two

Partly sunny, high today thirty-three, sang the local DJ while Marian downed the Hausers' fresh squeezed orange juice and read the paper. The lead story blared the latest wrinkle in the rumor that Hyundai was coming to Wade County. Elsewhere on the front page, Del Sperry, the police chief, stated that the investigation into the death at the Mission House was "proceeding," and anyone with any information about a J.C. Houston from Cleveland should please come forward. Which meant, Marian set aside the paper, the cops were stymied.

The six-foot Barb poured Marian's coffee, wearing a striped turtleneck, a jeans skirt, and a hairy sweater that depicted a small New England town. Marian could swear the print matched the one on the colorful border running the perimeter of the room. Barb called last night's Brecht play "creditable," then they spent ten minutes trying to work out transportation to Bella's dinner party that evening. In one car or two? If one, whose? The fine points of double dating. Marian begged off — "I have to beg off, Barb," she said, wondering if she'd ever used the term "beg off" before—on the chance that she and Charlie might go somewhere afterwards. Had she wanted to silence Barb for good, she could have said, "Go back to his place," but the idea felt absurd.

Barb, with her short, salt-and-pepper hair and oversized, blue-framed glasses, understood perfectly. She always understood perfectly. In fact, it looked to Marian like she approached human understanding with conviction, the way some folks take up good works. How well she understood their childlessness, or Cy's recent diagnosis of early Parkinson's,

Marian didn't ask. She pictured Cy Hauser's flat face, thinning hair, and stiff mustache. Add a bit of ruddiness, and he could be a retired officer from the time of the Boer War.

"Barb, you grew up around here?"

"Sure did."

She'd be about the right age. "Ever visit the Mission House?"

"As a kid?" She sat down.

"Well, teenager, say."

"It wasn't a—tourist attraction then."

Marian sat back, chewing her raisin toast. What she needed was someone who could tell her the contents of the Mission House around thirty years ago. Well, looks like another call to Cain or Girard—though, from where she was sitting, to do so was beginning to feel needy. "No," Barb went on, "we didn't pay official visits to the Mission House."

There was something in the way she slowed at the word "official" that made Marian look up. "Are you telling me you paid unofficial visits to the place?"

Barb grabbed her coffee and slipped into a chair across from Marian. "Plenty." Behind the glasses that covered half her face, Barb raised her eyebrows. "If you must know, the Mission House was the local indoor make-out joint. It was so popular you damn near had to make reservations to get in."

Leave it to good old teenage ingenuity. "Go on."

"Well, the place was packed with junk, but there were a couple of old couches—overstuffed, Victorian things—crammed into different corners. The windows were either boarded up or covered with flats —"

"Flats? You mean stage sets?"

"Right. Flats. And it was leaky and stinking and pretty awful, to tell you the truth."

"Cold?"

Barb threw her head back and laughed. "Not for long."

"How'd you get in?"

Barb shrugged. "You name it. Back door lock was busted, and half the time, the front door was unlocked. There was even glass missing in one of the rear windows, so if need be—"

"Someone could crawl through." So Bill Cain was right. *School kids have been crawling into the godforsaken place for years.*

"It was absolutely private—"

"Notwithstanding the other couple."

"Hidden in the far corner. It might as well have been the moon, for all we cared." Barb poured herself more coffee. "There were rules. A Walkman was okay. And flashlights, for what we called intermittent use. No food, booze, or tobacco. The idea was to leave no trace. And outside the Mission House, it was strictly forbidden to spread the word. It was just our group at the high school who used it."

"And no one ever found out?"

Barb shook her head, smiling. "Not that I ever heard," she said. "We used to call it 'studying Native American culture.' That was the code for going to make out at the Mission House. A friend would say, 'So what's up for tonight?'"

"'Tom and I are going to be studying Native American culture.'"

Barb laughed. "That's it. Our parents all thought we were a bunch of budding anthropologists."

"Lots of virginity gest lost there?"

"Some, maybe. Not mine." She took a sesame bagel from a silver bread tray.

Marian checked her watch. Ten to nine. "Tell me about the junk," she said, buttering another piece of raisin toast.

"The junk." Barb squinted, trying to recall. "Truly junk, believe me. Even then, I could tell good stuff. This wasn't it. They were municipal things, mostly. Disassembled grandstands, old school desks, broken rigs from parade floats. Little theater scenery, like I mentioned." Barb spread her hands. "Storage. That was it. Useless overflow from other places."

"Nothing you would have taken as original?"

Barb was interested. "What do you mean?"

"An original furnishing of the Mission House."

"From Chardin's day?" Her eyes went wide. "God, no."

"Anything that looked like it could hold something valuable."

"Like a safe?"

"A locked box. A cupboard. A desk."

Barb frowned. "Nothing like that."

"So it was crowded with junk."

"Packed. We had one little path to one of the couches. And we had to crawl over stuff to get to the other."

Marian stirred her cold coffee. "What happened, finally, to everything?"

"Well, around the time they decided to make some repairs, the Mission House got cleaned out. Some of the things were moved, and some were carted off to the junkyard."

From Mission House to Make-Out Manor. Personally, it appealed to her sense of anarchy. Maybe even Claude de Chardin himself would have approved. For she sensed he was a man who would have defined God's work with startling generosity.

Chapter Twenty-Three

Marian leaned against the Volvo, looking at the Mission House, figuring that if she stared at the building long enough, something might occur. Something did. She took out her phone and called Steve Grey again. "Hey, Steve," she tried to sound patient and chipper in the voicemail, "Marian Warner. I'd really appreciate talking with you about J.C. Houston. Please give me a call back." Snow was dripping from the roof Mags Oldham had made thirty years ago. The sun came out, weak and wintry, as Marian slipped her phone into her pants pocket and looked around.

Adjoining the Mission House property was a line of brick row buildings flush with the sidewalk that extended one long block to the center of town. A cornerstone put the one next to the Mission House at 1865. Just a few doors down was Mazeppa's Ride. The intervening shops sold vacuum cleaners, dinettes, and Bibles. In the window at All Makes Vacuum was a crooked Venetian blind and one of those snake plants that seem to have none of the same requirements as other living things.

On the other side of the Mission House, across Plum Street, was a Baptist Church erected in 1952 and more shops—bridal wear, bakery, New Age crystals. Around the Mission House, Carthage had happened, and the Mission House ended up looking like the one place that didn't belong on the street that shared its name. She could just about taste Bill Cain's frustrated desire for the property. But overriding it all was the torsion of fear felt by Jack Girard and Bella Murphy, and Alice Lowther, who, in the fate of the Mission House, were playing out their own complex needs. The Mission

House was an inkblot of wood and stone.

Marian looked. *I come in,* she told the weather-beaten Mission House, *on your side. I come in on your side. Only I am still uncertain about the company I keep.* A breeze curled by, creaking the sign outside Mazeppa's Ride. A man in a shapeless Army surplus coat and blue watch cap came down the street. From the looks of him, Marian figured he hadn't heard about the warming trend. When he stopped in front of Mazeppa's Ride and stuffed one mitt-like glove in his mouth, she recognized Tim Rinehart, the owner.

Fumbling for his keys, he called a garbled "Morning" to her.

"Morning."

He glanced at her. "Looking for inspiration?"

Marian grinned. "Something like that."

"I'm a little short on it, myself."

She pushed herself away from the Volvo. "What about some information?"

"If I've got it."

Marian went over to him. "How long have you owned Mazeppa's Ride?"

He squinted. "Almost nine years now. But I've managed it, on and off, for seventeen."

"Did you name it?" She looked up at the sign.

Rinehart seemed amused. "No, not me," he said. "The name's original. The place has always been Mazeppa's Ride. That's what makes it a local institution. One of the old photos inside shows the first owner—guy named Lemuel Prouty—in front of the place when it opened in 1865. He was the one who named it Mazeppa's Ride."

"What does it mean?"

Despite his size, Rinehart was looking cold. He shrugged. "I always figured it was one of those Greek myths."

"I wonder where Lemuel Prouty would have heard about it."

"From his wife, I guess. She was a schoolteacher." Rinehart made a face that stretched his thin mustache out even thinner. "Lemuel looks like he could tell you the difference between stout and ale, but that's about it. In other words," he laughed, tossing his keys, "not a whole lot different from me."

Marian smiled. "But you play jazz piano."

"That I do," he saluted. "Thanks for reminding me."

"And it's not just reflected glory."

He pulled off his cap, the lank dark hair falling across his forehead. "You mean Derry?"

Marian nodded.

"Thanks," he said. "Though I wouldn't mind," he added, "even if it was."

"Go have a shot." She jerked her chin at him. "You look cold."

Tim Rinehart unlocked the door. "Derry can sing for me as long as she likes," he said, his back turned. "And even though there are times I'd like to change the name of the place to Rinehart's, fact is I'd lose business over the public outcry." He turned to Marian. "You wouldn't believe it to look at me," he said, his arms open to show her his unpressed self, "but what I do best," he grinned, "is manage." He waved and disappeared.

Mazeppa's Ride. With the breeze gone, the sign hung motionless on its chains. The paint was dim, as though through the years it was sinking into the carved wood, showing a man, naked, lashed to a wild horse. It was grotesque and so much a part of the Carthage landscape that it became invisible. A scene of torture. Every day, every night, thirsty folks pass inside to their feeble flirtations and discontents—while overhead, flayed and pursued, the bound Mazeppa forever rides, a totem to human suffering. Maybe not such a bad moniker for a saloon, after all.

Marian walked through the ice and slush to the front of the Mission House, where she stood thinking. Alice Lowther did not skim from the repair funds thirty years ago. And municipal junk constituted the only furnishings in the Mission House around that time. So what the hell did the lady steal? If not the money, if not the contents, then what? There had been something of value about the Mission House that proved irresistible to Alice Lowther.

Could she have stolen a part of the actual structure? Was that it? Glass, board, brick, tile—something. Marian recalled her conversation with Lowther two days ago. It was the history of the place the lady cared about. Not for her the concerns of people like Girard and Bella, with their writing campaigns and S.O.S. meetings to save the old building on the corner of

Mission and Plum Streets. And now, a stalled process to call it a national historic landmark. Without something that would undeniably date the Mission House, nothing could save it.

What Lowther must have taken for herself from a derelict make-out joint crammed with municipal junk was a secret icon. Something signifying a history she could stroke, and have as her own, and preserve against whatever fate dished out. Husband gone, youth gone, the brick or board she stole was what remained. For it, Jesse Connor Hughes had died. And for want of it, the Mission House would probably be destroyed. She remembered the woman's face, her strange voice, "So you say," when Marian suggested that the fate of the Mission House was not her responsibility.

Lowther knew better.

For what she had stolen from the Mission House—whatever its other name, brick or board or tile—was the only chance to authenticate it. As a student of irony, Marian thought, climbing back into the Volvo, she was touched. The tale reverberates. She glanced at her watch. Later, after running the dogs with Bella, she would have to search for the stolen object.

And that meant letting herself into Lowther's home.

Chapter Twenty-Four

They took Bella's Bronco out to Wade Lake, with the four Honeymooners scrambling in the back, hampered by a stacking bin with two training dummies, a couple of frisbees, and what Bella referred to as "Norton's stick," a hunk of hardwood. Trixie curled up sensibly on a ratty blue blanket, cramped by the panting restlessness of the two black dogs, Ralph and Alice. Norton, stationed right behind Marian and Bella, looked impertinent. Marian found herself staring at his washed-out nose, which Bella called a dudley nose, a demerit in show dogs.

"So, how's the investigation going, Marian?" asked Bella, turning into the parking lot at Wade Lake.

"Good." Aside from an old Ford Fusion with masking tape and Visqueen for a rear window, the parking lot was deserted. Marian made out two slouched figures inside the clunker who looked like they were smoking a couple of joints. "The dead man was Jesse Connor Hughes, and thirty years ago he was married to Alice Lowther."

Bella blinked. "Why was he there?"

"I'm working on it."

"Did Alice meet up with him?"

"I'll let you know when I have proof."

With a tight nod, Bella swung the Bronco over to the far end of the lot and pulled to a stop. They looked at each other. Marian went on: "And I'm looking into the likelihood that Alice Lowther stole something from the Mission House."

"Stole...." Bella whistled softly.

Marian smiled. "I'm still digging."

"Good job." She looked Marian over and couldn't quite keep the surprise out of her voice. In the few moments before she let the dogs out the back, they stared intently at the tailgate.

"Stay," she told them, slowly lifting the door. Bella pulled Norton's stick from the bin and stepped aside. "All right, come on." All four of them leaped to the ground, dashing in every direction. They pranced and slunk around the familiar place. Trixie stayed close, but the others were off sniffing and peeing with abandon. Norton picked his way gingerly across a few feet of frozen lake, then seemed just as happy to poke around in the weeds. While Bella talked to Ralph about his burrs, Marian walked to the water's edge.

It was lovely, all of it, the thick ice white and creamy from a day's worth of higher temperatures. Below the surface was a lattice of gray fissures. There are, really, so many ways to melt. Bella came over, also silent, her green eyes stopping at distant things. From where they stood quietly together, Marian noticed that the Wade Lake Country Club was out of sight, obscured by two miles of curving shoreline and overhanging trees.

That end of the lake, Bill Cain had told her, was the "kept up" end, and in the summertime the club members used the sandy beach and the boat launch. Here, though, off the grounds of the country club, there was greater wilderness, solitary places for hiking and fishing. She and Bella headed toward an open area in a thicket of bare, sprawling bushes, where chevrons of snow ranged over the stumpy brown grass.

Bella found a hefty stick and walked to the edge of the clearing. She snapped her fingers once, pointing to the ground beside her, and the dogs quickly pulled themselves in and sat like dutiful little grunts. Slowly, Bella brought the stick back, then sent it flying with surprising speed. "Okay," she told them, and they sped toward the prize. From the rear they reminded Marian of those dusty Hollywood westerns where posses thunder out of town. Alice snatched the stick and had to dodge Norton, who was attempting an ambush, and then all of them trotted back.

What Marian saw in Bella was a master of quiet purposes. There were the well-trained dogs, the steady improvements in what had been the Girard home, the efforts in S.O.S. Probably her entertaining. Possibly even her relationship with Jack Girard. Underlying Bella's life was a sense of design, allowing in her life only what contributed to how she wanted to establish herself in the community, and she was already far more established than other twenty-three-year-olds, who struggle in shock with their own bad choices.

So how, Marian wondered, does she contribute in Bella's eyes? Was Marian just the latest champion for the Mission House? Was she a confidante? No, not likely, because at heart there is something guarded about Bella Murphy, despite her social ease. Marian watched her take the stick from Alice, bending over the dogs, scratching their muzzles, and offering advice. "Trix, you've got to get in there. Don't let the boys bully you. And Norton, no fair."

"How long have you and Jack Girard been together?" Marian crouched, clapping for Trixie, who padded over for some attention.

"Almost two years now," Bella said, "but, of course, I've known him all my life. He's the reason I left college." When Marian asked her where, Bella said it was Kittatinny College for Women, a small school tucked away in the hilly, northwestern part of New Jersey. Less than an hour from her cabin, Marian mentioned. They agreed it was indeed a small world and a funny coincidence and the prettiest part of the Garden State.

Bella had lasted three years there before returning for good to Carthage. It was time. College was feeling more like a delay of adulthood than anything worth doing for its own sake. Not for her the fraternal life of dorm and dining hall. At twenty-one, Bella found herself in sudden possession of the Girard home, a trust fund, and a career. She had been catapulted into a life most of her classmates were happy to defer for another ten years, their biggest frets having to do with meeting paper deadlines and not getting pregnant. But, for her, it fit.

When Marian asked how often she visits the nursing home, "Not often," Bella said and whistled for the dogs. A busy young woman, an inconvenient nursing home, a stroked-out guardian whose former life was unrecoverable. Is there a point we reach where we no longer respond to kindness, even?

Marian looked out across the lake. "Any plans with Girard?"

"You mean marriage?"

She shrugged. "I guess that's what I mean."

Bella answered carefully. "We're in no hurry," she said. "We have the house. We have each other. It feels—complete."

"So you have an understanding," Marian said. Whatever the hell that meant. Like Girard's teacups and sweethearts. Still, it was a way of keeping the topic afloat.

"We're free to see other people," Bella said, brushing the wet, stringy bark from her gloves. "We just never seem to want to," she smiled. Marian sat back. Gray, bony clouds sketched across the sun, a lambent thing in winter. Farther, surely, than the ninety-three million miles we're told. Around them in the silent clearing, the shadows rolled, graceful and gone, a surf of light and air.

It was winter at its most discreet, the season of veracity. When what we see is the true tree. The true sun, its borders indistinct, more truly a star. And ice is water's other name. In chevrons of melting snow and fissured ice, the things of this world are both broken and sovereign. *You, you of all people, Warner, should know that.*

Bella walked along the shoreline, her skirt rippling. The dogs trotted on ahead. Alone with Trixie, Marian nuzzled the sweet bristly face, and she saw—for the first time—that bliss and grief look a lot alike.

Chapter Twenty-Five

Back at The Briars, Marian found one of Barb Hauser's cryptic notes under her bedroom door, *Gn to Cin w/Cy. Bk 4 din. B.,* which made it a whole lot easier getting out of the place with some house-cleaning equipment and old clothing. Over her jeans, she put on a beige, three-quarter-length jacket she discovered in one of the Hauser closets, where a top shelf yielded the dullest kerchief she had ever seen this side of Murmansk. Marian tied the scarf over her hair and looked in the hall mirror. Well, the neighbors on West Fourth Street would take her for either a cleaning lady on a bad day or Alice Lowther on a good one.

She loaded two different kinds of mops and a bucket filled with germicidal sprays into the Volvo, then threw in a battered old Kenmore vacuum cleaner that was missing two of its wheels. From the spare tire well she pulled out part of her standard emergency equipment, two white plastic signs with black embossed lettering, MAID FOR YOU, and a fake phone number. The back adhesives still seemed sticky enough. Marian positioned the signs on either side of the Volvo, whacked them in place, and prayed they'd hold for about the next hour. Then she called the Wade County Historical Society and asked Lowther, "What are your hours, please?" in a soft soprano with a southern accent.

With Old Alice occupied for the next two hours, Marian drove directly to the block of West Fourth Street where, judging by the way the numbers ran, she figured she'd find Lowther's house, and stopped in front of #26. Around the property was a stone wall with wrought-iron spikes all along the top. What would Freud make of Alice's taste for spikes? Marian carted her supplies up the front walk to the house, where the window shades were only half raised, and the doe-colored clapboard siding shot two stories up to a flattened roof. The house felt austere.

At the front door Marian silently praised Old Alice for resisting anything wooden that says "Welcome Friends" and pulled out the duplicate set of keys. When the second one fit, she lugged the equipment inside, closed the door, and pulled off her boots. Then she slipped on a pair of thin latex gloves.

Be thorough—Marian checked her watch—and fast.

She stepped through the spacious archway into Alice Lowther's living room, where everything was painted off-white, including the fireplace, which starkly offset a coal-black facing. What she expected was a "branch" of the Wade County Historical Society—a kind of off-campus Alice Mary Lowther Room, complete with kneehole desk and Queen Anne chair, for Alice's eyes only, like a private stash of naughty postcards. Instead, the couch was a utilitarian piece with a dark wood frame and wine corduroy cushions. There was a chair along the same lines, opposite a wingback chair upholstered in pink brocade. The square, glass-topped coffee table came straight out of a Broyhill showroom.

It smelled stale, like a house closed up while its owners are away. A place where nothing is ever changed, the molecules hanging in a kind of deathly stasis. Even the motes of dust in the thin sunlight seemed to stagnate. The room was unlike The Briars, which was lively with antique clutter and owner-titans. Unlike Bella's, brilliant and empty, where pieces were added one at a time, with crocodilian patience. Unlike Girard's, simple and functional, less than the life it holds. Even Charlie's Dial-A-Decor had more life.

In the built-in bookshelves flanking the fireplace were just a few obligatory books, mainly hardcover Michener, blistering Hollywood bios, and references on collectibles. The shelves were lined with daguerreotypes and bisque figurines. Marian gently turned over a demure lady with a blue parasol, the companion to a gallant gent in blue breeches, and found a handwritten label. *Meissen, 1797, pair $35. 7/8/87. Estate sale, Cresco, PA. Real coup.*

On the far wall was a browned, framed page, from a Richmond shopkeeper's ledger in 1865. A white tag with Lowther's handwriting was stuck to the back. *N.B. entry for Pres. Davis. Especially love Col. B's bedsprings—ha!* According to the shopkeeper's spidery script, Davis ordered a rocker for eight dollars and Colonel Breckinridge bedsprings and a mustard plaster for a total of seven eighty-three.

Marian turned over photographs of Lincoln and Grant. *Church jumble, G'burg 8/10/90—imagine!!* Over the mantel was a campaign flag from the election of 1888 in a heavy gilt frame. "Protect Home Industry" was the motto, under bushy portraits of Benjamin Harrison and the unforgettable Levi P. Morton. Slathered to the backs of everything were Alice's handwritten tags.

What they recorded were Alice's triumphs—the thrill of acquisition and the commentaries on her own cleverness and luck. Careful to leave no trace of any disturbance, Marian straightened the framed campaign flag. She felt oppressed by the room, by the yeasty air, by the vain collection, and wondered where to search next. Marian looked down at the coal-black fireplace facing. It didn't fit its space very well, but it had a lot of intricate detail. She touched it. Cast-iron and beautifully wrought. The two vertical panels depicted the goddess Ceres, with sheaves of wheat in her arms, and the horizontal top panel depicted—Mazeppa's Ride.

"I need the exercise," Marian told the Hausers, who offered her a ride to the dinner party when Charlie's assistant called to say that he'd have to meet her there. Standing barefoot in the men's Woolrich robe she had bought secondhand years ago, the sleeves flopping down around her knuckles, she pictured the ride over, alone in their back seat, a Hauser tagalong. Barb and Cy made understanding noises about what sedentary work reading files is, and disappeared down the hall, dressed in his and her silver jacquard sweaters, leaving Marian five minutes to throw on the brown velvet tank top and wheat silk trousers—the theory being, if it's pleated, it's dressy.

She figured she still needed ten minutes to walk the few blocks to Providence, and five minutes in between to decide what to take from her backpack. No to the wallet, no to the checkbook, the makeup, the notebook, the trash. She stuck a slim lipstick and comb in the pocket of the long black flannel coat she'd put on her Visa that afternoon in Carthage's one department store and paused over the revolver.

Marian sat on the bed. That old feeling was back that she was never able to sort out—what came first, the gun or the anxiety? And why tonight? Soon she'd have to face writing a report for Joan, just one more document in the file on the Mission House in Carthage, Ohio. At that moment, all she could include in a report for the Park Service is the unyielding nature of the warring letter writers, whose positions seemed intractable. What would make a difference?

At least her investigation into the death of J.C. Houston was virtually solved. After tonight, Charlie would have the information, too, to do with what he will. Still, there was something intangible, the sort of thing that makes barnyard animals nervous long before the humans even have a clue.

Marian smiled.

It's a dinner party, where the worse that can happen is that someone spills wine on your pants. Some talk of football, some local politics. A chance, aside, to tell Charlie about Lowther and the theft from the Mission House. Three hours ago, she was nearly splitting to tell him. Now, showered, dressed, alone with a revolver in her hand, it felt like just another responsibility.

Finally, Jack Girard and Bella. Her hosts.

Marian put away the Chief's Special slowly, like any act where faith and judgment collide. Armed with a lipstick and a comb, she set out for Providence. The night air felt deferential, the constellations watchful.

Chapter Twenty-Six

There is a certain kind of cold on January nights that is hard and still, a beautiful unyielding cold that keeps you certain company, like death. Meeting Marian at the door to Bella's house was Jim Carney, the tall, graying coroner, who introduced Marian to his wife Jan. One of those skinny people who spends a lifetime just trying to stay warm, she had a fresh, tight perm, and the kind of intense listening look that made Marian feel like they were already in the middle of a conversation when in fact they'd only said hello.

Bella, her hair seeming to ride the air, came from the kitchen in a drift of Balenciaga, shaking water off her fingers, and hugged Marian with an elegant forearm. Like girlfriends. The one guest she could phone the next day to wring her hands about the mousse and complain about someone's gaffe. She wore a pale blue cashmere sweater and a calf-length navy skirt, which was dressier than Marian's outfit: more pleats. Satisfied her hands were dry, Bella took Marian's coat, explaining that the dogs were out back, and promised a frosty Sam Adams.

No Charlie.

Marian had to explain his lateness four times since each of the Carneys and Hausers apparently needed to hear it separately. They stood with their drinks in a small circle in the empty living room, where Bella had set out sturdy candles on wrought-iron stands that made Marian think of a monastery. Their light sent elongated shadows over a futon and several floor pillows. Jan Carney thrust her head forward as Marian explained once again about Charlie's unscheduled meeting with Hannah's science teacher, like it had all the complexity of Middle East peace talks. After everyone registered concern, Marian went to look for a beer.

Gardenias floated in crystal bowls at the center of the dining room table. Nearby, Jack Girard was crouching on the cold hearth, setting a small log over the others on the grate. Marian watched him strip a large, ragged square of birch bark.

"Tinder?" she said.

"Flavor, mostly." He glanced at her. "Here." He broke the bark and handed her half. With her fingernail, she scraped at the birch until the thin white paper came off in curls.

After a moment, he looked up. "How are you?"

"Fine. You?"

Girard nodded as Marian sprinkled the strips into his open hand. "How's the work going?"

"Which work?"

"Any work."

"Coming along." Then: "I'm not having any luck with Steve Grey. I've left him a couple of messages."

Girard added the birch curls to the logs in the wide, deep fireplace. "Steve lives in the garage apartment over the Carthage Pet and Garden Center. Straight down Main Street. Maybe you can catch him at home."

"Thanks."

"Did you see Bill Cain?"

She nodded. "He was helpful." Which was true. Only it was mostly true about the history of repairs at the Mission House, and the significance of that information wasn't something she wanted to share casually with Jack Girard. "He wined and dined me at the country club."

"What did you think?" He gave her a frank look.

What could she say? "I think you've got yourself a powerful enemy."

Girard seemed unbothered. "Do you like him?"

She inhaled. "Don't put me on the spot, okay?"

"You're a disinterested party, right?"

"Something like that."

"Are you?" He gave her a quick look as he stuffed crumpled newspapers under the grate.

"Not entirely." It was a big admission. And for this kind of foolishness, not even her Chief's Special would help.

"Only you won't say whose point of view you favor." He opened the gas valve with a crude key.

"No." She lifted her chin.

"I believe it's mine," he said, not looking at her.

Marian watched, irritated, as he held a lighted match to the papers. "I don't have to like Bill Cain, you know, to see his point of view."

"You don't have to like me," he countered, "to see mine. Either."

"But I'd prefer to," Marian said quietly.

"Holding me to a higher standard?"

"I guess so," she said with a small shrug. In the next room, Jim Carney was telling a lawyer joke that ended in a blare of laughter. Girard brushed off his hands, then rested his wrists on his knees. They watched the flames slither up the underside of the logs, finding cracks, looking for those dry, ragged places where they could thrive. Heat and light pressed out toward them, the ashes floating away in the chimney draft.

Girard watched them go. "I used to hide up there as a kid."

"From friends?"

"No one," he said. "Just hiding. I'd crawl up on the ledge of the flue. A few times, I brought a flashlight."

"What for?"

"Reading."

She took a shot. "Jules Verne."

His face creased, nearly smiling. "Jules Verne. Mark Twain. Whatever I could find. Poetry."

"Robert Louis Stevenson."

He shook his head. "Wilfred Owen. Rupert Brooke. Sometimes I think they're why I enlisted."

Marian watched the flames. "I don't think that was their intention."

"I wonder what they'd have to say about Haditha Dam."

"What do you think?"

He thought about it. "Nothing. It wasn't the occasion of poetry." Then: "Do you know Dylan Thomas?"

"Which one are you thinking of?"

"'Fern Hill.' That was my life."

Marian shut her eyes for a moment. "You were prince of the apple towns."

"Only without the farm." She glanced at him. Too close to the fire, his skin was reddening, but he didn't seem to mind. Then he squinted, trying to recall the poem. "'Oh, as I was young and easy in the mercy of his means, time held me green and dying.'" She thought of Bill Cain, savoring a cocktail onion and telling her that Girard's so tied up in the past he can't let go of a damn thing. As though mere letting go was the object of life for a child grown up, all of whose sins and frailties go unrelieved by memory. A dreadful passage into a dreadful zone. Forgetting the days when it was Adam and maiden. The nights when the owls bore the farm away.

What was left?

What was ever left?

It is better to know that time holds us green and dying.

Bella came over, handing Marian a bottle of Sam Adams. "What are you talking about?"

"A poem," Marian smiled. "Thanks."

"Oh." Bella leaned against Girard and rested her hand on his shoulder. Adam and maiden. All tenderness deferred until after the last dish is dried, the last stair climbed. To the place where fingers speak and voices stroke. Marian stepped away. It struck her that she didn't belong. For the first time since she arrived in Carthage four days ago, she wanted to be home. Go tonight. Now. Drive through the night.

"'Time held me green and dying.' I can never remember the last line," Girard said, looking up at her.

Marian was about to tell him—the English major in her never tired of supplying lines—when Charlie arrived. The others moved into the entrance hall, where Charlie shook hands and kissed a few cheeks. Bella slid his coat into her arms. Someone told him just wait until he tried the caviar toast. Someone else likened the pinot noir to nectar. Marian hung back, remembering the fight outside of Mazeppa's Ride. It was remarkable that they could still come together like this, undamaged. "Ah," he said. "My date."

He hugged her hard, and she knew it was something she never wanted to be without. "Hi, Charlie," she said into some useless place between his neck and his sweater.

"Marian," he said back, releasing her to shake Girard's hand. Cy Hauser and Bella stooped to pick up the wool muffler that had dropped from Charlie's coat. "I've got a message for you from Derry Wilson," Charlie said to Girard.

"Oh?"

"She wants to see you."

"I'll have to call her. I haven't had a chance since she's been back."

"In person."

Bella offered beer or wine to Charlie, who said he'd try the nectar, and the others drifted back into the living room and sat on the floor cushions. Any minute now they'd all begin to look shockingly attractive to each other, and there was no way Marian wanted to be there for that. She edged Charlie past the staircase, where she wouldn't be overheard. Slouching, he drove his hands deep into his pockets and listened.

She gave him only the essential facts—Hughes, Lowther, theft, blackmail—and he interrupted her twice, his journalism face stern, to question her sources. Then he leaned into her. "So, tell me," he said, "what did they steal?"

Marian took a long sip of her beer. "A fireplace."

They looked at each other. She could tell he was weighing his natural nosiness against editorial expediency. It was no surprise when he asked, "Are you sure?"

"I'm sure."

"So when Hughes met her at the Mission House—"

"His object was blackmail."

Charlie crossed his arms and looked at the floor. "A friendly little squeeze from a husband gone thirty years."

"Only, the stress triggered his asthma—"

"And she left him to die."

"Locked in—"

They looked at each other. "Making it altogether a different sort of crime," Charlie said softly. He was right. A capital offense had occurred. One that went beyond understandable human responses like panic and flight. One that, by turning a key in a padlock, demonstrated a chilling intentionality. A commitment to deed. It was one thing for Alice to want him dead and another thing to tell him so. But it was quite a third thing altogether to help him on his way.

"Have you told Bella?"

She shook her head. "Not tonight. She's too busy. I'll call her tomorrow."

Was she missing something? If there was some fact or piece of evidence that could explain the crime of Jesse Hughes's death in a way that did not also implicate Alice Lowther, then it was the elusive Steve Grey who might know it. Enough with the voicemail. She would have to pay him a visit.

Suddenly, over Charlie's shoulder, she saw Girard standing in the doorway leading to the kitchen, a glass of pinot noir in his hand. Marian straightened up. How much had he heard? "Here's your wine, Charlie," she said, feeling exposed. All she had wanted was to give Charlie the information and watch him take off with it like Norton after a stick. Get on the phone to the cops. Get on the phone to Donna Ardizzone. Do the usual, frenetic Levitan things.

Instead, he gave her arm a quick squeeze and followed Girard into the living room, where Jim Carney was telling a story he swore was true about the orderly who'd taken a snooze on a gurney and woke up with a toe tag. Charlie lounged, loose and quiet, by the others, holding his wine glass by the rim. Maybe, as crimes went, Lowther's lacked outrage. There was no perishable evidence at stake, and she wasn't decamping.

Maybe haste was pointless.

Or maybe Charlie was too preoccupied to care.

Lighting the tapers, Bella called them for dinner and seated Marian next to Jack Girard. Over the course of the meal, Marian learned that coulibiac was shrimp and scallops in a pastry shell, and Jan Carney was a tenth-grade English teacher who, with pastry crumbs sticking to her lower lip, called teaching her "fortay."

All Marian wanted was to eat, study the faces, and lose herself in the steady candlelight. Not forever would her beer stay cold. Jan blotted her lips and laid down her napkin like a gauntlet, declaring that Christopher Marlowe was every bit as gifted as Shakespeare. Marian very pleasantly called him a lesser writer and asked Girard to pass the pepper, please. Then she steered Jan into the Faust theme, which drew Charlie. And Bella. And for the first time, since they'd sat down, the conversation became general.

Marian drifted, Ulysses among the Sirens. It was the Debussy, she thought. Liquid and hypnotic. But where were the rocks? Where was the danger? She fingered her glass, enjoying the kind of animal stupor of a good meal. Beside her, Girard was quiet and watchful, his fingers tapping the edge of the table. Marian felt herself letting go. No, she wasn't Ulysses. She was just one of the stupefied sailors, lapping closer to death.

Ulysses saw the rocks.

Chapter Twenty-Seven

That chilly Manhattan evening all those years ago. Those were morbid days for Charlie, sapped by graduate school and girlfriend, savoring various methods of self-destruction. He told her he decided he preferred "the gas pipe" to hurling himself in front of the A train—he'd pass out from the smell of urine before he'd ever get to jump—or out the twelfth story window of some old hotel that still had windows you could open. Suicide, in those days, became his extracurricular activity, and since it seemed healthier than the time he spent either at Columbia or with Traci, Marian wasn't concerned. As long as Charlie was happy considering his options, she figured, he wouldn't exercise one.

He caught her at work one morning before she'd left for the NYPL to continue the photo research on the Bloomsbury group for a coffee table book her senior editor was handling. Not bad for the first full-time job after graduation. "This is it, Marian, I promise you, my life is over; she tells me she's pregnant. It's the gas pipe for sure." He sounded rattled—she couldn't bear it—so she promised to come over. It meant not stopping at the address Paul had given her briefly on the phone the night before, their only contact in months.

"You sound so far away," she had told Paul.

"Not so far, really. In the city."

"What have you been doing?"

"Working. Midwest, mostly."

"Chemicals again?"

"Some," he said. "Do you want to see?"

She felt sick. "See what?"

"What it is we do."

"You're involving me," she said. "No."

She heard him sigh. "Listen, Marian, this isn't easy for me."

"Then give it up."

"I mean seeing you this way." She should have known. "It's just that—I miss you, and I can't leave here right now. Please." He gave her an address in the East Village. "Basement. Any time tomorrow. Look, we can sit out in the back. There's a little courtyard. You won't see a thing, okay?"

It was the best he could do.

"We don't have to sit outside," she told him. "Just put away your toys when I come." But the next day, there was Charlie, and after spending a distracted morning at the library, cramming into four hours what should have taken eight, she found herself walking Charlie first briskly around the block—like clearing his head of a four-martini buzz—and then downtown to the studio apartment she'd taken in Chelsea.

She made him tea—wondered what the hell to do about Paul ("I'll go in a little while," Charlie said, "tell him I'm sorry I held you up")—and leaving him exhausted on the couch went out for some Chinese food. When she returned, Charlie had on the six o'clock news.

"Marian, come take a look at this."

Accidental blast ripped through the lower two floors where suspected members of the old FIAT Underground were living. *The package slipped from her hands, and she knew it all before she had even heard the rest.* Dead in the blast are two unidentified males and one female.

Chapter Twenty-Eight

After Bella's dinner party, Charlie dropped her off at The Briars. What followed was one of those tight-lipped kisses involving very little surface area, the kind that signals friendly feeling with no sexual content. She scrutinized him. It was okay, considering he was anxious to get home and have it out with Hannah. On the way home from Bella's, he explained that Waggedorn, the science teacher, had told him two things. One, that Hannah had an attitude problem. And two, that he suspected she was stealing from the lab.

"Can't be," said Marian.

Charlie shook his head. "I don't know." The teacher had been nice—very confidential—and was apparently hoping he, Charlie, and Hannah could work it out without having to bring in the principal. By the time Charlie pulled up in front of The Briars, the atmosphere in the Buick was grave.

Funny how the news about Hannah seemed so much worse than Alice Lowther's crime, Marian thought as she got out. "Call me tomorrow. And tell Hannah I'd like to spend some time with her." Then she added, "In the afternoon." He nodded, the engine idling until she let herself into The Briars. Marian watched through the fanlight until he was out of sight. She was back, even before the Hausers. But not by much. She heard the door at the rear of the house slamming open to the tune of "I've Got a Lovely Bunch of Coconuts."

Marian sprang up the stairs.

Inside her room, she switched on the lamp on the nightstand and undressed slowly by its sixty-watt light. Hannah. Nothing to do about it until tomorrow. If then, she thought, sitting weakly on the bed. If then. Never feeling this powerless since the day Paul died. When he altered his molecular structure forever in a moment of bomb-making inattention. Deciding rashly that his true self was some combination of gristle and brimstone.

Paul.

Hannah.

There is a wayward principle at loose in the world, seeding our lives with error and humility. So she folded her velvet tank more carefully than usual, and folded her trousers, placing them on top of the steamer trunk. She could do these foldings perfectly. Then she shrugged into her oversized robe.

Sunday, early, she'd leave for home. That leaves tomorrow for returning Lowther's ledger, getting a good start on her report for Joan, and seeing Hannah. And Charlie. And say what? It's okay about Derry, call me when it's over? About as good as anything else. And as true. But what she wanted most was to let it just roll on. Because for all these years, there had been a fine, rare poise between them.

And he knew it—although what she called poise he called inertia. Be that as it may. Come Sunday morning, she'd ease on down the road in her Volvo, plugging some Sarah Vaughan into her CD player, waving goodbye to the Levitans. Strangely content with one more missed opportunity. "Marian," he once told her, "you're responsible for more deferments than flat feet." *Fact is. Fact is,* she bit her lip, *since Paul, I can turn my back on anything.*

Damned if it wasn't her best quality.

Damned if it wasn't her worst.

Cross-legged on the bed, she was spreading out her notes on the letter writing vitriol about the nomination of the Mission House, when the call came. Marian checked the ID, then tapped the screen. "Hi, Joan."

"So," came her half-sister's voice, "are you in a cabin on the Delaware or a cabin on the Ohio River?"

Marian found herself smiling. "What's the dump *du jour*, that's what you're asking."

"I shudder to think."

"City girl." Marian put her phone on speaker and started to organize the scattered papers. "Actually, I'm still in Carthage, and it's an easy hundred miles from the Ohio River."

"But they've still got snakes?"

"Oh, King snakes, Queen snakes, you name it."

"All the snake royalty."

"You bet."

"I won't be visiting anytime soon."

"Promise?"

Joan laughed. "So you're still choking on that Mission House file. Anything you can share?"

"Not yet. Unless I can figure out an angle, Joan—" There was a knock at her door. She frowned. The Hausers?

"What? What are you saying? If you can't figure an angle, then—"

"Then I think the Park Service can expect more letters." And they'd refuse to consider the nomination. And Bill Cain will tear down the Mission House. "I need another day on the report, Joan." She flung open the door. Jack Girard stood there, his forearm on the door frame, a loose fist in front of his mouth. He was wearing a black, sleeveless down vest, unzipped.

"Hi." They spoke at the same time. Into her phone, Marian said, "Joan, I have to go."

"Call me." And she was gone.

She looked at Jack Girard, her arms hanging useless at her sides. All the extra material of her beloved robe suddenly dragged her down to the earth.

He straightened up. "Marian, can I talk to you?"

"Well, it's—"

"It's eleven-thirty," he said. "I know."

She looked him in the eye. Then stepped aside, making a small gesture. Deferment deferred. Charlie should only know. While Girard stood in the middle of the room, looking around at the chintz and festoons, Marian closed the door softly, wondering what the hell the Hausers might be thinking.

"Sit down," she said. But he didn't.

"Look, Marian," he said, facing her, "I'd like you to tell me what you know about the dead man in the Mission House."

She didn't move. "Why? It doesn't have anything to do with you." Not entirely true, since the reason Hughes died did affect Girard's interests.

"Why should that make a difference?"

She was silent. "It shouldn't. It doesn't."

"Well?" he said quietly.

What was she protecting him from? Nothing and nobody. Better yet: who or what was she protecting from him? Charlie? Lowther? Herself? Her eye caught a crescent of red backpack under the bed where she'd stashed it, armed, before the party. Maybe, she breathed, what we can erect against the wayward principle at loose in the world are these small occasions of faith. She looked at him, fire maker, flue hider, Cain tormentor, Bella lover, prince of the apple towns. "What do you want to know?" It was Marian who sat.

Hands on his hips. "Not why?"

She shook her head. "Not why."

"Thank you."

He's worked for two years to save the Mission House when, as far as she could tell, there was nothing in it for him. On the subject of the Mission House, she trusted him. Besides, once Charlie came out of his Hannah-induced torpor, the *Toiler* would blow open the whole story in a day or two, anyway. "His name was Jesse Hughes."

"Not Houston."

"No. Thirty years ago, he was married to Alice Lowther."

Thunderstruck. "Hughes," Girard said slowly, working it out. "Connie Hughes. I remember him." Like Moses at the moment he discovered plant life capable of speech. "How did you find out?"

Marian tried to describe the indescribable, those mental joints where things fit and make sense. How she concluded that the man calling himself J.C. Houston was a former Carthaginian with less than honorable motives. How his departure coincided roughly with the last set of repairs to the Mission House done by a trio of workmen, only one of whom was still living. How it happens that Connie Hughes was married thirty years ago to Alice Lowther, who was his mark when he arrived last Sunday by bus. How she eliminated money as the object of the theft—here she touched briefly on the pinched ledger, the duplicated keys, and the beauty of Maid for You—and settled on something part of the actual structure of the Mission House.

By this time, she noticed, Girard was sitting at the edge of the room's only chair, his elbows on his knees, staring at her with a kind of impassive attention. "What Lowther stole thirty years ago—with her husband's help—" Marian went on, "was a cast-iron fireplace facing."

Jack Girard lifted a hand. "Where is it?"

"In her living room. Where no one's ever invited."

His eyes wide, he almost laughed. "Were you?"

She lifted a hand. "I resorted to subterfuge."

"I see."

Marian went on to describe Lowther's tagged treasures, the vain notes to herself. "The fireplace facing in Alice Lowther's living room is the one from the Mission House."

"How do you know?"

"It shows Mazeppa's Ride."

"The saloon?"

Marian smiled. "The legend. On the sign hanging outside the saloon." According to the sources she checked at the library, finely wrought cast-iron fireplace facings fell out of favor at the turn of the nineteenth century—well before the date Temple put on the Mission House. And only two fireplace facings of Mazeppa's Ride in bas-relief are known to exist. There's a photo of one in a book called *Fine Old Ohio Homes.* It appears identical to the one in Lowther's house. That facing, Marian ran a hand through her hair, was commissioned by a wealthy Virginia landowner in 1769.

"Just five years after we're saying Chardin built the Mission House."

"Exactly."

"And the other?"

Marian opened her hands. "Location unknown. At least in the source I checked. And," she pointed at him, "the forge where they were made, near Blacksburg, Virginia, closed down in 1803."

"So, you're saying—"

"I'm saying I believe Claude de Chardin commissioned the first Mazeppa's Ride in 1765." A century later, she added, when Lemuel Prouty bought space in the new building next door to the Mission House, he needed a name for his saloon. In those days, long before it was demoted to municipal warehouse, the Mission House was a local beauty. Prouty admired its fireplace facing and borrowed the legend for his saloon.

"Alice Lowther's house was built more than a century after the Mission House. I can guarantee you the cast-iron fireplace facing I saw in her living room," Marian said, "is not part of her original house." She stretched. "It would just be a matter of checking the blueprints."

He was silent. Then: "Alice stole the one thing that could authenticate the Mission House." They looked at each other.

"That's right," Marian said. "But she didn't realize it. Thirty years ago, the Mission House wasn't in any danger."

His eyes were distant. "Poor old girl," he said finally. "She's worked so hard to preserve the place."

"So have you."

He dismissed it. "Not like Alice," he said. "She sees to it that the place is used. For her, it still has life," he said, running his hands over his face, weary. "And she's the only one who knows that it's because of her the place is at risk."

"We know."

"So did Hughes." Girard pushed himself out of the chair, then seemed undecided what to do next. With the backs of his fingers he pushed aside the white lace curtains, glancing at the street below. "Marian," he said slowly, without looking at her, "have you got any proof?"

The sides of her neck prickled. Went cold. Up to now, she realized, all she had given him was an account. A reasonable, Warner spin on events. Suddenly the profound loneliness of her situation struck her. For sixty-watt ambience aside, the facts were lined up as unequivocal as bowling pins: she was shut in a room with a man about whom the only thing she could say for sure was that he liked Dylan Thomas.

Proof. She looked at him, leaning on the steamer trunk, his thumb moving absently over her velvet top. If Girard figures in the crime at the Mission House in ways I've missed, then damn me. Proof was part of the story. Having come this far, she wouldn't back down.

"I do," she said. "For one, I measured the facing."

He seemed more alert. "You've got the dimensions?"

"I've got them."

"What else?"

"Hanging on the wall in one of the back rooms at the Historical Society are three framed sketches. Do you know them?"

"No."

"They've been there forever. The wallpaper behind them is discolored." Marian stood up. "The sketches were done by a Jesuit. Ink, lots of fine detail. They all depict Chardin." She pushed up plaid sleeves and crossed her arms. "One of the sketches shows Chardin and a Shawnee sitting by a hearth. Between them," Marian said, "you can see the fireplace facing. It's faint, but it's Mazeppa's Ride. You can make out the flanks of the horse and the man's—" she stuttered, "hips." A stupid word to stumble over.

He had narrowed an eye at her. "Is that it?"

"That's it." She raised her chin. Now the proof was his, too. To produce or destroy. Fact is, Warner, you don't know which.

"Right there on Alice's very own walls at the Historical Society," he commented. "On public display." Marian nodded. Then: "Let's go."

"Go?" She felt shocked. "Go where?"

"To the Mission House."

"Now?"

He nodded. "I can't talk our way out of the Historical Society, if a cop comes by. But I can at the Mission House." They sized each other up. Arriving, for her own part, at conclusions devoid of anything rational. It was already past midnight, a time when she was capable of creative thought. Capable of creative acts. Even procreative acts. But rational thought, no. While Girard waited out in the hall, Marian apologized to her pants and brown velvet tank for making them do overtime at the Mission House Make-Out Manor.

On their way out, they passed the Hausers, who were heading upstairs with two glasses of milk and half a dozen Oreos. At the sight of Marian leaving inexplicably with Jack Girard—at 12:20 AM—Cy and Barb seemed unquestioning. "You've got more energy than we do," Cy said, shaking his head.

Like they're going to tool down the highway looking for an all-night dance palace. At least if she doesn't turn up later, Cy and Barb will remember the time. And the company. Marian went out into the chilly night feeling like she was making her way along a subway tunnel.

Without a light.

Without a map.

Without a friend.

With only a distant vibration on the silver track.

Chapter Twenty-Nine

Jack Girard's jeep was a true jeep. Not the upscale model for suburbanites who dream about scrabbling over rock. Girard's looked like what the Allies drove at Tobruk. Regular Army issue, with only minimal protection against the elements. She held on to the half door as they rattled up Main Street: no shocks.

"Tell me," Marian said, feeling about as Nordic as she could stand, "what do you do when it gets cold?" She widened her eyes at him as he glanced over.

"Drive faster," he said.

They had parked around the corner from the Mission House, on Plum Street, out of the glare of the streetlights. Two weather-beaten boards were nailed across the back door, Marian noticed as they approached. Predating the death here this past week was her guess. As far as she could see, the area was deserted. Two doors down, Mazeppa's Ride disgorged stragglers to the sounds of hearty voices and a lingering piano, like an aperture in the seamless night.

"Here." Girard tossed her a key ring and turned back. "I've got a flashlight in the box in the back of the jeep."

Where she stood by the Mission House, set back off the street, Marian could see nothing. All she heard were the sounds of goodnights and high, aimless riffs. One of his keys released the padlock; the other opened the front door. She pocketed the keys and stepped inside, leaving the door ajar.

It was a dark, blank cold. The arc of mercury vapor from the streetlights dimmed to nothing just a few feet away from the Mission House. Girard closed the door behind him, then flipped on a high-intensity pocket flash. "Over here." He jerked his head. She remembered Bella, arrested in her golden poise against the fireplace, untouched by the fine rubble of mortar at her feet.

A glint of silver: Girard's tape measure. Marian held one metal end—shining the pocket flash where he worked—while he measured the space in the brickwork where a facing would fit. "Thirty-nine by fifty-two," he said, his voice low. "What have you got?" From her coat pocket, she pulled a folded slip of paper and handed it to him. "Well," he said with a kind of finality, returning the paper to her.

Kneeling then, Girard inspected the space where the facing had once been. Marian crouched, swinging the beam over his hands. As he leaned across her, their shoulders brushing, she smelled soap and old leather. "Look at this," he said. He took the flashlight from her, directing it at several places in the mortar. "See where it's been patched?" The patch covering the traces of the facing's removal was lighter than the original mortar. It had been feathered expertly.

"Hughes?" Marian asked.

Girard frowned, nodding, "I'd say." Then: "Take off your gloves," he said. Taking her right hand, Girard moved her fingertips over the old and new mortar in a kind of mason's Braille. "Feel the difference?"

Marian nodded. "The patch is finer," she said.

He sat back, draping an arm over his raised knee. "What I can't figure," he said, "is why the fireplace facing wasn't missed."

The flashlight dangled from his hand.

"Do you remember this place when you were, say, seventeen?"

"Oh," he said softly.

She started to smile. "Ever study Native American culture?"

He scratched an eyebrow. "Twice," he said. "With Barb Polson. Hauser now," he explained. "Occasions of great embarrassment—and no action. We couldn't get past being pals."

"Yeah," she said softly. "I know that one," came out before she even thought about it. Damn. She must have left her censor back in bed at The Briars.

Girard gave her a keen look, then, to his infernal credit, he looked away. What she'd yielded up to him over the past two hours—her theories, her larcenies, her proofs—felt puny compared to this bit of knowledge she was too sloppy to keep to herself. Damn. "In those days," she soldiered on, "the Mission House was packed with municipal junk. Flats. Collapsed grandstands. School desks. The fact is, no one would have missed the fireplace facing."

A small nod from Girard, who was staring into the firebox. "Tell me," he said, without looking at her, "what do you think happened here last Sunday night?" He listened quietly, only his dark eyes moving, while she described what she could picture as Lowther's meeting with Hughes. His threats, her anger. More than anger. All the strain of possible exposure, confronted after half a lifetime with the embodiment of a relationship gone sour. It was all too much. For both of them. The wheezing, the panic, the dreadful solution: in her flight, Alice turned the key in the padlock.

"For a two-of-a-kind fireplace facing."

"Of Mazeppa's Ride." Marian hunkered down in her long coat and told Jack Girard what she'd learned about the reference—that, three hundred years ago, Ivan Mazeppa had an affair with the wife of a Polish nobleman, who, in turn, had him stripped and lashed to a wild horse. Marian looked at him. "Mazeppa was rescued by Cossacks and went on to become a prince."

"Not a bad reward for a few hours of terror."

She watched Girard stretch out, leaning up on an elbow. "All we have of him," Marian went on, "is that image—naked, lashed to a wild horse, chased by wolves. For love."

"For punishment."

"No," she said, her voice suddenly loud in the cold, empty space. "The love came first."

His eyes slipped away to some point on the floor. Then back. "I guess it did." At the sound of voices approaching, Jack Girard switched off the flashlight. They sat very still. Two males, a female, their talk a familiar kind of boozy afterwash. It became apparent they were just cutting across the property. As the voices passed, Girard stood up. "We should get going."

Five nights ago, Marian thought, Alice Lowther met Jesse Hughes here. And somewhere on these sorry floorboards, he fell and died. Into this cold, still air, the spirit of Jesse Hughes vanished. It was not a nice spirit, but it was the one he was allotted for seventy-plus years. And he had hoped to ease both spirit and flesh on this trip to Carthage. Both got eased, all right.

The ride home was silent. Brief. The cold on her face felt necessary. Girard stopped in front of The Briars. "Give me a couple of days," he said, rocking the shift into neutral.

"What for?" In the absence of streetlights, she couldn't read his expression.

"Before you go to the police."

"I'm leaving Carthage on Sunday." It was a deadline.

"And I'm going to Zanesville for a couple of days."

"Well," she said, "then I may not see you. Goodbye." She held out a hand.

"Bye," he said, taking it.

Marian got out, then looked in at him. "I hope—"

"What?"

Say it. "I hope you can save the Mission House."

He nearly smiled. "Then I was right."

"Yeah."

She stepped away. Girard made a tight U-turn, one arm held out the window in a stiff farewell. She watched him go. Not down the alley, toward Providence, but straight up Main Street. Out toward Highway 8. The trailer, the space heater, the low metal bed.

We have the house, Bella had said.

We have each other.

It feels complete.

Overhead a skift of clouds moved across the moon. Looking for definition, like all things gray. Hand over hand in restless gesture. Like hearsay. Like hope. The moon was just past first quarter when the chip it held toward the sun was stripped white. If that was all we ever knew of the moon, Marian thought, we might find it enough. In the light from an elsewhere sun, it looked complete.

Chapter Thirty

Nearly three, Saturday afternoon.

Marian spent that morning making slow headway on the report for Joan. She was able to cover the basic sides of the argument, including the position of letter-writing high schoolers who took the stern position that if the old piece of crap building couldn't be turned into a teens-only community center, then it should be torn down and turned into a teens-only community center with a better sound system and maybe a hot tub. As for the heavy hitters Jack Girard and Bill Cain, she needed to touch on philosophical differences—so-called progress versus so-called history—only she couldn't bore Joan for more than half a page on that score.

Nobody would like it, but Marian would advise more patience on the part of the committee. After all, she'd tell them, new evidence has come to light (she cringed at the tabloid cliché) that might very well shake loose the unyielding positions of the past three years. Here she'd remind everybody that Carthage was a small town with all the old animosities of small towns. Marian read over her first draft, then frowned. She'd have to give Joan and the Park Service something more in the way of an action plan; otherwise, what was the point in sending her there?

She needed more time to think about the fireplace facing. And more time to research other options for the Mission House—like what? —that would keep it safe from demolition without all the rigor of an application for National Historic Landmark status. In the short run, she had some calls and visits to make. So she tidied up her papers, slammed herself into the Volvo, pushed the heater to Hi, and headed out of town.

At the stone sign for Carthage Pet & Garden, sculpted into the shape of what looked like a tombstone for a riding lawnmower, Marian swung into the parking lot. Toward the back of the commercial property was a large, gray garage, which was apparently where Carthage Pet & Garden housed their inventory. Bright, slightly rusted signs for Toro and John Deere lined the walls just under the eaves.

Somewhere on that second floor lived the elusive Steve Grey, and Marian pulled up close to the building and parked next to a black Kia that looked a few years old. Grey's? She ran up the stairs that had been shoveled and salted to the front door. The green, checked curtains on the nearest window were closed. She knocked firmly. "Mr. Grey?" she called. "Steve Grey?"

Then she waited, turning toward the sound of a large truck filled with stone slabs rumbling into the lot. Marian knocked harder. "Mr. Grey, it's Marian Warner. Can I talk to you about the body in the Mission House?" Pressing her ear against the door, she heard nothing moving inside. Just how sick was this guy? What had he missed, two days of work at MCG Construction? A couple of gigs? Deflated, Marian left. Whatever Steve Grey could tell her about Jesse Hughes's death and the scene of the crime, he wasn't willing to share. Not beyond the cops. If he was stonewalling her, she didn't know how to change his mind. Marian had done her due diligence, but she had gotten exactly nowhere.

By three o'clock that afternoon, Marian was lacing up a glamorous rental pair of men's hockey skates, which was all they had left. Hannah stashed her purple skate guards in a gym bag and made her way over to the ice in her stylish white Riedells, a birthday present a month ago from her mother, who was presently something called a polarity therapist in Kamloops, British Columbia. Rita was running a Petro Canada station, which appeared to be more in demand than polarity therapy.

The girl shrugged; the skates were nice. Even if Traci's part in the gift didn't go beyond mailing a check to Charlie to cover the pair, Hannah had chosen at the local sporting goods store. From her dad, she had received a sleeping bag—not just any bag, but the perfect bag: a zero-degrees quilted mummy bag in cadet blue with Quallofil insulation and six-inch loft from

L.L. Bean.

Cold Spring Municipal Park consisted of eight acres in downtown Carthage. The outdoor ice rink the city council debated every year whether to flood was near the street. A hundred yards away was Jack Girard's grain elevator and, across the street, Cindy's coffee shop. Today her business probably ran to hot apple pie and cocoa for shoppers who came downtown instead of driving halfway out of Carthage to the mall.

Four doors up from Cindy's, Main Street ended in a T at South River Street. A green '49 Chevy pickup pulled over to the curb long enough to let out a boy—Derry's son—who waved and ran inside the coffee shop. Out of the driver's window poked an arm swaddled in Army surplus, waving back. Tim Rinehart. As the traffic cleared, the old pickup went east on South River Street.

When Marian had arrived at Charlie's earlier, he was fulminating. And Hannah was stonewalling. "Apparently," Charlie finally managed, Hannah has been stealing —"

"Rescuing."

"Laboratory animals—"

"They're amphibians, Dad, not rhesus monkeys."

"From school and hiding them—"

"Housing them."

"—hiding them in her closet. For which she could get suspended."

Hannah shrugged. To delay her tears.

"What were you thinking?" he said finally. "Answer me that."

Answer me that.

Hannah deflated a little, suddenly given the floor. It was her chance to say why, to be eloquent. To be the champion for classroom amphibians everywhere. And she wasn't able to do it, even in front of just the two of them. What came home, Marian learned, were a salamander and a couple of frogs. Waggedorn, the science teacher, was doing a unit on regeneration, and Hannah was convinced he was going to hack off the salamander's tail. To prove what she called some stale, old scientific point to a bunch of seventh graders in Carthage, Ohio. Once you chop off one salamander's tail anywhere in the world and it grows back, why keep doing it again and again and again?

Marian couldn't defend it.

"These creatures," Charlie said, "are not your property, honey."

"I understand that." She was very dignified.

"They're not yours to save."

"I disagree."

At least the tone was friendlier. "Hannah," he said, "schools use protozoans to teach kids about regeneration."

"No."

"Ask your teacher."

"I won't take them back."

Marian stepped onto the ice. Overhead the sky was dense and low, a white slab before snowfall. Skating halfway around the rink, Marian glided around parents making slow progress with bundled toddlers hoisted by the underarms. Pulling on her gloves, Marian managed a two-footed turn and skated backwards, shifting her weight. At the center of the rink, Hannah called to her, "Watch." Marian, who saw her pull off a waltz jump, then grin, held up her hands and clapped.

Hannah, her face impassive, glided to a T-stop next to Marian. "I'm taking them back," she said. Expecting nothing—typical Hannah—not praise, not dismay.

A tight little nod. "I thought maybe you would."

"But I'm scared."

Across the street, Derry Wilson stood hatless on the corner by the coffee shop, her red hair tossing in violent peaks as she thumbed a ride. Through a scrim of cold air, Marian watched her: thin, lively, red, and pale all at once. All vision. No voice. Derry saw them, then, on the ice. Smiled and waved, her arm high. Delicate as frost on glass, a winter filigree. As perishable as breath in the granite air. A yellow Skylark pulled over. Marian waved back as Derry looked inside the Skylark and motioned the driver on.

"The thing is," Hannah was saying, "the risk isn't mine," and she skated slowly away.

Chapter Thirty-One

When the radio alarm kicked in at eight-thirty the next morning, Marian heard a snowplow and a voice like Liberace's telling her she was "spatial" in the eyes of the Lord Jesus Christ. Tack on at least an hour to the trip home, depending on the extent of the snowstorm. She opened her eyes. The room had the kind of supernatural brightness that only happens when what's outside has gone arctic. Ahead of her lay chopping at her ice-crusted windshield and creeping along the Penn Turnpike at forty miles an hour.

At noon, an appointment with Khartoukian. Thirty minutes, tops, to tell him, without relish, about Jesse Hughes. Lowther's act, finally, seemed only inept, and Marian had to keep reminding herself over the last two days that the original theft was a criminal act and leaving Hughes to die was a criminal act.

So what was it about the moral high ground, Marian wondered, that made it appear a post-nuclear landscape? Hell. Lay the facts off on Khartoukian, let him turn them over to the investigating officer on the city side, then make snowy tracks back to the cabin on the Delaware. Because if truth is something she can handle only when she likes its looks, then she'd better give up her license.

The ledger had been replaced.

The report on the Mission House roughed out and saved to the cloud.

Brief calls made yesterday to Derry and Bella. To Derry, she offered some time at the cabin on the Delaware, adding, "Bring Charlie." And the pang she felt when she invited him as half of a couple that didn't include her was unbearable. To Bella, who seemed a strange combination of shocked and thrilled, she provided her solution to the death at the Mission House.

Hannah had been hugged.

Charlie had been hugged harder—last evening, after a quick dinner at Friendly's, before he and Hannah went to a multiplex to watch something rated PG. The way Charlie saw it, swap classroom larcenies for more father-daughter time together. "What's going to happen to us, Charlie?" Marian blurted into some place between his collar and his ear.

"Not a thing." His voice was rough.

She couldn't look at him. "Yeah," she said. "Not a thing." About as comforting as Alice Lowther during an asthma attack. They said something about getting together during the spring, getting together during the summer—with or without Derry Wilson—maybe a beach house would be fun, maybe a canoe trip up north. The hollow, hopeful things spoken by the uncommitted.

She threw on her navy fleece pants and long red sweater. Given the road conditions, the sooner she could get in to see Khartoukian, the better. Marian phoned the Sheriff's office, and to the deputy who answered, she explained her need to move up her appointment.

"Move up? You mean come in sooner?"

"Right." Cradling the phone, she strapped on her wristwatch.

"Not possible," he said. "Fact is, you'll be lucky to see him at all today."

"Why's that?"

"He's on a homicide out Highway Eight. Called in about an hour ago."

"Homicide."

"At the pit."

The pit? Her mind raced. "The gravel pit?"

"Only pit I know of."

Her heart tumbled. "Who is it? Who's dead?"

"Next of kin has to be notified first."

"Look, I'm a friend—" Whose, she didn't know.

"Next of kin—" he repeated.

Marian hung up and scrambled downstairs, punching at the sleeve of her new dress coat as she ran through the back. The Hausers moved aside in a glint of apron and spatula. "Later," Marian yelled, already out the door. Six inches of snow. Shit. Everywhere. She made large sweeps across the windshield of her car, scraping the thin layer of ice with her fingernails. She pulled a set of keys from her coat pocket, and when they wouldn't work, she stared at them. Two keys on a metal ring. The Mission House keys. Marian still had them. When she found her own, she slammed the door on the hem of her coat, her foot pounding the accelerator, and blessed the Volvo for starting on the second try.

So much for safety of the road, she thought, setting the defroster at full blast, cold, her visibility about the size of a half dollar. Marian slid the car through the alley, erased by snow, fumbling at the buttons on her coat. Her nervous system had gone haywire, reduced to a strobe of neurons.

Think about bacon and eggs.

Think about the grand old flag.

None of it helped.

As she skidded out on to Main Street, her hands finally stopped shaking when she remembered that Jack Girard was in Zanesville.

Chapter Thirty-Two

By the time she pulled through the gate at MCG Construction, the defroster was working, sending jagged wafers of ice slipping down her windshield. And adrenalin was no longer squirting through her system. What was most likely, she told herself, was death by blunder: what she called the "oops" or "oh, shit" school of interpersonal relations. Too much passion, too much drink. Like waking up in a strange bed with a hangover and someone whose name you can't recall.

Only this time, he's dead.

A week ago, one of Cain's men took a knife in the hand. Chances are, last night, one of Girard's men had taken a knife in some pulpier place. The knives get longer. The drinks, stiffer. Convictions, stronger.

Oops.

Oh, shit.

Error.

Consequences.

Things strict and total in the waiting air. Nothing abandons like abandon. What remains, always, is some kind of brute object: the corpse of love, the corpse of everything else. The nameless, sleeping bedmate. The body in the snow. On Girard's doorstep. When it seemed clear to her the Volvo might not make it down to the gravel pit, Marian pulled over and set off on foot, skirting all the fresh tire tracks. Under the snow, the dirt road had vanished. What was left were the trees, snow-stacked and leafless.

She stopped. The road dipped to the final clearing and the crater she remembered. The trailer, the gravel mountains more alpine than ever, the

149

pit. The jeep was gone, but in its place were two black and whites, their lights blipping lazily, and a tan Land Rover. Backed up close to the gravel pit was the Squad, its rear doors standing open. From one of the vehicles, a radio crackled like frost.

No one was in any hurry.

Jim Carney was crouching in the snow over the body, his hair lapped by the wind. There at the water's edge, he looked uncomfortable, struggling to conduct an examination and keep his balance. Some poor turf warrior—barely a kid, judging by the size of him—had gone into the drink. Near Carney the ice was cracked into shards, the water as gray and implacable as rock.

The others stood around with the peculiar uselessness of the living. A black-jacketed paramedic was angling a cigarette into his cupped hands, flicking away match after match until he got a drag. The only one of them who looked warm in his sheepskin coat and hat was Khartoukian. "Go get yourself a drink," she heard him tell a baby-faced deputy. "Under the seat, passenger side." The kid looked miserable. As he heaved himself in the direction of Khartoukian's car, Marian got a better look at the body.

No doubt about it, death is one hell of a disguise. The jeans, the short jacket in soaked creases. Face dense as dough, Kabuki white. The short hair flattened in carmine streaks. Like old blood.

Red.

Red hair.

Dear God: it's Derry.

Derry.

None of it. Made. Sense.

Khartoukian came over to her. What she heard was a call for the stretcher, *I'm done here, shit it's cold, let's get her to the morgue.* What she saw was a monolith of sheepskin. "Marian?"

She looked at his unshaven face.

"You here to see Girard?"

Something about her felt dislocated. "He's out of town."

"That's what I hear."

"Zanesville."

"So, what brings you?"

Her words felt distant. "I'm not sure."

"Chiclet?"

"What?"

"Want a chiclet?" Khartoukian was shaking a small yellow box. She declined. Looking skyward, he tapped the box, three pieces of gum tumbling into his mouth. "Nice lady," he said, squinting past Marian.

"Yeah," she said. "Nice lady."

"Great voice."

She nodded. Nice lady. Great voice. And that, friends, concludes our service. A couple of well-meaning nouns grunted in a snowdrift. Christ, is this what it comes down to? Any minute now, she'd remember how to exhale. And when she did—when she did—she could count on anger to see her through the next few days. "Who found her?"

"Kid named Rodie Prescott. Works for Girard. Apparently, he's been out sick and made an arrangement to stop by here and pick up his paycheck. From the mailbox."

"How did she die?"

"Drowned, the doc says. Sometime last night. Looks like she was hit first."

"Raped?"

A small, tight shake of his head. "Carney's guess is no. He'll know more later. I can tell you one thing," he said, rolling the mangled chiclet box in one gloved hand. "Physical evidence is going to be crap. Just crap." Accessory after the fact: six inches of snow. When she said nothing, he asked, "You all right?"

"Yeah, I'm all right."

Only she wasn't.

"We're going to seal the area," Khartoukian said, working the gum behind his front teeth. "You have to go." Already he was looking elsewhere—taking in the terrain, the possibilities—his eyes denuding everything he saw. With something colder than the winter air. "You got anything I should know?"

Marian straightened up, the air searing her skin. She realized the sun had come out, high and bright as klieg lights. What bad grace. "Not a damn thing," she said. "Not yet." They watched the men lift the body. Crabbed wreckage. No longer Derry, maybe, but fucking personal all the same. Spongy and blighted. Only, which are you: the corpse of love, or the corpse of everything else?

Her first thought was for Charlie. Oh, honey.

Her second, for Cindy and Andy.

All the rest were for the killer.

Chapter Thirty-Three

The city room was empty. In a town with nearly three dozen churches, there was no Sunday *Toiler.* Amen to no news. A phone started to ring at one of the desks; no one got it. Not Charlie. Not even the cleaning lady in the shadows at the back, emptying out a wastebasket with a few sluggish taps, oblivious to grief. A banana clip was holding back her graying hair. What Marian thought was an absent-minded hymn turned out to be Ringo Starr's "I Wanna Be Your Man" sung to the beat of "Onward, Christian Soldiers." At the sight of Marian, one hand flew up in a pudgy wave, then snaked a rag over an empty desk.

"Charlie?"

She stood in the doorway to his office. He sat stretched out, stiff, in his chair, the back of his neck resting across the top. His arms hung loose over the sides. All the tension in his body seemed to collect at some point on his face: Pain Central. His eyes were closed. "I know," he said flatly, not looking at her. "I talked to Khartoukian a little while ago."

"I just came from there." She shut the door behind her.

"You saw?"

Marian nodded. Then, since his eyes were still closed, she said, "Yes, I saw. At least," she heard herself say, thinking of Paul Seeks, her voice squeezed into something tiny, "there was something to see."

Charlie nodded. He knew. "I sent Donna Ardizzone to do the story," he said. "I can't do it." Marian said nothing, saw only Charlie, his face tightening with pain. "Will you help?"

"Do you want me to?" *Give me a way in, Charlie. I don't know what to do for*

153

you.

"Yes." A sudden droop, like palsy, in his face. He covered his eyes. "I feel like hell, Marian." She couldn't stand it.

"I know." In an instant, she was beside him, pulling his hands from his face, pulling him out of the chair. Not knowing where to go, how to land. Falling against the wall in a languid hug. *All I know how to do is to hang on tight, and even that I can't do well.* They ended up sitting splayed against the wall, like wounded soldiers in a bunker. Suddenly, he struggled against her, his eyes wild as he looked around.

"What I need—" he cried.

"Say it." Derry Wilson, a double scotch, a little place in Florida. Even your sweet, sweet lovin'.

"What I need here is a couch."

Laughing, they slipped sideways in a sloppy, woozy shudder. With nowhere else to go, he rested his head on her belly. Derelict. Free. Fifteen all over again. No: better than fifteen. She stroked his hair. Something she had never done. A cross-hand piece, Charlie, that's us. When he started to shake his head violently, like casting off a bad dream, she pulled back. "What is it? Do you mind?"

He shushed her, reaching up blind, two fingers tapping her mouth silent. "That's not it," he said. "It's nice." Adrift. Strange. Their conversation floating into a grotto, a place where old words sound intimate in the blue light. His voice dark and low, caught in the wool of her coat. "I was thinking it wasn't Hannah," Charlie said. Her throat closed up; no, it wasn't Hannah. "And it wasn't you," he said, his fingers loose on her face. Making sure. A face his touch would know. Though she didn't see how. Didn't see how. She cried. A shadow lumbered across the frosted glass window of the office door: *Love you like no other, baby, like no other can.*

"Mr. Levitan?"

"Go home, Mary Ellen," he yelled into Marian's coat.

"I'm done."

"Go. Home."

"Is there anything else you want me to do?"

154

"Let me see now," he called out. "Why, yes, there is. Why don't you go home?"

"Are you all right in there?" Whatever obscenities he muttered seemed to satisfy her. "Well, then, I guess I'll be going." The shadow moved away.

Groaning, Charlie rubbed his face into Marian's coat. She shifted, rocking him with her hip. Asked if there's a Bob Evans in Carthage—to which he said hell yes, two or three—and she told him she'd spring for breakfast. Charlie rolled over onto his back and stared unblinking at the ceiling. What's needed here first, she thought, is caffeine, followed by a few nameless hot, fried, round things. Then, with her hand flat against his cheek, Marian looked at his face and felt completely inconsequential.

I can't give you Star Dust.

Chapter Thirty-Four

Certain things became clear later in the day when Marian caught up with Tim Rinehart at Mazeppa's Ride, where he was sitting motionless on one of the scuffed risers at the back. In the melancholy half-light, he stared at nothing. Derry had left work at Mazeppa's Ride, he told her, around 10:40 the night before. Finished a great set—sexiest goddamn "Up the Lazy River" you'll ever hear in this fucking life. Yeah, she left alone. No, no one followed her, not that he noticed. Yeah, she seemed in good spirits. No, she didn't say anything about her plans—just that getting a ride home shouldn't be a problem on a Saturday night. Was it snowing when she left? Rinehart shrugged, miserable. "What the fuck's it matter?" And he finished writing a sign for the front door in black marker: *Closed due to death in family.*

Which, Marian guessed, was how it felt.

Mourners found their way to Cindy Wilson's, a trim, aluminum-sided bungalow in the East End, where no one was ever more than four small blocks from the Conrail tracks. It was the neighbor Patrice with a jumpy little shih tzu named Danny Boy who first voiced the maniac theory.

"She got in the car with some maniac," Patrice cried, "that's what she did," making the murder seem as much Derry's fault as the maniac's. And with what was left of a lighted Tiparillo wedged between her fingers, Patrice pushed back her stringy hair. The room got quiet. Charlie, still in his coat though they'd been there over an hour already, sat lifeless on the edge of what Cindy called the divan.

Some maniac.

156

Derry got in the car with some maniac.

It seemed like one of those sudden, shared truths that quickly fill a space. One of the men poured himself a double from the two-liter bottle of Canadian Club on the coffee table. Dinner, she could tell, was going to alternate between whiskey and strong coffee.

Then the speculation started: not someone from Carthage, definitely. As though none of the local maniacs seemed to fit, somehow. Someone from the county, maybe. With a new car—maybe a truck—a pickup. And young. Maybe good-looking. With a smile like that Brad Pitt. "'Evening, ma'am,'" the double drinker imitated sourly, "'can I give you a lift?'"

Standing in the narrow hall just outside the light of the living room was the boy, Andy, in a Cincinnati Reds sweatshirt about two sizes too big, overhearing the maniac theory of his mother's death. Until he was noticed.

"Oh, hush, Ottie, hush."

"Go on, young man," the man called Ottie blared at the boy, "this is no place for you."

"Here, Andy, honey, take Danny Boy for a walk for me. He's gotta pee real bad. Will you do that for me?"

"This is no place for you, young man."

"It's my ma," the boy said quietly.

Patrice forgot all about the dog. "Your ma's in heaven, honey."

The boy shuffled. "If she is, then she had a hell of a time getting there."

"Oh, shush, Andy, you don't know."

"Jesus, Mary, and Joseph."

The doorbell. Two long, shrill rings.

Grateful for the diversion, two of the others jumped up to share the maniac theory with the newcomer, who turned out to be the local priest. Marian nearly collided with Cindy, her hair in careless spikes, coming out of the kitchen with a tray of coffee and Lorna Doones. *Fifteen minutes more*, Marian thought, *is about all I can stand*. After the next good opportunity to speak to Cindy, alone, she'd leave.

She touched Andy's shoulder, turning him back toward the bedrooms. "It's my ma," he said, his blue eyes narrow under the dark, lank hair.

"I know. I'm sorry."

He gave her a long look. "I can stay if I want."

"When they act like that," Marian said, "why would you want to?"

"They don't know what they're talking about."

"Probably not."

"They don't." Not plaintive, even. Just matter of fact. *Who am I to tell him they mean well?* Besides, she wasn't sure they did. Marian watched him shuffle back down the hall and close himself in his room. Maybe Derry's death was just an opportunity for neighbors to drink Cindy's whiskey and eat her cookies—and scare themselves silly with their talk of a handsome homicidal maniac from the farther reaches of Wade County.

Marian slunk into the kitchen as Father Kenney launched into a psalm. "I will lift up mine eyes unto the hills," he prayed, the others murmuring whatever they recalled of the words. From the green and gray squares of linoleum came a faint smell of ammonia, a task Cindy found to do for herself after Khartoukian gave her the news. And left her alone in a household reduced violently by one. Get out the bucket, get out the mop: murder is as good a time as any to do the kitchen floor.

When a wall phone next to her rang, Marian picked up. Jim Carney, looking for Charlie, who seemed relieved for a chance to leave the divan and the prayer meeting, even if it meant having to hear the report on the post-mortem. "So?" he said into the line, pulling a notebook and ballpoint pen from the inside pocket of his sport coat. He scribbled a few words, then closed his eyes tight. "How many?" he asked. "Where?" He had stopped writing.

"So what does it mean?" he said, resting a hand on Marian's shoulder, shaking his head as he listened. "Okay. What else? Any sign of sexual assault?" Charlie put away his pen. To Marian he mouthed 'no.' She felt relieved, somehow, that Derry's death just included one less act of violence. "Right. Thanks, Jim." He hung up, staring at the phone for a moment, and turned to Marian.

"Tell me," she said.

He moved her out of earshot, then shoved his hands into his pockets.

"Carney's putting time of death before midnight. His best guess is eleven-thirty."

"Go on."

"Based on contusions on the back of her head, he says Derry was knocked out—"

"With?"

Charlie raised an eyebrow. "For now, with apologies, he's calling it a 'blunt object.'"

"The blow didn't kill her?"

He shook his head. "She was alive when she went into the water," he said. "Out but breathing."

"Could she have fallen in when she was hit?" Back to the "oh, shit" school of interpersonal relations. Maybe Derry Wilson's companion that night hadn't reckoned on anything quite so final but hit her with enough force to send her through the thin ice of the gravel pit. Out of reach of any rescue. From an impetuous blow to a mess of the first magnitude. The stupid, sloppy sort of crime that takes on its own unpredictable life. Exerts its own perverse power.

Leaning back against Cindy's kitchen wall, Charlie shook his head slowly. "She has bruises on her, Marian, here—" he touched the side of her ribcage, "and here," he touched her waist, "and over the pubic bone," he said. "Several."

Marian felt confused. "What are you saying? She was beaten up?"

"Carney thinks she was kicked into the gravel pit."

"Kicked."

"The worst bruises are here—" he pressed his fingers first into a place between her shoulder blades, then at the base of Marian's skull, pulling her closer. "Someone kicked her into the water," he said, "and held her head under until she died."

She thought of Derry, the hands at her neck, her back, letting the frigid water enter. A strange heaviness in a place accustomed only to air and song, things unsuited to mortal struggle. Leaving her mother with a plate of Lorna Doones and a grandson to raise. Letting Father Kenney console her, giving him some purpose. Letting the neighbors dredge up fond reminiscences of the dead Derry, giving them some purpose. Shoring them all up with coffee, whiskey, eats.

Marian dragged her fingers through her hair. Maybe, for most people, death is never entirely unexpected. Even violent death. Grief is always available, just another form of disappointment, upped a notch or two. Layoffs, unpaid bills, fevers of all sorts, busted dreams, tepid marriages, smoldering lonelinesses, and a God whose distance one can never entirely calculate. Compared to these, death is something meaner than layoffs but not as final, even, as some unpaid bills. One last cosmic heel ground into whatever's left of the busted dreams.

Marian caught Cindy by the elbow and steered her into a bedroom. As it turned out, hers, a place of latch-hooked throw rugs and wall hangings—amazing how much of a living space can be made into shag carpeting—and needlepointed picture frames. Marian kept her questions simple. How had Derry seemed lately? Happy? Secretive? Fearful?

Cindy looked at her. "Like always," she said, "just herself." Any complaints? Did she enjoy her work? "She never complained, not her, and she was grateful for the work, I can tell you."

Had she received any threats? Any out-of-town mail? "No, no," Cindy scratched the side of her face, "nothing like that," she said, "nothing like that." Any more or less money than usual? "Nothing different," Cindy dismissed it without considering the implications, "just as broke as ever." Aside from Charlie, Marian asked, finally, feeling strange, was there anyone new in her life?

Cindy frowned. "No."

"Don't just say no," she caught Cindy's sleeve. "Think about it." Like an assignment. Inhaling mightily, Derry's mother lowered her chin and pulled herself up straight: a stance of recollection, reviewing day by day the last month of her daughter's life. Calls received, names mentioned, places gone.

Marian waited, her eyes straying to the family photographs crowding the highboy. One, a black and white enlargement whose frame Cindy had needlepointed in an ivy motif on a white background. Two men, forever smiling into the sun, their faces creasy, past their youth. They were hatless, leaning together against a fence post, grass ranging behind them in flattened spikes. Fond and motionless in early summer daylight. Though they both wore shirtsleeves and work pants, the taller man looked patrician.

"A real eye-catcher," Cindy breathed. Her husband and Clayton Girard, outside MCG. "Of course, one's passed away now, the other's in Sparta Vale, but those were some times." Marian didn't need a guidebook to tell her that Derry's father was the shorter man with the proud chin and rounded nose. She saw in his tight-lipped smile a kind of feudal certainty that his contribution to MCG Construction mattered. In their eyes squinting into the sun, there was nothing of cancer, nothing of paralyzing stroke. Girard and Wilson were snapped during that fine, ineluctable period of good health and hard work. *Those were some times,* Cindy said, sharing her husband's loyalty.

It still hadn't sunk in that twenty years later, her only child turned up murdered on the premises of MCG Construction, a few hundred yards away from where her husband and his boss stood smiling in their Kodachrome innocence. "There was no one," Cindy said, finally. "I've thought about it, Marian. And I know why you're asking. But there was no one new in Derry's life. Except for Charlie," she added. "No one new at all."

Chapter Thirty-Five

"I just came from Bella's."

"She told you?"

"She told me," said Jack Girard. Monday morning, 7:35. Marian rolled over. When the call came, Barb Hauser had brought her the *Toiler,* mouthed something unintelligible, and closed the door softly on her way out. While Marian struggled to make sense to Girard, she wondered which looked more like it had been left out in the slush and manhandled—the newspaper or herself. *Local Singer Slain,* ran the headline. "Are you sticking around?" he asked.

"Looks like it."

After a moment: "Good."

"I still have your keys. From the other night."

"I know."

"I can drop them by later."

"Any time tonight. I'll be in."

"Did you just get back?" Pretty high-level conversation, considering the hour and her general condition: a sort of boneless lassitude without the benefit of either drink or sex.

"Less than an hour ago. Look, I can't talk now."

"This was your call," she said, irritated, "remember?"

"I'm at the sheriff's office."

"Oh."

"Apparently," he sounded wry, "I interest him. See you later." He hung up.

She had too much stuff to carry on the school bus, Hannah explained on the phone, and Dad had already left for work. With no time to brush her teeth or hair, Marian had picked her up. The girl was wearing fake Uggs, a secondhand pea coat, and a red plaid golf cap. The "stuff" turned out to be a small aquarium covered with a tattered yellow baby blanket. Hannah seemed composed, a little distant, interested in everything they passed. Seeing, she would have you believe, stop signs and donut shops for the first time.

"Taking them back right away?" Marian asked.

The girl jumped. "What? These?"

"Those."

"Oh," she said, biting her lip. "Right."

Marian glanced at her. "How are you doing with it?"

"It isn't heavy." Hannah's eyes didn't quite meet Marian's.

"That isn't what I mean."

"Well," the girl said, looking straight at her, frank and tearless, "it isn't Derry, is it?"

No, it isn't Derry, Marian agreed. Even the part of her that argued for the integrity of any creature's suffering had to admit that it wasn't Derry. *At least it wasn't Hannah*, Charlie had said, *and it wasn't you*. Maybe it was one of those necessary human things, placing our sympathies in order like a poker hand. They rode in silence the rest of the way. As she got out of the car, Hannah slung the backpack over her shoulder and—completely without emotion—picked up the aquarium. Like she was bringing in her project for the science fair. In the girl's impassive look, Marian could tell she had entered a place where the act and its consequences could no longer touch her. "Good luck," Marian said.

"It doesn't matter."

"It does." She leaned over. "Derry matters," Marian said. "This matters, too." Fine words, Warner, considering how many relationships had a better chance of identifying you from the back.

Hannah's lip twitched. "I can't have everything matter," she said, her voice quivering. Then she turned away and walked heavily up the sidewalk to the school. On her spindly little pre-teen legs, everything on her frame seemed too big. She had a shapeless pea coat, a golf cap that obscured her eyes, and boots that Carthage princesses could tell at a glance were not the genuine article. And Hannah Levitan had a heart that didn't quite know what to do with a world that lops off tails and fills lungs with freezing water.

It was a point Marian understood. So well, in fact, she sat staring at the steering wheel until a school crossing guard told her she was parked in the crosswalk and had to move along.

Chapter Thirty-Six

At The Briars, she cleaned herself up more ruthlessly than usual and silenced her stomach with Barb Hauser's French toast. The prospect of going to Bill Cain's felt good. Even downright essential.

What she discovered was a new, blue, vinyl-sided "farmhouse" on the corner of South River Street and a quiet side street called Creekbed, on the fringes of the commercial district. One block, she noticed, past the turnoff to County Highway 8 leading north out of town. And maybe a dozen blocks away from Derry's night job at Mazeppa's Ride. Farther still from the bungalow, she had shared with her son and Cindy. Derry definitely had a transportation problem. Apparently, a fatal one.

To its credit, Cain's building had what Marian was coming to see as a rare commodity in Carthage, Ohio: off-street parking. She plowed noisily through the slush, spattering the man's new radials as she swung alongside the honey-colored Audi. It was the first she noticed the license plate: CAINDO.

Past the row of box elders on the property line was a trim brick house serving as offices for a podiatrist and a C.P.A. Just beyond was a larger brick house, whitewashed, with a long, low porch, housing the Wade Chapter of the American Red Cross. Down the street ranged more homes turned into commercial space with signs offering massage therapy, insurance life-health-auto, espresso, and tanning beds.

Inside the Carthage Development Corporation was an Ethan Allen showroom, what with glistening cherry furniture and blue satin wingback chairs. On the grass-cloth walls were framed prints of leaping spaniels and flustered pheasants. The place felt like a satellite of the Wade Lake Country Club. The gray Kerastan carpet throughout the office sucked noise right out of the air and neutralized it: telephones purred, voices evaporated. Standing in the reception area were Cain, a young man wearing a necktie with mallards, and a middle-aged woman in a Dress For Success business suit with a pink rayon bow tied under her lowest chin.

From the looks of Cain and his crew, the week had begun with a crease. Derry's death left them shorthanded. "Call a temp agency, Evelyn," Cain was saying to the woman, who was telling him that she couldn't possibly be expected to do "the Wilson girl's job" in addition to her own. And the mallard man was struggling to appear part of the generalized anxiety but not so integral to it that he'd be willing to substitute for "the Wilson girl." A difficult position. The fact that he managed it so slickly was a tribute to why he was hired in the first place.

Bill Cain spoke slowly, as though Evelyn depended on lip reading. "Call a temp agency, get someone out here ASAP, and go back to work." Then he saw her. "Marian." He stroked his Dior-shirted chest. "You find us at a disadvantage," he said, guiding her past him. "How lovely." Whether he meant it as a comment on her appearance or the fact that she came in on them with their perfectly creased trousers down around their ankles, she couldn't tell.

On the door to his inner office was a brass sign with a matte finish: *William Henry Harrison Cain, President.* He closed the door and motioned her to a chair. More country club, with a flawless leather couch and chairs, where you could lose anything from loose change to simple motor control. On the walls were framed glossies of Cain shaking hands with business acquaintances. The one who wasn't Japanese was Ted Turner. There were photographs of Cain accepting a Lion's Club Award, Cain accepting a Rotary Club Award, and Cain presenting an award to Ronald McDonald.

Bill Cain sat, crossing his legs, showing a length of Cardin "hosiery." She watched him choose an attitude. He couldn't count on her tolerating some harmless flirtation, so he decided to go with ministerial and folded his hands.

"What can I do for you?"

"Derry Wilson."

"Terrible thing." And thinking maybe it wasn't enough, added, "Unspeakable."

She nodded at "terrible," nodded at "unspeakable." Then she explained to Bill Cain that she was making some inquiries on behalf of a friend—in truth, Derry, although this she kept to herself—and watched his eyebrows draw together into a bar of interest. "When did you hear?"

"Ten minutes ago," he unfolded his hands. "You saw."

"She was found yesterday morning."

"Apparently," Cain said, "no one thought to let me know." He shifted his seat. "I was just her employer," he said with saurian hurt.

"And friend."

"That too." He lowered his head, still looking at her. "When she was forty minutes late for work this morning, I had Evelyn call her home to find out where she was." Cain tugged his earlobe. "I found out," he said flatly.

"Forty minutes late. You start at eight-thirty?"

"I start at seven-thirty," he corrected. "I'm up. And it gives me two full hours before the banks open." He clasped his hands around his knees. "Derry Wilson started at eight-thirty. As do the others."

"Tell me about her work here."

What he went on to describe was what Marian expected. Answering phones. Scheduling appointments. Greeting clients. Filing, typing, purchasing. Making coffee. "Then we all helped ourselves," he added quickly. A twenty-first-century fella.

Marian sat up straight. "Anything of a sensitive nature?"

Cain blinked. "Like what?"

"Contracts," Marian groped. "Accounts. That sort of thing. Did she have access to anything confidential?"

He thought about it. "Access, I suppose," he said finally. "Although nothing of the sort was expected of her. It wasn't part of her job."

Nail it. "But she had access."

"I suppose."

"Did you trust her?" Forgive me, Derry.

"Trust her?" Bill Cain smoothed his blue and gold silk tie.

"Yes."

"I suppose."

"Didn't you ever think about it?"

"Not—the way you mean. She wasn't in a position of trust."

"So you didn't trust her."

With some spirit, he said, "I wouldn't have hired her if I couldn't trust her. If only to make a good cup of coffee. Not now, not then."

She caught it. "Then?"

He flung a hand. "Back then. Before she left town. Years ago."

Marian was careful not to lean forward. "Derry Wilson worked for you ten years ago?"

"That's right. Same drill. I'll save you the trouble. Only her coffee got better, and her typing got worse." It was during the decline of MCG Construction—John Murphy was dead, Clayton Girard seemed determined not to prosper, and Cain himself was fed up.

He hired Derry as his personal assistant. To shore up his interests during what he called "those bleak times." It didn't sound in the least sexual. And when he said she was "at liberty," Marian took it to mean available for work, if not for painting each other's toenails. If she'd been looking, in that sense, she found it shortly thereafter in spades—and, as Derry herself had put it, "landed up with Andy." *Some guy on the road.* End of conversation.

End of liberty in quite the same way.

End of lots of things. Including life.

Chapter Thirty-Seven

A ndy Wilson.

Paternity as a motive for murder. If so. If so, what a shitty deal. Marian looked briefly at the wall behind Cain's chair. How likely was it that Ted Turner had come to Carthage, Ohio? Even given the times the Braves played the Reds, what were the chances he'd make a two-hour side trip to Carthage to be photographed shaking hands with Bill Cain? Slim. What seemed more likely to Marian was that travel came with the territory as president of the Carthage Development Corporation. That William Henry Harrison Cain enjoyed a certain amount of time—as Derry herself might put it—on the road.

Away from Corliss.

Away from the other Presbyterian elders.

Away from everything he had worked hard for—although she could certainly imagine him working hard at a once-in-a-lifetime pop with Derry somewhere in Amarillo. In a spirit of homesickness and altruism: hers. When Marian asked who else was in Derry's life ten years ago, Cain stroked his throat. He was a man, she noted, who spent a lot of time touching himself. "As to her friends, I couldn't say. But if memory serves," he came out with finally, "she was babysitting the Murphy kid and singing nights. Different places."

"And working for you?"

He shook his head. "She quit me a few months before leaving town." Spread his trim hands. "This was all ten, twelve years ago, Marian, you understand."

She asked about Tim Rinehart—and Alice Lowther—ten years ago. Nothing. That would be during the time Rinehart was gone, and Lowther, well, he's not sure she ever had much to do with the Wilsons. Marian let it go. Lowther's erstwhile husband and Derry's father had worked together on the repairs of the Mission House thirty years earlier. For now, she could buy the possibility that any other connection between the families was nonexistent. For now. "What about fifteen years ago?"

"How old was she?"

"Nineteen, say."

Hanging around MCG Construction. Seamus Wilson was sick by then and Derry kept an eye on him. When Marian asked who else was around, he shrugged, "All of us. Myself. John Murphy. Clayton Girard."

"Not the son?" she twigged him. With a straight face.

"No," he said wistfully. "Those were the good days. He was gone out West. Maybe still in the service. I don't make it a practice to follow the early career of Jack Girard."

"The later career is challenge enough."

"How true," he said softly, mistaking her look. "Lunch?"

"Lunch?"

His eyes narrowed. "Today's special at the club is scrod."

He was the only man she'd ever met who could make a menu item sound like a sex act. She shook her head. "I'm working." He made a face and let it go. After all, what can you do with someone who declines the opportunity to listen to Ronald describe the daily special at the Wade Lake Country Club? "Tell me how she spent her time there."

"At MCG?" He looked bored. "Clayton kept her busy."

"Doing what?"

"You'd have to ask him. He handled employees."

"Typing and filing, I'd imagine."

"I'd imagine."

"Are old personnel records available?"

"Again, you'd have to ask him," he said.

Marian stood. "From what you tell me," she pointed out, suddenly weary,

"I wouldn't get much of an answer."

She filled the tank at a corner Sunoco station, where about the most you could buy was a quart of motor oil or new wiper blades. Any hankering for Doritos, smokes, and soda pop would go unmet. It was her kind of station. She smiled at the stiff old man who ran the place — "Art" was stitched on his pocket—a regulation cap pulled down almost to his two hearing aids. She called Charlie, and when he got on the line, she asked how he was doing.

"I'm doing." He sounded brisk. "That's about all."

"Question."

"Okay."

"Who's Andy's father?"

A beat. Then: "I honestly don't know."

"She said it was someone on the road."

"Then I guess it was." His voice slowed, interested. "What are you thinking?"

"Give me a time frame." She watched Art squeegee her windshield. "Andy's nine?"

"Right."

"And Derry took the out-of-town job when?"

"She wasn't pregnant when she left, if that's what you're wondering." From what Charlie had been able to put together, Derry had been away from Carthage well over a year before Andy was born. "So, give."

Marian lowered her voice. "She lasted a month, Charlie."

"What are you saying?"

"After she got back," she went on. "When Derry left Carthage ten years ago, did she leave for good?"

"I think she thought so." Except for the fact that he was still making sense, Charlie sounded strung out. "From things she said, Andy's what brought her back."

She took a deep breath. "And maybe Andy's what got her killed."

Charlie was quiet. "So I take it you don't think much of the idea of a deranged county man in a pickup."

"No."

She could almost hear him smile. "You just don't like Ottie and Patrice."

"That, too."

Charlie needed to get back to proofing the auto classifieds. "Therapy," he explained. "In fact, I might branch out to proofing the Legal Notices this afternoon." Marian promised to keep him posted.

Her search of Derry's desk had yielded little. Bill Cain seemed agreeable when she asked. "Be my guest" was how he put it. Truth was, she'd have preferred some resistance, which might have indicated something worth finding. Bad enough she had provided him with a scintilla of pleasure when he asked her where Derry had been killed, and she replied, "the gravel pit." Despite Cain's hasty air of detachment, it was clear that nothing Ronald could say that noon about the scrod would approach his present pleasure at the possibility that Jack Girard could, at the very least, be inconvenienced.

Marian parried quickly, saying she hoped the sheriff would find Cain's alibi "in order"—whatever the hell that meant, she thought, like we're talking transit papers in *Casablanca.* Cain was unassailable: he and Corliss had spent Saturday evening up at The Branch, where the Heidelberg Quartet was performing in a concert series. Pachelbel's "Canon," he added, waving her out toward Derry's desk, was especially splendid.

Leaving Marian with a new appreciation of the term slim pickings. At the back of Derry's workstation was a recent school picture of Andy in a wooden frame that was clearly a product of wood shop. Rough joints. A first attempt at wood burning — "Andy." Taped to the backboard was a candid, backstage shot of Derry in a green sequined top with Branford Marsalis. "As good as it gets," someone had written across the back.

Only the top drawer held anything personal. And that consisted, at first glance, of a battered bottle of generic aspirin, half gone. Some orange Tic Tacs. A small box of Tampax. A moody postcard of Joshua Tree from a friend named Lily in Oxnard, a few letters, bills, and a brand-new Ann Geddes date book. Finally, tucked under the Tampax, an art card. A black and white photo, dusky and erotic. Nude male and female torsos, entwined, their heads and feet cropped out. The artistic effect was one of a vast and shifting landscape. Printed in the lower, white border was the word "Sahara."

She opened the card. Inside was a familiar dash of black ink. *I don't remember the guy with the camera, do you? Charlie.* Funny. Leave it to Charlie. She replaced it with an obscure sort of regret, wondering what Khartoukian would make of it. When she asked, mallard man brought her an empty printer paper box, and Marian transferred all of Derry's belongings. Then she called the sheriff.

"So?" he said when he finally got on the line.

"You want some help?"

Silence. For a moment. "I'll take it," he said. "So long as you don't get underfoot."

She felt a flare of irritation. "I'll give it," Marian said, "on the same condition." She heard him chuckle. "What do you say we meet tomorrow morning?"

"Fine."

"How early's too early?"

"Any time after seven. My office."

"I've got some old business." By the name of Alice Lowther and Jesse Connor Hughes. Had she waited too long? All her fine work on the Mission House felt just about as far away as Pluto, in a firmament recast in the image of the dead Derry Wilson. Tomorrow, early, she would tell Khartoukian. She pulled herself back. "Cain's got an alibi."

"How nice," Khartoukian said. "That makes one."

"One?"

"I had Jack Girard in here this morning."

Meaning? "He was in Zanesville."

"No, Marian," Khartoukian said, "he wasn't. Not on Saturday night."

"Did he tell you that?"

"Actually, I told him."

"And?"

"He agreed."

Chapter Thirty-Eight

When she hung up from Khartoukian, no place seemed possible. The Briars, the library, Mazeppa's Ride, the gravel pit, the floor of Charlie's office. Nothing satisfied. She felt sick. Confined. The closest she had ever come to the same feeling was standing, that night almost twelve years ago, outside Paul's blown-out brownstone. Glass, wood, stone unfurled. Windowpanes, still dangling from upper windows, falling with a tinkle that was very nearly sweet. There's no mistaking death, so she had turned away. Whatever blood and bone she missed that night, she took away with her. In that part of the mind that's awake and feeding only at two AM, they thrived.

Twelve years ago, she took on the detonation. It pressed her lungs outward and peeled back her heart. To others, those who asked—truly, few—she called it restlessness, and laughed. Called it being uneasy in her skin. It wasn't that. *There was nothing you could do,* Charlie had said, two years after the blast, when he was done being ungenerous to the dead Paul. Marian never bought it. There is, she believed, always something you can do.

The feeling was back.

And all she knew was that she needed to put some miles on the Volvo. She shoved the box of Derry's stuff into the back. Northwest of Carthage by an hour and a half, was a town called Sparta Vale. She could go east, toward home, or west, toward Clayton Girard. East toward safety and ignorance. West toward—more broken glass. She paid Art for the fill-up she could have pumped for herself and headed toward Highway 53. Enough of rifling through Derry's things, sprawling under Charlie's desk, strafing unarmed

174

books and ledgers for their meager yields. Time to bloody my feet.

Alibis be damned.

Or lack thereof.

According to Khartoukian, it was the night clerk at the Travelodge in Zanesville who remembered Girard, registering, their scrupulous records showed, at 1:48 Sunday morning. He had yet to check with the day clerk, who had changed the original reservation for a day earlier to one marked "Hold for late arrival." Girard admitted the point and stonewalled the rest.

Such as where, in fact, he had spent last Saturday evening. If not in Zanesville with disgruntled union reps, with Bella would be the obvious. Only Marian couldn't figure his unwillingness to go official on something that was already pretty public. Neither could Khartoukian. Let it come from Bella, he concluded—give Girard his fire sale chivalry—and was on his way over to see her when Marian called.

It didn't fit. Not for Marian. Jack Girard didn't strike her as a man of such useless gallantry. It wasn't because he was with Bella Murphy during the critical times that he stonewalled Khartoukian. It was because he wasn't. An observation Marian kept to herself. Should be interesting, the interview on Providence.

From there, the sheriff planned to work his way down the list Tim Rinehart had provided of all the customers he could recall who'd been at Mazeppa's Ride that evening. And he was waiting to hear back from the gruff folks at DMV who were running down a plate on a hit-skip early that evening involving a Camaro and a parked car just three blocks from the saloon. Marian was relieved to hear he had doors to knock on and calls to make. It gave her time.

For one, to discover the identity of Andy's father.

For another, to learn why Derry Wilson had died just a month after her return. Without knowing why. For Marian was convinced that in her last millisecond of consciousness, Derry herself didn't know why. Nothing Cindy Wilson had been able to describe in the last month of her daughter's life gave any indication that Derry felt in any way threatened. Maybe she herself was the threat. If the answer didn't lie in the life she led ten or fifteen years ago, then the idea of a cross between Clint Eastwood and Ted Bundy in a black pickup was looking pretty damned appealing.

A local fifth grade chorus, equipped with recorders and Orff instruments, had come to entertain the residents at the Sparta Vale Skilled Care Facility. A piano-playing mother, struggling with disintegrating sheet music, was half a measure ahead of the music teacher. The children worked gamely through Disney's "Let It Go": "Let it go, let it go! Can't hold it back anymore." What the audience might know about ice queens getting their groove on, Marian wasn't at all sure, but if they were waiting to hear some Stephen Foster or Irving Berlin, they'd have a long wait.

Marian stood near the back of the large, bright hall. A table of cookies and punch had been set up for some post-concert fellowship. Ambulatory patients had come in wearing crepe soles and fluffy sweaters draped over their shoulders. Some wielding walkers. Some carrying purses. Whether out of a fear of thievery or a sense that they were "going out," she couldn't say. A few, wheelchair-bound, had been brought in by aides. In their slack faces and reduced bodies, she felt fully what it meant to be so profoundly infirm.

Clayton Girard was one of these.

And after an aide pointed him out to her, Marian had to sit down for a while and pretend to listen to the fifth graders to collect herself. What she saw first was the white hair and clean blue bathrobe. Then she noticed the paper slippers. The dangling hands. His body, a bony jangle without the symmetry of beauty and youth. Hell. What was left were uncooperative muscles that tug at the cheek, hitch the shoulder, knock the knees.

Father of Jack.

Guardian of Bella.

Partner of Bill Cain.

Employer of Seamus Wilson. And Derry.

These things now far away, like a train whistle at night. Having, finally, no more call on his heart or memory than which aide has the warmest hands or whether he'll find rice pudding on his tray that evening. What possible meaning could the death of Derry Wilson have for this man? She pulled over a chair and took his cool, unresponsive hand. "Mr. Girard, my name's Marian Warner." His eyes—dark like his son's, only yellowed around the edges like antique lace—had a fixed look. He appeared to be watching the concert.

She knew it, then.

The man in this wheelchair was no source of information. What she had pictured was the patrician from Cindy's photo. The noble paralytic. But there was nothing romantic about this man. Not the thin dribble from the corner of his mouth. Not the faint smell of urine. If anything, he reminded her of a cardboard carton that's been bumped off one truck and sideswiped by another. Without thinking, she pulled a crumpled tissue from her pocket and dried his chin. "I've come from Carthage to talk to you."

His eyes slewed around to her.

Marian sat back, surprised. It was a keen look, without curiosity or feeling. Just a kind of concentrated intelligence. A self, distilled into a few areas of cerebral activity unaffected by a disabling stroke. What must it be like, she wondered, to be a human transistor? To cast an intelligent and impotent eye on the world. She looked closely at the man's face, past the popped capillaries and ragged brown age spots, at the shapely nose and intense eyes. The basically good bones. She removed decades like dead skin, picturing Clayton Girard, erect and powerful, in the house on Providence when it had furnishings and Elinor and a young son, a place flaxen with life.

He was watching her with interest.

Marian put a hand on the padded arm of the wheelchair. "Do you remember the Wilsons?" She asked him. "Seamus used to work for you." No response. Not negative, just watchful. She wanted to be precise. "Fifteen years ago, his daughter Derry worked for you, too, for a while. She did typing and filing." His eyes blipped, having pulled up the information for himself. Marian inhaled. Her voice dropped. "Derry was killed two nights ago. At the gravel pit. She was drowned. What I hope you can tell me —" She stopped. Make it a yes or no question.

"When Derry was your employee, did she have access to any sensitive information? Contracts, personnel records, accounts. That sort of thing."

After a few moments of imperceptible review, his eyes dipped briefly and closed. A squint against the breezy sunlight, like smiling into the camera twenty years ago, with Seamus Wilson at his side. *Nothing like that,* the look seemed to say. Nothing like that.

What she felt was a vague disappointment, which, it occurred to her, she would have felt either way. For had she sensed his answer was affirmative, how in hell could she get any specifics out of him? In the short run, Girard's negative response was easier to handle, only it didn't help her on the subject of Derry's death. Then she surprised herself. "I've seen your hometown," she said to him. Telling him was like speaking a dangerous truth in the noncommittal wilderness, undisturbed by her puny voice falling to the ground. "I've seen your house, your son, your ward, your place of business." Marian zipped her jacket. "I move about in all those places. Only I can't explain why."

Chapter Thirty-Nine

How much longer could he hold out?

Steve Grey's fingers clutched the curtain at his front window. Carthage Pet & Garden had closed an hour ago, the pickups wheeling out of the employee lot, the exhaust just white puffs like his own breath outside in the January cold. Good, normal folks heading home to what he imagined to be fried chicken and mashed potatoes with their families. Helping the kids with their science projects. Falling asleep with mates that maybe they still even loved.

He let the curtain rustle back into place.

No point looking.

It was a life closed to him.

It's not so much that he had carefully constructed this life in this southern Ohio town. On the job at Jack Girard's, or lost in his own beautiful sax riffs on the risers with the Second Shift Band, or giving those middle schoolers free sax lessons. Sometimes even a date—preferably with someone just passing through. Even a few sweaty hours in a dimly lit room in the Motel 6 on the outskirts of town seemed inexpressibly sweet. He had developed a special fondness for strangers. Because he himself was a stranger everywhere.

All those years ago, in his moment of fright, Carthage was a life he chose when he didn't even know he was choosing. He had come to find his mother. That was all. Find his mother the way kids do when they fall off their bikes or get pushed down on the rough playground. And when he found her, he realized right away that she was just one more loss. What you hear on the news as collateral damage. He could no more tell her that he was her son than he could open the door to Marian Warner, who had knocked.

In his early years in Carthage, his mother became a private little hobby for him. She lived alone. She drove a silver Honda. She watched WWF on TV. She liked pork chops, sometimes with apple sauce. She poured herself the occasional Harvey's Bristol Cream. She could tell you the names of all the generals in the Civil War, both sides. She colored her own hair with Nice 'n Easy. She had no friends and maybe a couple of enemies. And whenever he found himself standing next to her in line at the Kroger, she'd look right through him. Not knowing who he was. And maybe that was fine. For anyone else that Steve Grey could ever find himself next to in a line anywhere on the planet, he had to shave his head and bulk up by fifty pounds and hope to hell it was enough.

But his mother never knew him beyond the first week of his errant life. In some ways, he was at his safest with her. Without her even lifting a hand, the skinned knees and purple bruises of his heart got tended. Just the way they should. The way mothers do. And for some reason—it must be a good one—she was calling herself by her own mother's family name.

Lowther.

Chapter Forty

"Pour us both something." Tapping the razor against a basin set in the sink, Jack Girard made upward strokes through the shaving cream under his chin using a small, frameless mirror set on a narrow ledge. He was wearing jeans and a faded blue University of Michigan sweatshirt. Marian draped her down jacket over a chair and opened the dorm-sized refrigerator. Seltzer, cranberry juice, Dos Equis, and a pitcher of something she couldn't identify. At the back, behind some store-bought hummus and wedges of Jarlsberg, was a bottle of wine. Given the last two days, it was unreasonable to expect too much from Ocean Spray.

She reached for the wine, which turned out to be dry, white, and Italian. "This okay?" She held it up.

He glanced sideways. "Fine."

She poured two half glasses. Girard splashed away a few frothy lines of Barbisol and grabbed a towel. The lamplight, the Turkish rug, the radio tuned low to a folk station—the trailer was a good place to be. Even if, Bob Dylan, a hard rain's a-gonna fall. She sipped. On the footlocker near the bed was an open duffel stuffed with clean, folded laundry. Bath towels, jockeys, khakis, what appeared to be the white polo shirt from the dinner party the other night.

On the desk chair he had set a black nylon carry-on bag, still unpacked. Stashed in a side pocket was a thick manila envelope with a Department of Labor return address. "Just move that stuff," he said, drying his face. Sticking out of the waste basket was a length of black and yellow plastic: Police Line Do Not Cross.

"Must have been satisfying to take down the tape."

Girard set aside the towel. "It was."

"When did they let you back in?"

He looked at his watch. "Less than an hour ago."

Marian swiveled around the desk chair to face him. "Ten years back," she said slowly, sitting, "where were you?"

He seemed curious. "Denver," he said. "Why?"

"Derry Wilson was on the road then."

"That's right." He was waiting to see where she was going.

"Did she come through Denver?"

He picked up his glass. "As a matter of fact," he took a drink, "she did, briefly."

"Did you have an affair?"

Girard gave her a small smile. "You're getting personal." Marian waited, her look steady. Finally, he sidestepped it. "We had her over for dinner."

"Who's we?"

"Claire and I."

"I see." When she didn't see a damned thing.

He shot her a challenging look. "What do you see?"

"Who's asking the questions?"

"We both are."

"Who's Claire?" she blurted.

"My ex."

Who lasted five years. "So Derry came to dinner."

"We had chicken."

"I think you're laughing at me."

"Partly."

A beat. "Partly's okay."

"Where are you going with this, Marian?" he said softly.

She leveled. "Andy Wilson."

Girard gave her a long look. He got it. The full reach of it. "So it's paternity you're after." He studied a point on the low ceiling. "Aren't you afraid of the answer?"

"I'm not even afraid of the question."

He measured his words. "But is it smart," he said, "to ask it?"

"Smart? Yes."

"Safe, then."

"You tell me."

Girard swung a chair around and sat on it backwards, facing her. "Marian," he said, crossing his arms over the back of the chair, "an old friend turns up murdered on my property. Do you think I'd admit I'm her son's father?"

It was just another wrecking ball. She was sure of it. "Yes," she said, "I do." Her heart flopped. "Are you?"

His eyes narrowed. "No."

"Did you have an affair?"

"No." They were silent, his hands folded into a tight knot. "We can have a drink, you can give me the keys, and we'll say goodnight. But don't challenge me. Please. Not tonight."

She heard it.

Trouble was, Derry Wilson was dead on Carney's stainless-steel table—her internal organs stuffed back into her body like it's a goddamn gym bag—Cindy Wilson was mopping lickable floors, and Charlie was looking over Legal Notices with a magnifying glass.

She needed information.

But she'd start small.

"I saw your father today."

Not small enough, apparently.

"My father." His face was stony.

Something.

Went powerfully wrong.

"I went to Sparta Vale."

"Now, why did you do that?" he said softly. Gone, in a dreadful shimmer, to some murky place twenty feet underwater. What she was looking at was anger.

"To find out about Derry's work history with MCG," she went on. "What I found was an old man wearing paper slippers. In a wheelchair."

He stared hard at her. She didn't look away. "My father—" he said, scraping a hand through his hair, "can't talk."

"I know that now."

"He can't chew his own food. Can't pee without help. Can't wash or dress himself," Girard said. "He can't turn over in bed, he can't change channels, pick his nose, brush his hair, or cry. And don't—" he held up a hand, "say you're sorry."

She waited, breathless.

Jack Girard inhaled, tucking his head down between his bent forearms. Then he rested his forehead on two curled fists. "Ten years ago," he said, extending an arm toward her, "my father sexually abused his ward." He looked up at her. "Bella." His face changed. "She was thirteen." It started in July. He'd come in at night and lie down beside her and pull her nightgown up to her chest. Calling her his own sweet little girl. At first, all he did was touch her. She was petrified. Finally, he penetrated her. Eight. Nine. Ten different nights. After that, she lost track.

Girard's voice was quiet. *See it, Marian, feel some small part of it,* was what he didn't say. Only it was there. And all she could give him was her attention. "It hurt. She cried." His voice was flat. "She bled." Not just from her vagina. But her arms. Bella had to bite into her own skin just to keep from screaming. He called it part of his responsibility. That's what he told her, there in the dark. After a while, she believed him. By then, of course, she was truly fucked. She hated him, she loved him, she cried in the dark all the same. And took to wearing long sleeves in the summer heat. Until she lost track. Then her arms started to heal. And her cries shrank.

Along with the rest of her.

Soon after it started, she stopped seeing her friends. Their talk of volleyball and YouTube and Miley Cyrus seemed distant to her. Like a weak transmission from a faraway place. By then, night terrors and untreated yeast infections were more in Bella's line, and these she couldn't discuss. She passed whole days at a time sitting alone in the air-conditioned ranch on the hill, the shades drawn, looking at soaps and reruns of *I Love Lucy*.

There were evenings when Clayton would take her out. For a walk downtown. Or to Mazeppa's Ride for a Coke. When his friends admired her, he'd squeeze her shoulder and tell them she's getting to be a real woman. In the fall, he sent her to boarding school. That, too, he saw as part of his responsibility as executor of John Murphy's will.

Don't look away.

If you look away, Marian, he'll take the shame as his own.

What else does he have?

Teacups.

A lover in beautiful ruins.

A riverbank folly called a grain elevator.

A story.

What surrounded them was no longer air, but some other element—the leaden water of pain. Like Derry Wilson, caught in the purpling cold. *Time holds us green and dying.* Ice holds us. Memory holds us. She looked at Jack Girard, his hands rough with wear. The furrows around his mouth. The lines around his eyes—a grid of age and disappointment. Iraq. The death of Elinor. The violation of Bella. His father. She covered her eyes. Then pulled up her legs, hugging her bent knees for warmth. And for something else: the reassuring feel of herself, intact. "Did she get help?"

"Not until later. At college."

"Who knows?"

"Just me. Now you."

"Why did you tell me?"

He thought about it. "Because I want you to stay away from my father. He shouldn't see you. He shouldn't hear you. Nothing good should come into that old man's life. Don't feel bad about his paper slippers, Marian. As far as I'm concerned, he's lucky he isn't in jail. I pay his bills. And that's all."

"I'm sorry."

This time, he let her say it.

"That's how Bella spent the summer she was thirteen," he said, getting up for more wine. "How did you spend yours?" No answer necessary. Nothing could compare. They both knew it. Certainly not the horror of finding a decomposed cat under Aunt Mirelle's cabin porch. Not the languid pleasure of writing in her locked diary, her body her own. The thing that was becoming Marian elongating into warm and dreamy afternoons by the Delaware. Still, she wanted to answer.

"Learning to stern a canoe," she said. "And wondering if I'd ever get breasts." She held up her glass for a refill. For her, the moment had come. She had witnesses: the open duffel, the piled footlocker, Dylan's jazzy bass line—*I should have left this town this morning, but it was more than I could do*—and Bella's secret, filling the space with a raw and inviolable calm.

The question felt easy. "Where were you?"

"In Denver. I told you."

"The other night." She looked up from her glass as Girard turned away. "And please don't say Zanesville."

"I wasn't going to." He leaned against the sink, his arms crossed. "You spoke to Khartoukian."

"I did," Marian said. "I know about the Travelodge."

"Then you also know I had nothing to say."

"Is that still true?"

His mouth thinned out. "For now, it is."

She felt shut out. How can he tell her about his father and Bella and shut her out now? "Why won't you tell me?"

"Because you're better off out of it."

She stood up, queasy, setting aside her wine. "Then why did you call me at seven-thirty this morning?" He inhaled, looking over her shoulder.

They stared at each other, frowning. Finally, he opened his hands. "Okay," he said. "I was in Carthage."

"So I assume."

"With Alice Lowther."

"Lowther." She couldn't figure it. "Why?"

"I helped her return the fireplace facing to the Mission House."

She felt herself stagger. "You did what?"

"Saturday night," he said. "I put it back."

Her arms tingled. "Of all the damn fool things."

"Why?"

"It's called tampering —" she felt incoherent, "—with evidence. Obstruc-
tion—" *what the hell were the words?* "—of justice." Jesus.

"She didn't lock him in."

"What are you talking about?"

"Hughes. She says she didn't lock him in. I believe her."

None of it mattered. "You deceived me."

"How?" His hands on his hips.

Marian fumbled for her jacket. "You know how."

"Tell me how. How did I deceive you? Where are you going?"

"You said you were leaving town for a few days—"

"I thought I was."

She cut him off. "—and then you pull this. It was my proof, goddamn it."

"It still is. Only it's back where it belongs. It was a chance to put something
right."

She shook her head. "You should have asked."

"Asked? Asked permission? Whose? Yours? It may be your proof, Marian,
but it's not your fireplace facing."

"You should have asked."

"What's the matter with you?" He tried to touch her.

She pulled her arm out of reach. "I have to go." Where the hell were her
gloves?

"Is this about Bella?"

"It's about you," she said, pointing violently at him, her voice fierce and
unfamiliar. Then, broken: "It's about you." Almost from the start. About
him. Her feet were bloodied long before she made the drive to Sparta Vale.
Only getting the hell away from him could clear her head. Give him that
sleek, swift view of her: the back.

Hurling the Mission House keys onto his desk, she flung herself outside,
where the air was so bracing she nearly cried. Loping to the Volvo, Marian
slammed herself inside and started the engine.

Chapter Forty-One

Ten lurching feet across the gravel and she knew the right rear tire was flat. Shit, she pounded the steering wheel, shit to the ninth power. She left the car door open while she pulled the jack and toolbox from the back of the Volvo and landed them in the snow next to the goddamn tire. She stared at it, all the wickedness of the world embodied in a Michelin.

When the jack slipped for the third time, Marian sat back, feeling small and hard with anger. To the left was the road out. It was all she wanted, and she couldn't have it, not fast and easy. She pressed the heels of her hands into her eyes. Behind her was the dim light of Jack Girard's trailer, and overhead an abrasion of stars as useless as everything else. She refused to look. For if she looked, she'd have to consider that what she was feeling wasn't anger.

Wasn't anger at all.

When he came up behind her, she heard in her sigh a mighty inevitability, casting her back through centuries, collapsing the alarms of human history into the space of a fingernail. She stared at a place on her fender where someone had keyed her but good. She could still fight. If she could fix the flat herself—and if she could keep from looking at the stars—she could expand those centuries again like a goddamn concertina, and she'd be safe.

He set the flashlight down, its beam slanting off to the left, and crouched beside her. She continued to stare at the flat. "Here." Jack Girard handed her the flashlight. "I can help." He pulled off his gloves.

She thrust the flashlight against his stomach. "I can do it myself."

"I know you can," he said reasonably. "I just want to help." Handing the

188

light back to her set her off balance. "Is that all right with you?" When he reached for the jack handle, she went crazy, a burning, hurtling thing, a meteorite. She cried out and lunged at him, the flashlight and jack handle crossing yellow and silver in the night air as they went sprawling. The struggle was one of those fierce, blank things, and she knew it wasn't about the jack handle she was straining to grab out of the snow.

Girard raised himself up on his elbows, supporting her weight. She slid back until they were nearly face to face. His hair and cheeks were wet from snow. The struggle, suddenly, was gone, and in its place were the scant lessons of human history. Something about roundheads and cavaliers, something about flossing twice a day. She looked. The only thing darker than the night were his eyes. Don't just move away. Don't just brush off snow.

She kissed him.

Discovered the perfect feel of his mouth.

Then kissed him again.

"Is that so?" he said quietly, rolling her over, her drenched jeans clinging.

"That's so." Pinned. Breathless. More from the truth than his weight. *That's so.* All of her soldiers were gone. Her voice, her nerves, her feet. In all of her life, Marian had never felt herself so entirely in another's keep. She started to shiver.

With the backs of his fingers, Jack Girard slowly brushed her hair from her face, watching his own gesture. Then one finger traced a soft trail from her cheekbone to her jaw. With an effort, he looked her in the eye and nodded. *That's so.* He pulled Marian to her feet, then walked slowly around to the driver's side of the Volvo. She watched him kill the headlights, remove the keys, and lock the doors. He came back around, held out a hand, and they walked wordlessly to the trailer. All we can manage in this life, Marian thought, are small acts.

Kissing in the night snow.

Lifting his sweatshirt over his head.

He stayed expressionless as she touched his collarbone, her fingers sliding to a stop over his heart. He pulled off her boots and placed them by the

189

heater. Her sweater. His jeans. In slow ceremony. The last of the clothing set aside, she sat at the edge of the low bed. Girard knelt before her, their hands strong on each other's shoulders. Frowning, he bent his head, rubbing her hand with his chin. When she turned her hand toward his mouth, he kissed her palm. Then she reached under his arms and drew him up beside her.

Marian touched the side of his face. Prince of the apple towns. "Look at me."

"I do."

"Let me see you." *In more ways than I can name.*

"You do." It was a whisper.

Later they slept, Marian suddenly wakeful at what the clock on the floor said was two-twenty. She scratched her head. Smiled, fuzzy, sore from love and use. Outside, the wind was picking up. The trailer was cold. Girard lay half curled on his side with his back to her, the blanket down around his hips. She pulled it up, wanting badly to spoon herself up against him, but maybe she didn't know him well enough. Funny. When she touched his back with her forehead, he grunted—a sleepy, feral sound she liked—and reached around, pulling her hips in close. She slept again, safe in a place she had never reckoned on, and woke up again just before dawn. This time for good.

Dressing quietly, Marian let herself out of the trailer and set to work on the flat tire. Only in winter, she thought, were dawns indistinguishable from dusks. Stark, polar, the cold so complete it was like solid geometry. She needed this sudden plainness as she tightened down the final bolt. It pulled her back to the investigation. Made her look down toward the gravel pit and imagine what Khartoukian had seen: Derry Wilson, floating face down, wedged against unmelted ice.

She wondered whether the hands that just hours ago had touched her own inner thighs had also drowned the redhead with the coppery voice. Sitting in the snow, she snapped the hubcap into place with her boots and started to put away her tools.

"Good morning."

190

Her stomach lurched. She looked up. Jack Girard stood on the steps of the trailer, his short hair uncombed, hands in his pockets. "Morning," she said, replacing the lug wrench in the toolbox.

He frowned. "Are you leaving?"

"I think so."

"It's not even seven."

She folded the jack. "I told Khartoukian I'd help with the investigation."

"At seven?"

"No," she said slowly, "not at seven. I'm anxious to get going on it, that's all."

His eyes narrowed. "The pay's lousy, but you get to fuck the suspects, is that it?"

They looked hard at each other. She wanted to go back into the trailer with him and find the same speechless place as last night. She wanted to emerge in about a week, but by then, she'd be no good at all to Charlie. She stood up, wiping her hands on her jeans, and looked at him. The man was waiting for an answer, his arms folded across his chest. She slammed the toolbox and jack into the trunk of the Volvo, then kicked her hubcap for good measure. Flinging herself into the driver's seat, she shifted into first, let in the clutch too hard, and lurched gracelessly until she picked up speed and drove away.

Chapter Forty-Two

"Custard or jelly?"

"Custard."

"That's the right answer. I prefer jelly."

Marian smiled. "What a team."

Khartoukian tore off an old page from his Week-At-a-Glance, set the doughnut on it, and pushed it over to Marian. She raised an eyebrow at him. "It's clean," he said, wounded. "October seventeenth. I took a personal day." From a desk drawer, he pulled out a shoe box top containing freebies from half a dozen fast-food joints. "You give me such a hard time, I guess I'll have to break out the good stuff. Here."

He fished out a yellow paper napkin and a wooden stir and then hesitated over two packets. "A less classy guy would give you just the coffee lightener—personally, I think this outfit cuts corners on their nonfat milk solids—but since I like you," he tossed her the other packet, "all the way to whitener."

"Duly noted." She sampled the powdered sugar on the top of her doughnut, wondering whether Barb Hauser would still provide a breakfast, if her guest hadn't used the bed. The fine points of hostelry. She'd find out when she stopped back at The Briars later to shower and change her clothes. Khartoukian, whistling the Trocadero through his teeth, jiggled a geriatric coffee maker, bullying it into trickling faster.

Even without his sheepskin jacket, he seemed like a craggy Mongol from some part of the map nobody can ever identify. Everything in the office was metal. The file cabinets, the desk, the chairs, the framed portrait of the

President (still Lyndon B. Johnson, apparently), and Khartoukian himself. She wouldn't put any money on the likelihood there were fifty stars in the flag pushed into the corner. "Won't the taxpayers spring for some decent furniture for you?"

"They did." He waved the glass carafe. "This is it." He poured two cups of coffee, handing her the mug imprinted with Thank You and a local dentist's name. "I think metal is very underrated," he said. "It's shiny. It's durable." On the floor next to his desk were a shoeshine kit, a stack of old *Toilers*, and a Saul Bellow paperback. "What can be more American?" He gave her a flat smile, his eyes glinting, and sat down across from her.

Marian scraped her chair over to his desk, setting the mug on a preexisting ring. The doughnut wasn't bad, the coffee, almost good. Khartoukian was dunking with an absorption she could imagine him bringing to an interrogation. They ate in silence for a minute, looking each other over, listening to the hiss and clang of the radiator. Then Khartoukian wiped his mouth. With precision. "You go first," he said.

"I'm still eating." She wanted to disappear into a carbohydrate reverie. Feel the weak sunlight slant down from the high window. Hear the slow rumble that in Hank Khartoukian passed for speech. She leaned back, cradling her coffee. *What I need right now is distraction.* Courtesy of the man across the desk. "Tell me about the interview with Bella Murphy." Shame on you, Warner: eating the man's doughnut, drinking the man's coffee, eliciting information only you know is worthless.

Khartoukian settled back in his chair, clasping his hands behind his neck. "Girard wasn't with her Saturday night. According to her, he was supposed to be in Zanesville. That was the plan. The last contact she had with him—before he stopped by the house early yesterday morning—was at a dinner party Friday night."

"I was there."

"She mentioned." One eye squinted in recollection. "Along with Charlie and a few others. Nice party?"

She wiped her fingers carefully. "I enjoyed myself."

"Was Derry Wilson invited?"

"I guess not." Where was he going?

"Did her name come up?"

"No." Although.

"So you went—with Charlie."

"That's right," she said.

"Tell me about the fight last Tuesday night."

So Khartoukian had heard them arguing outside Mazeppa's Ride, after all. The doughnut was reassembling itself inside her stomach. "It was absurd."

"What was it about?"

As if he didn't already know. "Derry Wilson."

He nodded. "Why is that absurd?"

"He thought I didn't like her."

He leaned back. "Did you?"

"Yes."

"By Friday night—" Khartoukian ran the rim of the mug over his lower lip, "had the two of you made up?" Eyebrows up.

"Not the way you mean it," she said, sounding starchy.

An innocent shrug. "How do I mean it?"

"Charlie and I are friends."

"That fine with you, Marian?"

"Perfectly, Sheriff."

"Fine with him?"

"You'll have to ask him."

He sipped with a faraway look. "It's on my list."

Don't get rattled. End it. "By Friday night," she said, "we were on good terms."

"What about Saturday night?"

"What about it?"

"Did the terms improve?"

She sat up. "Sheriff, are you investigating—" she set down her mug, "—or peeping?"

He kept his smile at bay, his eyes still on her. "I'm not sure there's much of a difference." She watched his fingers play a scale on the edge of the desk.

CHAPTER FORTY-TWO

He asked again, "Did the terms improve?"

"I didn't see Charlie on Saturday night. At all." Then it struck her. "If you want to know what I was doing Saturday night, why don't you ask?"

"Because I'm having fun just watching you."

Shit. Who called this meeting, anyhow? Who left Jack Girard's bed at daybreak to get here on time? "I was at The Briars all evening. Most of the time, I spent writing. From about ten to midnight, I played a game with the Hausers. Scattergories, if you must know. We had cocoa. After which I went to bed. Alone." She looked at him. "Match that for excitement, if you can."

He leaned toward her. "Marian," he said, "you came to Carthage about a week ago. I know less about you than I know about Tunisia." He ticked off on his fingers, "Capital city, Tunis. Official language, Arabic." His eyes slid away for a moment. "Offhand, I like you better than Tunisia. But you'll have to bear with me if I don't just take you on faith."

She was silent. Then: "Any more doughnuts?"

"It just so happens." From a lower desk drawer, he pulled a white bakery bag.

"And the coffee's cold." She was beginning to sound like one of those icy, thin-lipped people who send back entrées.

"No, it isn't," he chuckled. "You're just mad." He pushed himself out of his chair. "Still," he said, "we can pretend. Give me your mug. I'll get you a warm-up." Glaring, she held it out. "I'm bringing Charlie in for questioning."

"Charlie." Not Charlie. Couldn't Khartoukian see what he was? Marian stared at her lap. All she wanted was to bundle Charlie off for good to some warm place with songbirds. Where talented girlfriends sang endlessly. Where radical boyfriends plotted overthrows.

"Just so you know."

She felt alarmed. "Charlie was at the movies with his daughter."

"Late show?"

Oh, Charlie. "I don't know."

Khartoukian made a gesture: well, then. He topped off her mug. "After all," he said gently, "he was Derry Wilson's—"

"I believe the word is lover." A little too quick.

He nearly smiled. "I'm familiar with the term."

"Current lover."

"You can see why I have to ask." He seemed apologetic.

"What about back issues?"

"Meaning?"

"Old lovers."

"Talk." He handed her the mug.

"She has a son." Let it sink in while she whitened and stirred, hoping to hell Jack Girard had been telling the truth. Otherwise—whether or not Khartoukian could tell—she had just emptied her pockets, and Jack Girard was tangled up with gum wrappers, lint, a broken yo-yo, and a length of fishing line.

"The kid called me yesterday."

Bells and whistles. "Oh?"

"Saved me a lot of legwork." Given the size of Khartoukian's hands, dunking the remains of the doughnut into the remains of the coffee was becoming problematical. It was like watching the Yeti build a ship in a bottle.

"How do you keep the jelly from falling in?"

"I don't," he looked up at her. "It's what I use instead of sugar." She nodded as if it made perfect sense. "Before the boy called, I was working my way down the list Tim Rinehart provided."

"And now you're not."

"I can be more discriminating."

"Why is that?" Where was he going?

"His mother only took rides from folks she knew."

"So she said."

"No, Marian," he said, "the boy was quite clear on it. Hitchhiking scared her. Although she never admitted it to the grandmother. So until she could afford a secondhand car, Derry Wilson only took rides from friends." It fit. Marian recalled the yellow Skylark, Derry's looking inside and waving it on. Preferring cold or trek to uncertainty.

Feeling claustrophobic, Marian pushed herself out of the chair. With

Rinehart's list shelved, Khartoukian had sprung into Warner territory. They were scratching the same patch now. She could almost feel it. "So tell me," he said with friendly interest, "what have you learned?" Like asking Hannah what she'd done that day at school.

She mentioned paternity.

Khartoukian called it a worthy line of inquiry.

She mentioned the trip to Sparta Vale and Derry's work history with MCG. "Unproductive," she finished.

"Ah," Khartoukian murmured, twirling a wooden stir.

With what she hoped sounded like naive perplexity, she mentioned Bill Cain and Derry's work history with him. Possible motives and opportunity. Might be worth a closer look at the concert alibi, she tossed out, expecting to see Khartoukian peel off, baying, over a hedgerow.

He suggested she ask Corliss Cain. Rocking slightly in his squeaky metal chair.

Marian folded her arms, her heart pounding. It was all smoke and mirrors. Only it was Khartoukian, damn him, who was blowing the smoke and arranging the mirrors. She had watched him make her meeting his. Her agenda his. All for the price of a doughnut and a cup of coffee. When it came right down to it, she had come pretty cheap.

"What about Girard?" he asked, his eyes ancient.

She was careful not to straighten up. "He's not the boy's father."

"You asked him."

"Yes."

"And he answered you."

"Yes."

"And you're satisfied."

Silent. Then: "Yes."

Khartoukian looked skeptical. Three fingers were laced around the slender wooden stir. "Marian," he said, snapping it in half without so much as a look, "I have a witness who saw Jack Girard's jeep in town Saturday night." His lips thinned out. "Late," he added.

She kept her look mild. No small feat, considering her bones were liquefying. "What a breakthrough," she said. Next stop, Alice Lowther.

"In fact," he said, craning his sizeable neck to check the clock on the wall, "by five this afternoon, I'll have a warrant to search Girard's trailer and the company files." He folded his hands across his uniform shirt. Tan, starched, pressed. She should have noticed. "The place is small, and my deputies are thorough." He tucked his chin into his collar. His eyes were like fissures. "They're just not very neat."

Marian set her mug—nearly spilling it—next to the coffee maker. "Thanks for the breakfast," she said, smiling.

"Don't mention it." Then: "I thought you had some old business."

"Not old enough." She needed to get out.

"Marian," Khartoukian said, getting up with glacial slowness, "there's one thing you should know about me."

"Really? Just one?" Downright sunny.

"I don't like heroics."

She looked him in the eye. "Define heroics." He inhaled. No answer. "I thought you told me there are some things you uphold besides the law."

She had him. Only it wasn't so sweet. What she saw on his face was concern. He opened his hands wide. "I've got a badge and an attitude," he said quietly.

"I've got a license and a bigger attitude."

"You better work at keeping both."

Chapter Forty-Three

A shower. A change of clothes. Fresh orange juice. Barb Hauser, discreet, feeding orange wedges into a juicer that had all the vicious power of a woodchipper. To Marian, coming through the back door to The Briars at something after eight, she flashed a confidential smile, like working gal roommates. How Cosmo girl. Then she went back to singing *Non dimenticare che t'ho voluto tanto bene.* Dragging her jacket behind her, Marian started upstairs. "Juice and waffles in twenty," Barb called after her.

By ten-forty—showered, changed, and Vitamin C'd —Marian arrived at the Wade County Historical Society.

"Can I come in?"

Alice Lowther stood in the doorway. When she saw it was Marian, the opening got smaller. "The building is closed," she announced, using her body as a doorstop.

"I don't want to see the building," said Marian, moving closer. "I want to see you."

Lowther's chin went higher. "You'll have to make an appointment."

"I could do that," Marian said patiently, "or—" glancing at her watch, "I could come back in twenty minutes when you have to open up." She raised her eyebrows.

Alice Lowther stiffened. Marian watched her make a quick review of her defenses: her stature in the community, her tenure at the Historical Society, the repellent quality of her personality—all proof, maybe, against the next few minutes' unpleasantness. But, beyond that, Alice, not much more. The time for realizing that craven behavior was unbefitting the recipient of the prestigious Markworth Award was gone. It ended the night she ran out on a crumpled Jesse Hughes.

Lowther stepped aside.

The south parlor, Alice's command center, was the site of considerable activity. All solitary, except for Lowther's companions, pink, plastic, and pert—three of the mannequins from upstairs. Two were female, one male. One of the ladies was clothed all the way from her satin bonnet down to her white kidskin gloves, but the gentleman was naked and surprisingly smug, considering he was about as anatomically correct as a Ken doll. On a card table alongside the mannequins were three beautiful old hat boxes, stacked, and a box of big dolly underwear and accessories. A rolling metal clothes rack held an array of antebellum costumes. Alice was preparing for one of what Bella called the Carthage equivalents of State Days.

Lowther herself was wearing a white cotton shirtwaist dress with vertical pink stripes—a peppier number than her tan interlock, Marian thought. Must be exhilarating, dispatching unsavory exes, replacing illicit fireplace facings. Alice had been having adventures outside the purview of her job description. And they agreed with her. Led to such extravagances as peppermint stick shirtwaists.

"I could have you arrested," Lowther remarked.

"Oh?" Marian said, stuffing her hands in her pockets. "On what grounds?"

"Criminal trespassing." From her kneehole desk she took a pin cushion meant to look like a ripe tomato, and a pink brocade sash.

"Is that what I did?" Had Jack Girard told her? Marian picked up the small metal stand on the card table. Lucy Luckinbill Martin, it read, wife of Rep. Thaddeus Martin, and it went on to give a description not of her accomplishments but her clothes.

"You know it is." Lowther spoke with two pins between her lips. "Lucky for me, I have nosy neighbors, and you—" she said, fussing at the second female mannequin, "have Jersey plates." Marian waited. "Naturally," Lowther went on airily, "it's not in my best interests to press charges." Marian watched her pin tucks at the back of the ample bodice. "Every time I do Lucy I have to make these alterations." Her face softened. "She had a huge bosom and a midriff that got worse every year, poor dear, what with having Thaddeus's babies—" she jerked her head at the overgrown Ken doll, "so when I fit Lucy Luckinbill's dresses to these skinny models—" she smoothed and fluffed, "I feel I'm improving her. Doing something nice for her."

"Diddling history."

Alice gave her a flat look. "It's harmless."

"It's a fraud, Alice," Marian smiled. "When you improve on history, you make it fiction."

The woman started to bluster. "It's a costume, for heaven's sake, not a—"

"—fireplace facing," Marian cut in. Alice caught her breath. "Not a man wheezing to death in the Mission House."

"I didn't lock him in." Her eyes big. "I told Jack Girard."

"Then who did?"

"I swear I don't know. But someone else was there—outside, in the dark. I saw something move when I ran out."

Try it a different way. "Why—" she leaned against the kneehole desk, "would someone else—not you—turn the key in the padlock?"

"I don't know," she said, agitated, "I don't know."

"Who else knew he was coming to Carthage?"

"No one. I'm sure. He said I was the only one he'd look up in this—sinkhole, is what he called it."

Marian nearly smiled. "Maybe the Chamber of Commerce turned the key."

Lowther made a disgusted sound. "He was vile. He was always vile." She went on to say that she never should have married him. He should have stayed just a one-week fling, but then three years later, he was back. "I had already made plenty of sacrifices, believe you me, to have this life—" With that, Alice Lowther flung out her candy-stripered arms to demonstrate the grandeur of the coveted job. There at a historical society nobody visits in a small, economically depressed town in southern Ohio. Dusting the shelves, winding the clock, setting out weak lemonade. *Plenty of sacrifices, believe you me.* Marian felt speechless.

"So why I consented to marry a pathetic cretin who thought mound builders were ants—ants! —when he came around for more is the great mystery of my life." When Alice Lowther's hands began to tremble, she clutched the skirt of her shirtwaist. "After two years, I got out of it. I got rid of him," she finished with an airy wave, as though he was a three-legged chair. Suddenly her expression changed, and she seemed to forget she wasn't alone. "At least when I got pregnant by that piece of shit in the very first week I met him, I knew enough to give it up—" she started to shake her head, "because there was no future in it. Not for someone like me."

It. The baby was It.

After a while, they looked at each other in silence. Finally: "You heard about the murder of Derry Wilson?" Marian said.

"The singer. Yes. I read about it."

"I understand Jack Girard was with you the night she died." She watched Alice Lowther incline her head. Either failing to make the connections ahead of Marian—or waiting to see what Marian could provide in the way of information. Say it. "That gives him an alibi."

The other woman blinked. "Does he need one?"

Hat, more or less, in hand. "It would be helpful."

"Has he been to the police?"

"The police have been to him. She was killed on his property."

"Yes, that's too bad," she said vaguely.

"Up to now," Marian said, crossing her legs at the ankles, "he's admitted he wasn't in Zanesville, where he was supposed to be, Saturday night. That's all."

"I see." Lowther looked away, fingering the pink brocade sash.

"A witness saw Girard's jeep in town late Saturday night. Now the sheriff is having a warrant issued to search his trailer."

"How unpleasant," Lowther said, rooting through a sewing basket for some thread. She held a spool next to the brocade sash. "Too rose." It was dropped back into the basket.

"How long was he with you?"

She considered. "From around three in the afternoon until nearly midnight, I'd say."

"The entire time?"

"Around four, he left to rent a dolly, but he was back in half an hour." She held another spool to the sash. "Too salmon." She held up the tomato pin cushion. "The pins will just have to do."

"After that?"

"After that," she shrugged, "we were together the entire time."

"Did you help?"

She got defensive. "Some. It was heavy, dirty work. And I'm not a mason."

"Neither is he," Marian pointed out.

"Which is why it took him hours." She closed the basket. "I was sure he was going to damage the facing, the way he was chipping away at the mortar."

"Did he?"

A beat. "No."

"Which is why it took him hours." Marian folded her arms.

Lowther gave a small shrug. "Then there was the weight of the thing. I'd forgotten." No wonder: it's been thirty years. When Mazeppa's Ride made its first covert trip, from the Mission House to the living room on West Fourth Street, Lowther was more strapping and more motivated. Object lust was like a trial of anabolic steroids. "Then came the problem of getting the thing on to the dolly," she went on, tipping her head in mild boredom. "Then into the jeep. Then out. Then getting the thing into the Mission House."

The thing.

Now that she'd been persuaded to give it up, the fireplace facing had about as much appeal as Jesse Connor Hughes—either dead or alive. "It felt endless." Lowther's shoulders heaved.

"Imagine how it felt to him."

Lowther lifted her chin. "He didn't complain."

"What time did he finish up?"

"Sometime after eleven." Even though he used a quick-drying cement, he had to be careful with the light from the lantern, what with all the activity on the street at that hour. Waiting it out slowed him down. "Then there was the clean-up. I helped with that."

"That's nice," Marian said with a straight face. "The time together," she said, "yours and Jack Girard's. There were no lapses? However small?"

"No."

"How do you know what time you got home? Did you look at a clock?"

Lowther gave her a pinched look. "I watched a program on TV."

"Namely?"

"Wrestling, if you must know," she said. "It relaxes me." She flipped half-heartedly through a stack of unopened mail on her desk. "Why so many questions?"

"When you go to the sheriff—"

"The sheriff?"

"To alibi Girard."

A breathy laugh. "You must be joking."

"Why do you say that?"

"If Jack Girard hasn't brought me into it already, why on earth should I implicate myself?"

"Because he helped you."

"He helped himself," she snapped.

"Make no mistake, Alice. You are the one he helped." Like explaining complex moral truths to an eight-year-old. "And now he's in trouble."

"If you don't think it would all come out about Jesse Hughes, you're a fool."

"It wouldn't have to."

"Absolutely not. I have a reputation to consider."

"So does he."

"Jack Girard is resourceful. He'll find a way out."

Apparently, finding the limits of Alice Lowther's self-interest was like putting a final number to pi. "Let me understand you. You're going to leave him twisting in the wind, is that it?"

"He'll find a way out," she said shrilly. "Only it will have to be without me."

The man had risked personal injury, public embarrassment, and arrest on a murder charge to help this woman. *To put something right*, he had said. But for Alice Lowther all his help meant was an end to her personal discomfort.

She looked at Lowther, at the blank, stubborn face and concave body, over the years its moral insulation thinning out. The discomfort the lady had felt wasn't guilt, just a fear of discovery, and her frustration that the theft of the fireplace facing thirty years ago jeopardized the Mission House. When Jack Girard came to her Saturday, it was comfort over covetousness, so out went the stolen object. What he offered her was heart's ease, and Marian would be damned if she'd let Alice Lowther purchase her personal comfort with his safety.

"No, Alice." Marian shook her head. "No. That's just not good enough." There was an edge to her voice she had never heard. "These are your choices. You have until—" she looked at her watch, calculating how fast Khartoukian could get a warrant—"three this afternoon to tell the sheriff that Jack Girard was with you on Saturday night."

With a short laugh, Lowther breezed by her, sash in hand. "I will not."

Marian caught her arm. "How you color in all those hours together is entirely up to you." She let her go. Violence and gravity were beginning to feel an awful lot alike. "But if I hear the sheriff's department sets so much as a regulation toe inside his trailer —" She backed Lowther into the unfinished Lucy, who fell stiff as timber, taking down Thaddeus and the box of frilly accessories.

"Now look what you've done—" Lowther cried, unable to stop the cascade of plastic and frippery. She sank to her knees. Lucy Luckinbill Martin lay like an obscene log, her hooped skirt springing up around her demure face.

"—I will go to Khartoukian myself—"

She shrieked. "You're on her hem. Get off her hem—"

"—and give you to him one hair at a time."

"Are you threatening me?" Lowther jerked around to face her.

"With full disclosure. You bet."

"Damn you," she said with spirit, "damn you."

"And I will not spare the details."

A sly look. "Let Jack Girard ask me."

"You know he won't."

"Then why are you doing this to me?"

Marian held out a bone corset and pink brocade sash. With a furious sob, Lowther snatched them where she sat in a garish wreckage of costumes and dolls. Hers to dress. Hers to champion, with her primly lettered signs, *Please Do Not Touch.* "Because you owe him," Marian said. And let it go.

Chapter Forty-Four

"I 've got Miller's and Molson's on draft," Tim Rinehart told her, his hands on his hips.

"Anything," Marian rested her arms on the bar. He was wearing a yellow Oxford dress shirt, only slightly wrinkled, and a green paisley tie for the occasion. In the window of Mazeppa's Ride was a handmade sign in thick magic marker: *Open to Friends of Derry Wilson—All Proceeds Donated to Funeral Expenses.*

When Marian asked Rinehart about it, he explained Derry had no burial policy, and he figured he could take it on the chin better than Cindy Wilson. Besides, folks were overpaying on everything: he was selling twenty-dollar beers and forty-dollar fish and chip baskets. And nobody wanted change. Keep it, keep it, never mind the change. That's what they all said. Maud and Donald Jimson, sniffing, pressed a Benjamin into his hand and said they'd pay it ten times over if they could only hear her do "Georgia on My Mind" just one more time.

Friends of Derry Wilson.

There were the darts players near the door, the regular drinkers, the jazz fans, the Second Shift Band, slowly unpacking their instrument cases. Still no sax. Everyone was returned to the time before Derry came, when they were just pumpkin and mice. There were all the same people doing the usual things, only tonight with restraint. What they shared was a self-consciousness that heightened all their activity—made it sharper, made it duller, made it savory, made it tasteless.

Smokers were scrutinizing the tips of their cigarettes. Drinkers were turning their glasses in circles. Musicians were discovering new things to do with chamois. She watched a darts player in a railman cap nod solemnly to a lady in Ralph Lauren wools, when all they had in common, she suspected, was the absence of Derry Wilson.

It was a night for acknowledgment.

Of a different kind. One, at least, that excluded her. *I, for one,* she thought, *am done with acknowledgment, thank you.* Marian lifted her glass to all things peripheral in Carthage—herself on a bar stool at Mazeppa's Ride headed up the list. Made her feel secure, sovereign, a little principality of proud, square shoulders and long legs. This blessed plot, this earth, this realm, this Periphery. An easy, slippery place where she can do the work of investigation without explanation. And without grief. For, on the whole, she would rather do than grieve. Because the latter included more than the death of Derry Wilson. But she wasn't about to enumerate griefs.

She checked her watch. Past eight-thirty. Charlie would be along soon, and she'd recount her day. Khartoukian in the morning, followed by Lowther—only she'd leave out her own fury. After Lowther, her visit to Polly Gundersen of the primitive bowels. From Polly, she got no information but a good deal on a terra cotta cream and sugar set she'd present to the Hausers when she paid the bill. Over the phone Derry had seemed happy—new job, new man, kid healthy, no long shadows from what the potter could tell and was going to pay her a visit real soon. They agreed they'd have a howl over some old photos from the summer they went to King's Island, before Derry left town.

Then in the afternoon, Marian had seen Toby Mainwaring, who "does hair, nails, and facials" out of her home. "Chez Tobée" said the sign outside a west-end version of the Wilson bungalow: add one carport, subtract three metal awnings. From Toby, who pushed at Marian's cuticles with a kind of touching fervor, she heard that back then, Derry only made it with serious musicians "the way I—" she grinned, "only made it with serious truckers." Like a pact, she laughed.

It kept their friendship simple, with no real chance of romantic overlap. Derry's rep was better than Toby's: few bands, lotsa highways. "Soak," she said, pushing Marian's fingers into the warm, soapy water. So, Marian thought, admiring her shapely fingernails, maybe the father of Andy Wilson is just what Derry described. Some guy on the road. Some shaggy, itinerant drummer who can make beer come out his nose.

Finally, she made a return trip to Cindy, there at the coffee shop—still officially closed—swabbing the one remaining floor in her possession, having just come back from making final arrangements for the funeral Thursday. She was wearing jeans and an Ohio State Buckeyes hoodie. Running the string mop through the wringer, she shook her head at Marian's questions. She didn't know. It's been so long she's stopped thinking of Andy as even having a father. "He's done all right without," she shrugged.

She gave Marian a cup of lukewarm coffee—free, with her thanks for all Marian's fine efforts and with her apologies at not having any oatmeal available, since "I know how much you like it." Most expensive free cup of coffee Marian ever drank. After an awkward hour, all she came away with from the half-lighted coffee shop on Main Street was a caffeine jangle and a sense of utter futility.

When all else fails, Warner, line up beer nuts. Only the bowl in front of her was empty. It was then she saw the boy, while she was cadging more bar freebies from a fellow three stools down. Andy Wilson, his lank hair slicked back, dressed in dark pants and a green cable knit sweater, standing near the brokenhearted Jimsons. He shook Maud's hand solemnly, his lips pressed tightly together, and moved to another table. And other friends of Derry Wilson. A nine-year-old host at the benefit for his mother's burial.

The trombonist tried a dispirited half-scale.

That just about sums it up.

Damn.

Chapter Forty-Five

Tim Rinehart refilled her bowl from a bag. "Draft okay?" he said.

"It's fine," she said. True, her beer appeared unloved. "I'm slow."

They looked at each other, a little weary, judging whether a bit of conversation was worth the rappelling equipment it required. "Are you playing tonight?"

He shook his head. "Not tonight. Not tomorrow night. Not, for that matter, lots of nights." Marian slung a look at what was left of the Second Shift Band. No keyboard, no vocalist, and still no sax. The clarinet launched into a soft, downbeat version of "Up a Lazy River." Nobody seemed to care. Tim Rinehart folded a bar towel. "There was a time," he said, "when I was a serious musician."

"Meaning what?"

With one long finger Rinehart pushed his loose eyeglasses back up his nose. "Meaning I thought more about the keyboard than food, sex, and money put together. Which they often were."

A serious musician. "What about now?"

"Now?" he smiled. "The way I see it, sex goes. Money goes. Even music goes." He evened out the beer nuts in the bowl. "Only food stays. Help yourself."

She grabbed a handful. "You bought Mazeppa's Ride eight years ago?"

"That's right."

"Before that?"

He looked down. "Oh," he said, "I bounced around."

"In town?"

"And out. Tending bar. Doing gigs."

A beat. "With Derry?"

"Some," he said, not looking at her.

"In Austin, say, ten years ago?"

He leaned his elbows on the bar. "It was Amarillo." Finally, he gave her a long, frank look. His mustache, trimmed unevenly, rippled over the mobile mouth. Behind the old black glasses, an earpiece held in place with a small safety pin, his eyes were blue. "I'm not much of a person," he said.

Marian smiled. "Andy Wilson could do a whole lot worse."

Rinehart shrugged, then took a slow look around Mazeppa's Ride, his eyes stopping at some point on the other side of the saloon's wall. "It's okay sex and music go," he said. "But I feel an urgent need for more money."

"Put in karaoke." She made him laugh. "He's only nine."

"There's college." He tightened his necktie.

"Does he know?" Marian felt absurdly happy for the boy.

"Not yet."

"You should talk."

"But not tonight."

In a draft of winter air from the open door, Marian leaned away. Moving through a tangle of darts, players were Jack Girard and Bella. Over a long gray skirt, she wore an oversized purple wool sweater cut deep across her flawless breast. Marian looked around. With Tim gone, Charlie yet to come, and Andy too distant to engage, there was no cover. The smoke was light, the music irregular, and the conversation reserved. Turn down the lights, electrify the damn band, and she might stand a chance. She was rereading a golfing joke on her cocktail napkin for the sixth time when she felt an arm resting on her back. It was Bella, delighted to find her.

Marian explained—from some part of her brain that could still pull off small talk—she was waiting for Charlie. The glance from Girard was cold and fleeting. "Excuse me," was all he said, leaving Bella with her as he made his way to the back of Mazeppa's Ride. There she watched him shake hands with Andy Wilson, the boy's eyes wide.

"Why don't you and Charlie come back to the house with us later?" She laid a hand on Marian's back. "We'll have a fire."

"I don't think so, Bella, but thanks," she said. "I'm pretty tired." Pumped full of every stimulant known to man, she'd still decline this one.

Bella pushed back one side of her hair, which just tumbled slowly back, infiltrated with light and air. "Just as well, I guess. We have to turn in early—I've got to be at Cold Spring State Park for a field trial at eight in the morning. And then I'm taking the dogs out for a shoot."

She had to ask. "What's a shoot?"

Bella smiled. "Another name for a walk in the woods with a shotgun," she said. "Actually, it's my insurance against gun shyness. I use a twelve-gauge to simulate hunting conditions."

"Who's competing?"

"Just Grady, the yellow male from North Carolina."

"The hammerhead?"

Bella laughed. "That's the one. I want to get him started on his field championship before I send him home." She crossed her arms. "It's good for business." Marian wished her luck. Bella went on to describe her purchase that afternoon in Columbus, a white eiderdown for their bed. Expensive, she breathed, but they've been needing something new to liven up the room.

It sounded so domestic.

So very long-term.

"It sounds lovely, Bella." But a new eiderdown was a far cry from a green Army blanket that seemed barely to cover them both unless they made a delicious tight package of themselves. Perhaps the fleetness of joy is in direct proportion to its intensity. For now, she sipped her beer.

"Good job on Houston, Marian."

"Thanks." She forced a smile.

"Any chance you can stop by the house sometime tomorrow afternoon, just to—" here she winced.

Marian understood. "Fill you in on what I'm going to report to the Parks Service?" Nodding, Bella folded her arms. "I think so. I can text you when I'm heading over." Even as she spoke, she knew there was no way she'd chance running into Jack Girard coming downstairs rumpled and groggy for his first cup of coffee. She'd have Bella meet her somewhere.

"Good," said Bella, "Afternoon's better. I'm tied up in the morning, what with the field trial. But for now," she said, touching Marian's shoulder, "come sit with us when Charlie shows up."

Marian smiled, noncommittal, as Bella pushed up her purple sleeves, revealing a glint of golden forearms, her skin restored. Her beauty, imperturbable. She was poised and purposeful everywhere. Standing at Marian's side, walking through the crowd at Mazeppa's Ride, and lying in her lover's arms. Down the languid ravel of years, their attachment held in place by an ingot of passion and duty that allows for very little freedom of movement.

To the discontent of neither. Truly. Neither.

Marian's cheeks burned. It soothed her to watch Tim Rinehart mix a dry martini, cutting a lemon twist. When Jack Girard came up beside her and ordered two shots of Chivas, Marian sat very still, her fingertips deployed around her beer. With a smile, Tim Rinehart plunked down two cocktail napkins, commenting that they hadn't been around for a while. "Bella's choice," said Girard, as Rinehart tipped the scotch into shot glasses. For Marian, the moment felt brief and excruciating. When Jack Girard handed him a check, Rinehart thanked him and moved away with the martini. After a moment, Girard said, "Alice Lowther alibied me."

"I'm glad to hear it." Not looking up from her beer.

"You have something to do with it?"

She looked longingly at the dartboard. Why had she never learned to play? "I guess."

"Yes or no." His voice was low.

"Yes."

"Thanks."

"Is that it?" She still couldn't quite look at him.

A beat. "No."

With a sigh, Marian sat up straight. "Say it."

"If you thought I killed Derry Wilson," he said, "what the hell were we doing together last night?"

Her hands felt heavy in her lap. Upturned and still, cupping a truth only she could see. "I can speak for myself."

"Go on."

"I was making love." The words glittered. Abandoned. Her skin tingled.

"With a killer."

Silence.

And there it was.

Girard shook his head. "You had no faith."

A bad moment for a play at the dartboard to erupt in laughter and scattered clapping.

She had to take it. "I had no faith." He was right. And she was lost. "Can I explain?"

"Actually," he said, with a small shrug, "you can't."

She swung around to face him. "Then I guess I'm not the only one." Marian looked at Jack Girard across what felt like oceanic inches of air. Both of them powerless to make the crossing. As he turned away, her fingers flew to her eyes, pressing them shut. The word *bereft* came to mind. Old English, past tense, bereave.

Chapter Forty-Six

*W*eeks after the blast, Charlie told her they got there by taxi. She couldn't remember. All she could pull up was the sight of the brownstone, missing half its roof and nearly all of its windows. They pushed through the crowd and started up the steps, past a couple of cops who were still taking statements. "I want to go in," she said to one of them, who caught her arm. "My friend's in there," she yelled, pulling away.

"Oh, yeah, who's your friend?"

Just then, an older man in an open all-weather coat came down the steps. "Let me in," she said to him. "I have to go in. I can identify one of them."

He shook his head. "Not likely, miss."

She had to get inside before she started to cry. "But he has—distinguishing characteristics." Ontario. Quebec.

"Like no face?" A young cop, hatless and unsteady on his feet, passed them on the steps, his eyes slack with what he'd seen.

"They're gone, miss," the older man said, "coroner's van came first thing."

"Where? Where did it go?"

"Honey," he sighed, "it doesn't matter. The shape they're in, even God can't identify them."

New skin.

New bones. New blood and organs. The list, Paul, the list has become too long. She wandered away from Charlie, who was trying his student press pass on the unyielding older man in the all-weather coat. At Battery Park she watched a garbage scow make its way slowly upriver, smooth and silent in those minutes between sunset and nightfall. What was left of the sun was only its pallor, *darkening the water and browning the foam. Near the water's edge a gull settled its wings. How white the bird looked to her, a place where suddenly all warmth and sense resided.*

Behind her, distant, a woman's laughter, and Marian turned to see two nicely dressed men and a woman crossing the mall, on their way to drinks and dinner. They passed an old man in a battered fedora rummaging through a trash can. They were held, all of them, in a terrible poise, occupying the same space with a vast and cheerful disinterest. Across the river were the lights of Staten Island, other houses, other roofs, other men intact.

And Marian knew then—as her eyes slipped past light and water and darkening shore, looking for Paul — that what we inhabit, what we inhabit, really — he was nowhere, not anywhere she could see or feel or go—are great, loose parabolas of worlds defined by our own wayward experience, slinging through space and time.

An unidentified male.

It broke her heart. She should have tried harder, back there. To see. To name. To place relentless hands on whatever was fugitive in herself and Paul and the young hatless cop and the older fed—and Charlie. Charlie who, while she was trying to get past the older fed, was saying into her hair, "No names, Marian, don't give them your name, if they get your name you will never get a civil service job, you will never hold public office, you will never get a gun permit—"

She listened. Told him to shut up, but listened, because violent death offended her. And she had nothing to offer against it but her wits and a sharp insistence on the truth. She had no interest in civil service or public office. But she left the way open for a gun.

The gull flew out over the dark water.

Chapter Forty-Seven

A imless.

Without even getting out of bed. Her brain registered a two-beer turgor. Right—lay it off on the beer. The sheets felt like tentacles, the air stifling. She wondered if, in a fit of midwinter dementia, Cy had bumped the thermostat into the stratosphere. Kicking off the covers, she peered at the clock. Six-twenty. Entirely too early to get out of bed, considering she lacked anything resembling a plan for the day ahead. At roll call this morning, only muscle and will are turning up.

What you need, Marian....

What you need is discipline.

Which begins with tough sights.

Charlie, subdued last night, their forearms twining on the bar, their fingers loosely laced. No drama, no flirtation. Something plainer. To Marian, their hands felt old. Felt old, were old. Through the years ahead—on other bars in other places—drier, cooler, bonier. Until the day when only one hand remains. Unclasped. Its griefs, perhaps, unremembered.

Khartoukian, his resources better than hers. Beginning with the history he shares with these people. Their habits, habits of mind, dispositions, predispositions—piling up like silage. All these were available to the sheriff during those rare seasons of criminal activity. No outsider's efforts can compare.

Jack Girard, released from suspicion, and Bella, asleep under the billowing eiderdown. Bought for their bed. Such simple English words, each of them: bought, for, their, bed. So harmless, separately. Marian lay her arm over the empty space beside her with a new appreciation for the power of the phrase.

And finally, herself.

Her faithless self, returning to the world of Joan Fleck and the weekly supply of scammers and cheats. At 6:30, with any luck at all, Joan's phone was still turned off as she squeezed out another half hour of eye mask, white noise machine, and silk sheets, dead to the world. The call went straight to voicemail, and Marian left a quick message about the murder of Charlie's girlfriend, the Work in Progress report for Parks, the need for more time.

Not a good start to Joan's day.

Flat on her back in the darkened room, Marian felt like she was steaming slowly upriver on a scow. Detached from the garbage-making mainland. Detached from the lesser rubble from lesser bombs. Detached from the benched Marian sitting alone and dazed at Battery Park, a spectator to the queer majesty of the untimely. The thing that rustles in its dim habitat, before error, before act, even before desire. Paul's deadly sculpture of wire and plastic. Derry Wilson, her death untimely to everybody except one. In all things, there is one source. A yearning that survives disaster, that survives the vacated arms, the torso sprung in a burst of bloodied glass, the voice trapped in water.

We are all the corpse of love, Derry.

There is nothing else.

Marian pulled the gray flannel trousers and blue sweater from the back of the chair where Girard had sat five nights ago. Jack Girard. Over the occasions together, appreciating her facts, but not her faith in telling them. Accepting her help in the investigation, but not her faith in giving it. It wasn't a lack of faith that made her wonder whether he had killed Derry Wilson. That was just fear, all along. It was faith, damn it, that put her back in the trailer in the first place. Despite fear. Even despite desire.

You are wrong, Jack.

You are unfair.

You are unforgiving. But these things you will feel only as disquiet, cold-blown white across the frozen pit, not quite vapor, not quite snow. Through the years. As the house on Providence grows emptier with each piece added.

218

The pleasure becomes less in each faltering landmark saved. And the last lines of poems go unsupplied.

Marian washed up. Then she made up the bed with a zeal that was damn near military. Grabbing her backpack and down vest, she went quietly downstairs. In the kitchen, on the west side of The Briars, daylight had no particular quality, only made itself felt as a lessening gloom. Turning up the fire under the tea kettle, Marian pushed a couple of frozen croissants into the Hausers' toaster oven, then pulled a jar of homemade apple butter out of the fridge.

Corliss Cain, worth a shot. Even if Khartoukian had shooed her in that direction, like telling her to go play nice outside. She'd go, but not at the crack of dawn.

Also later, as a kind of mental spackling, Tim Rinehart. The question of Andy's paternity settled, Marian watched dispassionately as her pet theory went under like a paper boat. Besides, Rinehart had as many alibis for the time Derry was killed as his saloon had patrons, but even he might be able to fill in some cracks about Derry Wilson that could present what Khartoukian might call a worthy line of inquiry.

For the same reason, back to Toby, back to Polly. For some cell shedding, platter purchasing, and—without a doubt—straw clutching.

Finally, call Charlie.

Call Cindy.

For no other purpose than to offer support.

Meeting up with Bella would have to wait until later in the day.

In the meantime, the best thing to do was just about anything not related to the investigation—excluding sleep and sex, since neither seemed to be presenting itself—for about two hours. Preferably outdoors. She'd drive by Bella's, snag one of the Honeymooners, and take off to Wade Lake. Marian slathered one last wedge of croissant with apple butter, chewed, drank, wiped her mouth, and cleared everything away to the sink.

Remembering, suddenly, the field trial.

She sagged. Bella wouldn't be home. And she'd be damned if she'd get Jack Girard out of bed to ask his permission to borrow one of the dogs to see her through the loss of her crime-solving capability and her two-beer capacity.

Field trial as alternate plan. Its virtues: canines aplenty and less opportunity for reflection. Done. Marian zipped up and was out of The Briars before Barb could greet the day by liquefying cantaloupes—what she termed "the queen of fruit," high in vitamins A and C, beta-carotene, bioflavonoids, and silicon.

Marian would just have to miss her RDA of silicon.

Chapter Forty-Eight

Field glasses, check, in the glove compartment. Wade County, blue and bright on her Google maps. Empty coffee cups, Carthage tri-folds, the box of Derry's stuff, the *Toiler* issue from a week ago. She'd toss what she could before heading to the field trial. Grabbing the coffee cups and tri-folds, Marian slid the *Toiler* closer and turned it over. A smiling Polly Gundersen. Then another page one piece caught her eye. ANNUAL POLAR BEAR PLUNGE was the headline that Charlie managed to hold to a single exclamation point. A quick scan for content: *Nine hearty souls gathered at the gravel pit at MCG Construction for their fundraising plunge for the Special Olympics. The rules of the Polar Bear Plunge require. . .*

And then she saw the photo that captured the moment after the plunge. Bare-chested men, women in tank suits, all leaping through the high, frigid splashes to get out of the water. Some onlookers, well bundled, were pumping their fists. Everything from happy shock to stunned relief showed on the plungers' faces. Marian studied them. One looked like Tim Rinehart, flabby, wearing classic black swim trunks. A quick check of the caption named plungers left to right. Tim Rinehart, third from the left. Her forefinger touched each Polar Bear plunger, staggered in the photo as each of them headed separately for dry land.

Her eyes stopped at the name of Steve Grey. Three to the right of Tim. Jack Girard's man. Tim's sax player. The finder of Jesse Hughes's body. The man out sick her whole time in Carthage. The guy who never returned her calls. Unseen, unseeable. Nearly an abstraction. He was bald, with a long face, and he looked like he was carrying an extra fifty pounds. His head was turned to his right, and through the splashing as they all headed for dry clothes, his mouth was open, his arm outstretched, pointing to someone bundled up. Shouting his commitment. Urging the others to plunge. The radical arm of the annual Carthage Polar Bear Plunge.

Her eyes slipped below his face. To the bare chest of the man known as Steve Grey. She stared hard at all the scarring. The scarring. Chemical burns that made his chest a map of Canada. Ontario. Quebec. With a strangled cry, Marian fell out of the car, still gripping the paper, and buried her face in the welcoming snow.

It was Tim Rinehart who told her over the phone that she could probably find Steve Grey—if he was feeling any better—in the gym at Jefferson Middle School, giving sax lessons to seventh graders during study hall. Corner of East 10th and Mulberry, Rinehart added before she hung up. She sailed through a stop sign in a state of white blindness. On East 10th she skidded around the slick corner and drove on with her mind a fierce blank thing. At Mulberry she didn't slow down at Jefferson Middle School and careened into the parking lot of the gym.

All these years later, she was about to see the man whose fate she had grieved every day of her jangled life. That blast had sent her, Marian, higher in a spray of relentless, bloody images than it had Paul. Swinging the wheel hard to the left, Marian jerked the car into Park alongside the curb to the plowed sidewalk leading to the gym doors. She strode to the doors, both hands tugging hard, eyeing the sign VISITORS MUST SIGN IN AT THE OFFICE. Locked. She pounded them once in frustration, then loped to the other set of doors.

One opened easily, and she heard the sound of a squeaky scale on a saxophone as she stepped inside. At the center of the brightly lighted gym were two figures. Metal folding chairs, open instrument cases, a music stand. A lanky, dark-haired boy in jeans and a yellow t-shirt was red in the face from blowing into the sax. Next to the kid, there he was, the sax loose in his grip, wearing a black and white checked shirt. As she started toward him, he caught sight of her. "Marian—" Her name filled the space. She started to run. "Marian—"

He made a move to stand up, his chair scraping, which was when she flew at him and took him down. "Whoa!" cried the kid as Marian and Steve Grey hit the floor, where the sax clattered on the polished wood. "You son of a bitch!" she yelled, tearing his shirt open with both shaking hands. Exposing the life she thought he had died for all those years ago. New skin? By the time she got finished with him, skin would be the least of his problems. When he started hollering, the kid ran to get help. Steve Grey tried to push her away, but she had him pinned. "Goddamn you, Paul," she screamed as she hauled off and punched him in the nose, liking it so much, she punched him again. A right jab, a left uppercut, her fists coming at him fast, pounding the flesh of a guy she had only ever wanted to protect. She cursed him with every blow.

Tiring, she could hardly look at him, at the bald head, the extra weight, and now the broken, bloody nose. She pushed herself up from him, bent over double. "Marian, listen to me—" he pleaded as she wheezed at him, moving off. "Listen to me—" he said again, his voice thick, as she kept stumbling away from the dead Paul, which, of course, was nothing new. He was incoherent as he followed her, trying to tell her he was there that day, the day of the blast, there in the crowd. He'd gone out for condoms. And then the world exploded, and all he could do was run. All the way to Carthage and the mother who didn't know she was his mother. And the father who was dead in the Mission House, so couldn't appreciate that it was his son who found him. All the price of a new identity. A new life.

"Oh, really, Paul?" she said fiercely. "Well, I've been busy living the old one." She pushed hard at the gym door.

Footsteps came hurrying toward her. "Ma'am!" someone called. "Can we help you, ma'am?" bounced voices in a space meant for basketballs and cheers. Not this.

"No!" she yelled back. "I'm leaving."

Paul dropped back, blood smeared across his cheeks. "Marian, are you going to tell?" His face was tight with pain. Steve Grey, the guy who does the Polar Bear Plunge for the Special Olympics, the guy who gives free sax lessons to twelve-year-olds.

"Stay away from me," she hissed, "stay very far away from me." Marian hurried out into the sunny cold. Let them keep coming at her if they like. Let them keep right on coming. Before the gym door closed for good behind her, Marian heard Steve Grey say something apologetic to the school principal about his "ex."

Chapter Forty-Nine

Marian headed south out of town and picked up Highway 12 toward Cold Spring State Park. In the east, the sky was violet, slashed by steely winter clouds. Driving helped. Also Sarah Vaughan, scatting her "No 'Count Blues" as smoky as the January sky. But for some things, there was no help in sight, not for her, not unless she could have her memory scoured clean of Steve Grey pulling at her arm as she stumbled toward the exit of the gym.

It was a twenty-minute drive.

And it took every one of those minutes for the nausea to pass. Her hands felt like rubber.

At the entrance to Cold Spring State Park, a sign had been hammered into the ground: Quad Counties Retriever Club Field Trial, plus the dates and the advice to follow arrows. Passing picnic areas, hiking trails, johns, and a maintenance yard. The parking lot she reached was nearly full. Marian looked around, then grabbed the binoculars and got out of the Volvo, wondering if she'd stumbled into a paramilitary camp. There's something about human beings who make camouflage a fashion choice. Its rival was the weekend squire look, squashed hat, chinos, and canvas field jacket.

The dogs seemed content simply to hang out, standing bored or sitting on one haunch like old cows, while their handlers regaled each other with training horror stories, advice about brood bitches, and the merits of high-voltage dog collars. Registration was taking place in the open-air shelter house. A quick look around yielded no Bella and Grady, but Marian paid two bucks for a cup of coffee—black: dog people tough it out, apparently—and picked up the field trial equivalent of a program. She found a listing for Bella Murphy, Trainer/Handler, showing a dog called Sir Walter Raleigh O'Grady His Nibs—date of birth, sire, dam—in an event called Derby Dog.

Derby Dog, a haughty official explained to her, was in progress. Past the shelter house, follow your nose, you'll see signs just over the hill. Marian trudged, passing a chocolate Lab, panting, on a short lead. His handler was giddy. "Wouldn't do a damned thing," she announced to Marian, then, after she passed, "not a goddamned blessed thing, you dear old donkey boy, would you? Would you?" she said with an affectionate laugh. The hill the official mentioned sloped down like a natural amphitheater to the place of the trial. Spectators ranged over the hillside, some sat in the snow on folding camp stools, some held their steaming coffee bundled against their chests. Marian looked up. Cloudy, the sun absent, the temperature dropping.

At the bottom of the hill, the landscape broke up into a flat river in a wide glen with tall, leafless trees. Three streams converged. A yellow dog was swimming against the unhurried current. Marian raised her field glasses. It was Bella at work, the lanyard whistle between her lips, an open beige field coat over brown flannels. That woman, Marian smiled, could make mud a fashion accessory. She watched Bella signal the dog, who swam more toward the low, right bank, finally snagging the duck. One whistle blast, and he started back toward his handler. "Excellent work," said a man standing nearby. The woman with him reached for his program. "Murphy again?" she said. He nodded.

Murphy again. Reaching for golden apples: house, Girard, field champions. She had an eye for excellence that Marian admired. The dog, its nose aloft, neared the shore. Marian looked through the field glasses. She saw Bella, statuesque, the wind snapping her hair, rippling the water as the dog lumbered out. She saw a pleased official marking a clipboard. She saw the dog tuck in regimentally at Bella's side, sit, and release the duck to her hand. Heard the scattered hillside clapping.

She saw the dog.

But it wasn't Sir Walter Raleigh O'Grady His Nibs.

It was Norton.

Thought, fresh out. And all Marian had in its place was a kind of disturbance. When she had recognized the pink, Dudley nose and impertinent expression that could only be Norton's, she started backing out of sight. In the matter of the dog, she knew what she was looking at—what, if anything, it signified, she needed solitude and more information before she could say. She had come uninvited; now, let it work to her advantage.

Unless I'm mistaken, she thought, *a golden apple has fallen into my lap.* Something to turn over and consider, free from the explanations of Atalanta. In the shelter house she strolled around the registration desk, killing a minimum of time, casually asking the registrar in a buffalo plaid jacket if there had been any substitutions in today's program.

"Substitutions?"

"Oh, you know," Marian said, paging through a catalog of dog-related products, "one dog out sick, another dog in its place, that sort of thing."

The registrar adjusted her glasses. "This isn't school," she drawled. "No. All the entrants are here."

Marian located the Bronco in the parking lot. A quick look—for what, she couldn't say. As if Bella's car would suggest a perfectly reasonable explanation. The inside of the Bronco was tidy. At the back was the faded dog blanket she remembered—and in the plastic stacking bin, two Frisbees and two training dummies, one rubber, one canvas. But no stick. Marian slammed herself into the Volvo and took off. On with the heater, off with the jazz. She hit the highway, but not exactly running. When a semi blared her over into the right lane, she checked her speedometer.

Bella had switched dogs, Norton for Grady, the Carolina hammerhead. One yellow retriever, roughly the same age, for another. There was no way around it. She'd swing by the house on Providence and check the kennel on the chance the real Grady looks a hell of a lot like Norton. The shoot that afternoon: Bella's insurance against gun shyness, she had called it. The switch: her insurance, it would seem, against failure.

Get "Grady" started toward his field championship before he's shipped home to his well-paying, duck-shooting owners. A future field champion can pull down nice stud fees, earn some ink in *dog magazines*, and help pass the time for the proud owners, crouched for endless hours in a duck blind with some companions they want to impress.

And if the champ disappoints, well, chalk it up to the vagaries of dogs and inexperienced owners. After all, he's got credentials, documents that attest to his performance in the field. So send the backslider back to the trainer for a refresher course. It was beautiful, really. In fact, any discrepancy between the dog's credentials earned in Bella's care and his true performance at home really only work in Bella's favor. Giving her, as a trainer, a patina of the miraculous.

It was a scam Bella couldn't work often—the frequency with which the same people turn up at trials made it risky—but she could work it judiciously. Save it for the hammerheads whose owners are particularly gullible, moneyed, or well-connected. And work it preferably at a distance from Carthage and the local dog network.

Marian turned slowly into the alley along the north side of the old Girard property. She saw the kennel and dog run—what appeared to be Ralph and Alice nosing around—but, nowhere, the jeep. Pulling close to the chain link fence, Marian whistled for the dogs. Over they came, prancing, colliding, and pushing for room. Ralph, Alice, Trixie, two chocolate males, and, presumably, Grady. Except for the black nose leather and a more phlegmatic expression, a ringer for Norton.

As Marian drove slowly past the kennel, the dogs followed along inside the fence, waiting for her to come across with a treat or a walk. In the rearview mirror were five uncomprehending faces—and Grady's, still expectant, the last to catch on that Marian was stiffing them. She parked in front of The Briars.

Bella had lied.

Call it fraud, call it hoax, call it scam. Strip away all the details—the ingenuity of the plan, the nerve behind it—and what you find at the bottom is a lie. The sky was low and ashen, winter heavy. The day had lost something. As if the things around her had been scraped clean.

The UPS truck double parked across the street, the distant siren, Cy Hauser shuffling down the front walk, library books tucked under his arm. Everything seemed made out of paper and sticks, as insubstantial as a Chinese dragon. This is what a lie does. Makes you question even the commonplace.

Chapter Fifty

I nside The Briars, Marian found Barb in the parlor, paying bills at her cherry desk. She was wearing a blue velour warm-up suit. On a seven-inch TV, Hoda Kotb was shocked by tales of amorous schoolteachers and the teen boys who love them.

Barb looked up with a quizzical smile.

Marian said nothing.

"You all right?" Barb toyed with her pen.

"I don't know." Was she ever going to be all right?

"Maybe you need some juice, you Philistine."

"What I need," said Marian slowly, "is some information." Then she stretched out on the Victorian horsehair sofa and stared at the ceiling. "Talk to me about the Girards, Barb. And the Murphys."

"Why?" Setting down the pen, Barb Hauser pushed herself back from the desk.

"I need to hear you talk." *I need a story that isn't my own.* For hers was a story about how a serious jackass's trip to the corner Duane Reade for a pack of condoms saved his life, possibly at the expense of parts of her own. Hers was a story about how, when it came right down to it, she couldn't even assume the condoms were for use with her. When the world exploded, and all Norberto Sartre could do was run, she found it so very comforting to know that all along the way, he was practicing safe sex.

"How far back do you want to know?" she asked Marian. "Twenty years? Forty years?"

Marian rubbed her face, unsure of the answer. "Not forty." Figuring it out as she went. "Not even twenty." To the place where the monster heart lies, possessing its own coiled intelligence. "Tell me about Jack and Bella."

Jack and Bella.

Barb recalled blankets spread for picnics and fireworks on July fourth in Cold Spring Municipal Park. Bella at two in a yellow sundress, toddling around after Jack in uniform, home on leave. Tumbling into his lap. Bringing him a book, a toy, a handful of grass, an apple while he lighted green and gold sparklers for her brother Ben. Bella at six in a devil's costume on a warm Halloween night, watching the parade on Mission Street from Jack's shoulders, her forearms tight around his head. Her father, John, laughing, showing a honeymooning Cy and Barb how the child won't come down. *No!*—she pushes at her mother's reaching hands—*No!* to her brother who asks isn't she coming as he scrambles with other kids to pick up candy tossed from the parade queen's car.

Bella, reckless at nine in a lime green swimsuit at the municipal pool, flinging herself off the board, calling Jack's name. Jack, discharged from the Army, visiting from Colorado, nodding at Bella's efforts. Returning to a thick paperback and the conversation of women his own age. Bella, at ten, in a black coat, standing between Jack and Clayton at the graveside service for her family. Jack grim, his arm around her shoulder.

Bella, at twelve, standing miserable with her bike just outside the tennis courts where the Hausers were playing doubles with Jack and the pretty wife he'd brought with him from Denver. Finding a role handing out cups of ice water from the Coleman thermos they'd brought, begging Jack for a lesson, teasing him with a towel yoked around his neck. Bella, at thirteen, outside The Golden Scoop with Derry Wilson, sad to get such a short letter from Jack, saying he wouldn't be coming back to Carthage very soon, citing work and plans with Claire, but he hoped she was having a good vacation. "I get one back for every three I write," she said softly.

Bella herself, off to boarding school, returning at fourteen, fifteen, sixteen with her beauty sprung. Winter break coincided with one of his rare trips home, fresh from a divorce. With the house on Providence rented out and the hillside ranch with only two bedrooms, Jack booked in at The Briars.

Barb remembered Bella and Clayton arriving to share dinner with them on Jack's first night back. Bella, sixteen, no sooner out of her coat than her arms went around his neck, her face flushed.

"Aren't there any boys at that boarding school?" said Jack, laughing, as he freed himself gently. "Plenty of boys," she remembers Bella saying. "No men." "Give them time," he added. Her eyes bright: "They don't interest me." Bella, set aside, as Jack hugged his father. All her best attempts at flirtation unobserved or misunderstood. "The child's infatuated with Jack," Cy announced to her later in that oratorical way of his. Barb didn't answer, remembering a six-year-old in a devil's costume, riding Jack's shoulders.

Bella, at nineteen, timed her spring break from Kittatinny College for Women with one of Jack's trips home—bringing with her a very presentable boyfriend, a Princeton senior who couldn't figure the purpose of the trip—he had wanted the two of them to go to Vail—but bore the change of plans with conspicuous good grace, considering he didn't seem to know very much about Bella or her family or Carthage. With the practiced ease of a nineteen-year-old letting her family know she's sexually active, Bella explained to Jack that she and Princeton would be more comfortable staying at The Briars. Jack was understanding and asked Princeton if he'd be interested in some tennis in the morning.

Bella seemed distant.

Princeton never returned.

But Bella did. When she left college —"More books just aren't in the plan"—she bought puppies and moved into the house on Providence. Her house, finally. Her own. "The sentimental favorite for Jack when he comes back," she told Barb one day when they met at the hardware store. Barb commented that she hadn't heard he was making a trip home. "I mean for good," Bella said, collecting free color charts. "After all," she added, "his life is here."

When Clayton nearly died, Jack came back—to see the business through the first couple of months until his father's condition improved. His help, Barb thought, which he provided cheerfully, was meant to be temporary. But two months after the stroke, things changed—Clayton was moved to Sparta

Vale; Bella thrived; and Jack, who returned to Denver just long enough to close out his life there, resumed a life in Carthage that seemed long on duty and short on joy.

Bella was patient.

Jack was attentive.

At some point—about a year ago—Bella went public. She started S.O.S. as an adjunct to Jack's own efforts and hosted elegant dinner parties at the house on Providence. She was establishing herself as a presence in Carthage the way a thoroughbred vies for position along the backstretch. And books, she was right, didn't figure in the plan. But Jack Girard did. It seemed to Barb that he more than figured: he was the plan. Everything else—the dogs, S.O.S., entertaining—was ornament.

It must have been around this time that they started sleeping together, for Bella changed pronouns—our plans for the house, our feelings about the grain elevator—and let drop unmistakable messages. How he takes long showers, how he wakes her up when she's having a nightmare, how they have to get to bed early because he's got to go to Cincinnati in the morning. Watching it happen, Cy had huffed to her, was like learning in school about the nitrogen cycle—you can see why it happens, only you wish you didn't have to hear about it.

We're free to see other people. We just never seem to want to.

We have the house. We have each other. It feels complete.

Marian wondered how much was true relationship and how much was just masterful marketing. The creation of a group perception. Norton for Grady. Half Jack—or less—for all Jack. She knew how the first perception was created: the bold and purposeful lie at the field trial. About the second, she wasn't sure. Images tumbled like the two-year-old Bella into Jack's lap. The yoked towel, the clasping arms. Bella, nodded to, her grip loosened, set aside as he embraced his father, or Claire. Or a life elsewhere that in no way seemed to require Bella. Her frustration must have been vast as she felt only punishment at the hands of Girard men.

Chapter Fifty-One

"Duncan here."

Upstairs in her room, Marian got the general number from the Kittatinny College for Women website and explained herself to the operator as a PI for the DOC, calling with some questions about a former Kittatinny student. The operator put her through to Dean of Students, Jo Duncan. It was a warm, ironic voice, the kind that belongs to someone who has one foot in academia and the other as far away as possible.

Marian said, "I'm calling for information on a former student."

"The name?"

"Bella Murphy."

Silence. "What's the nature of your interest in Bella?"

Did she hear a stonewall coming? "You remember her, then?"

"Very well," the dean said neutrally. "What do you have to do with her?"

Deciding to come reasonably clean, Marian explained that she's calling from Bella's hometown, where she's been sent to look into a building nominated for National Historic Landmark status. Now she's looking into a crime, and "Bella's name came up."

It flew. "If I can help you, I will."

Where does she start? "She left Kittatinny in her senior year?"

"You might say," Duncan said. "She was one step ahead of the Honor Board."

Marian's arms tingled. "How so?"

"Bella was playing paper broker."

"What does that mean?"

"She had a bunch of hirelings she paid to write papers for what you might call the scholastically disadvantaged." Pay three hundred, charge five—depending on length and complexity—and pocket the difference. She was clever enough to keep the local operation small to avoid detection. And where she had it all over Internet paper mills was that she offered truly customized service—very hard to detect—and quick turnaround. And because the papers were one-of-a-kind, no worries from software like Turn It In. "Now, of course," Jo Duncan sighed, "we're grappling with the likes of ChatGPT, which appears to be running its own paper mill as a community service."

At its height, Bella's operation involved half a dozen colleges and universities in northern Jersey and eastern Pennsylvania. Bella was selective, hiring quick, smart, cynical college writers who needed more pocket money for coke or ski weekends. And selling only to two types: one, the pragmatic cheats who preferred to spend their time cramming for the organic chem test than writing a paper on *The Sun Also Rises*; the other, the weak fretters with one nostril barely above the academic waters and pushy parents exhorting them to bring home honors they would never in this lifetime see.

"I take it you don't like her," said Marian.

"There are lots of things I don't like. Bella's right up there somewhere near liver with onions." It was the weak fretters, Duncan went on, Bella squeezed twice. Poor souls. One was a Taiwanese student at Kittatinny called Tai-Jue Su. Not only had Bella purchased her soul for a few pithy thesis statements, but she then turned around and worked a neat bit of extortion. She sent Su anonymous letters—the "I-know-what-you-did-and-you'll-have-to-pay" sort of thing—and when Su came crying, Bella claimed to have received some herself.

They'd have to pay up and keep quiet. Su finally came unglued and wound up babbling in the Infirmary. In two different languages. Nonstop. About money and Daisy's green light and Queequeg's coffin, and the women who come and go talking of Michelangelo. And Bella. "Which," Duncan finished, "is how the operation came to my attention. And I called Bella into my office."

"What happened?"

"I told her we were going to throw her out on her very lovely ass." Duncan was enjoying herself. "Never have I made a shorter speech that brought me more pleasure."

"What did she say?"

"She threatened to bring me up on charges of sexual harassment," Duncan laughed. "Well, the girl has nerve of the first magnitude. I said the head of the state Civil Rights Commission was a personal friend of mine. If she cared to wait, I could get him on the phone for her."

"Did you?"

"I was bluffing," said Duncan. "But so was Bella. Only she blinked first."

"Why?"

Jo Duncan's voice changed. "Because I had some kind of moral authority. That's what I think."

Another tack. Remembering Jack Girard's comment that Bella didn't get any help for the sexual abuse until later. At college. "Do you know whether she ever got any counseling?"

"What an image." Duncan laughed. "Bella on the couch."

"Still."

"The only way you'd find her there," said Jo Duncan, "is if she was working a scam on the shrink. No. There's nothing in her records about couch time."

Marian wanted to know whether the college contacted Bella's guardian to let him know about the charges. Bella, Duncan replied, preempted them. Before the case came before the Honor Board, Bella withdrew from school. According to her letter, Kittatinny College for Women was no longer meeting her particular needs. What she told friends, Duncan later heard, was that she was returning home to go into business and get married. There was a moment of long-distance silence. "Now it's your turn, Marian Warner. Ante up. What's the crime?"

Suddenly the dog fraud slipped away. "Sexual abuse."

"Who'd she abuse?"

"She was the one who was abused," Marian said.

Duncan's laugh was short. "Bullshit."

CHAPTER FIFTY-ONE

"She was sexually abused by her guardian."

"Bull. Shit." The dean was almost merry.

"You don't know the facts." All she could picture was Jack Girard's pain as he told the story.

"I don't have to know the facts. I know her."

"She was thirteen."

"So was I once," she rejoined. "And I wasn't sexually abused. Either."

Marian sat back. "You don't see her as a victim."

Duncan snorted. "Bella's less likely to be victimized than anyone I know."

"Why?"

"There's no way of getting to her," Duncan said. "No way in hell."

"She blinked." Marian reminded her.

"Only because I knew her for what she was."

"Which was—?"

Duncan got serious. "Something between the devil—" she paused, Marian thought, trying to name what was worse than the devil, "and a sociopath."

"But at thirteen, virginal, a ward in someone's keep—"

The dean was delighted. "How Gothic of her. I wonder what she'd been reading before she came up with that one. *Uncle Silas*, maybe, with a sexual twist."

"So you're not sympathetic."

Duncan came in fast. "I damn well am when it's the truth."

But Bella's experiences—everything from the sexual abuse by Clayton Girard to the double squeeze on the paper scam—aren't necessarily mutually exclusive. Marian put it to Jo Duncan. "Can't she be all those awful things and still have been sexually abused at thirteen?" A pause. "Maybe even all those awful things because she'd been sexually abused?"

She heard Duncan inhale. "I suppose." Tempering her own doubt with an attempt at being fair. "But," she went on, "I have one bit of advice for you about Bella's story. Assume it never happened."

Marian looked around the room, keenly, the way a field commander looks around the camp before the battle is enjoined. "I hear you."

"Do you like baseball?" asked Jo Duncan suddenly.

Marian was grateful for the diversion. "Like doesn't even come close."

"Then come see me in May. After exams. We'll go into the city and take in a game."

"New York?"

"Of course New York."

"Mets?" The moment of truth.

"Of course Mets. I'm strictly NL."

"Then it's a deal," Marian said. "And thanks, Jo."

"One more thing," Duncan kept her on the line. "If you go up against Bella—"

"Go on."

"Cover your ass." Adamant, like a coach at halftime when the score's close.

Marian smiled. "What did you teach before you started deaning? Girls basketball?"

"I'm dead serious, Marian Warner. Cover your ass."

"Okay."

"Brit lit." She could hear the smile in Duncan's voice. "I taught Brit lit. And girls' basketball."

"Listen," said Marian, "don't worry about me."

A pause. "I'm thinking of Tai-Jue Su, the Taiwanese student."

"What about her?"

"When I blew the lid off Bella's operation, Su's parents pulled her out of school." Her words tumbled together. "All the way back home to Taiwan. In disgrace."

"That's too bad."

"It gets worse," Duncan said. "She killed herself."

The phone felt loose in Marian's hand. It was worse than a college crime. Tai-Jue Su went home to death. Bella Murphy went home to shrimp in pastry shells.

Duncan's voice crackled.

"Yes, bye," Marian said, detached. And for the life of her, she couldn't say how long she had been sitting there before setting down her phone.

Assume it never happened, Jo Duncan had said.

If that's the case, then Bella told Jack Girard one hell of a damaging lie. More than a lie. It was a false and wicked tale filled with elaborate detail and affecting passages. Sonorous with truth. Powerful in reach. A specious epoch Bella had inserted into her personal history for the purpose of—what? — isolating and binding the object of her desire. Jack. Elusive not by his nature but by circumstances: the age difference, the distance to Denver, Claire, and custom—his affection for her only brotherly. Bella, tolerated. Bella, nodded to. Bella, advised in matters of the heart while never recognizing his own sovereignty. Bella, released, set aside.

What she lacked was opportunity. A fair and sufficient chance to pull Jack into her own orbit. Not just for a week or two. The matter required whole seasons at her disposal, in a climate of attentiveness. Lovely and frequent occasions of contact. Then Clayton Girard had a stroke, a global and debilitating one, bringing Jack into range. And at some point during his extended stay it came to Bella.

The way.

The wicked, daring tale designed to isolate Jack from people he loved. Designed to lash him to a place and a smoldering girl he had left behind. *For love,* Marian had said of Mazeppa's torment. *For punishment,* Jack Girard countered. Quiet together in the dim, cold Mission House. *But the love came first,* she said. He seemed to see it. Of Mazeppa. A torment of love—like a unit of measurement—a horror of love, a punishment of love.

Until finally Bella spoke it. And it came out in words that described episodic rape at the hands of his father. And Jack stayed. *It was a chance to put something right,* he had said about returning the fireplace facing. Maybe in the matter of Bella the same principle applied. To Bella, it was his staying that was imperative; his reasons were unimportant. Let him spend time with her first out of grief and guilt; over time, that attention would bring them both pleasure. This was Bella's gamble.

And it worked.

She pulled it off.

For a chilling moment, Marian didn't know which possibility felt more dreadful. That the patrician smiling into the camera with Seamus Wilson had systematically violated his ward. Or that Jack had accepted Bella's lie without a ripple of disbelief. And for the first time since she woke up at six-twenty, Marian discovered a task.

Only first, she had to get back in the Volvo.

Because there was still the matter of proof.

Chapter Fifty-Two

She found Clayton Girard in the solarium, a room with a southern exposure at the Sparta Vale Skilled Care Facility. There were a few split-leaf philodendrons and several white wicker chairs—and, against the far wall, a fifty-gallon aquarium with a colony of flickering fish. What the solarium was missing was a television, which was probably why it was empty. Except for Clayton Girard, whose wheelchair was by the windows.

Only he wasn't looking outside at the towering blue spruces, their branches laden with snow. He was reading. From a book on an elevated tray snapped to the arms of his wheelchair. What slowed the process was the time it took him to turn the pages. He had to angle a useless finger between the pages, then stretch himself practically out of the wheelchair, pulling the page along until air and gravity took over and let it sink to the left.

"Mr. Girard?" She dragged over a wicker chair and sat. He was regarding her with interest. And perfect recollection. The paper slippers and blue bathrobe were the same. The pajamas were different, although she couldn't say how, and he was wearing reading half-glasses, placed by other hands. His page-turning hand lay quiet on the great, short works of Joseph Conrad, his body arched away from her. His chin was still wet. "Two days ago," Marian said, "I asked you some questions about Derry Wilson. Today I'd like to ask you a question about Bella. Is that all right?"

What she saw on his face was relief. Strange. She'd expect almost anything else, but relief was hard to explain. Unless, of course, ten years ago Clayton Girard did to Bella precisely what his son had described. And now, caught in those moments of page-turning suspense—would the page drift to the left or the right? —the old man had arrived at a place of regrets. She looked straight at him. "Did you sexually abuse your ward?"

Clayton Girard didn't blink. He didn't look away. Marian felt riveted. With a speed she was unprepared for he jerked his body violently, sweeping the Conrad book from the tray with stiff fingertips and battering the tray with his forearm until it clattered to the floor.

They looked at each other. She spoke quietly. "I take it your answer is no." His look was steady.

An aide came squinching along in her rubber-soled shoes, and Marian reassured her that Mr. Girard was fine. When they were alone again, she said, "You're not fine, are you?" The relief she had seen on his face looked new. But the anger wasn't. Why? How in hell was she going to sort it out? She told him about the dog scam and paper brokering and ended with the tale of sexual abuse. Just as she had heard it two nights ago in the trailer. Give him the details, give him the affecting passages—the whole elaborate stink of it. From the nocturnal fondling of his "own sweet little girl" to Cokes at Mazeppa's Ride. It was a tale that had damaged him worse than a stroke. They watched each other in silence. Finally, he gave her a quizzical look. "From Jack. He's told no one else."

Clayton Girard managed a dismissing look. If his son believes the lie, then he didn't give a good goddamn if the whole town believes it, too. Here again, it occurred to Marian that what she was seeing in the old man was a feeling of some longevity. And then it struck her. The reason for his relief. The reason for his anger. "You've known about it for some time," she said suddenly, "haven't you?" Where it lay on his thin leg, Girard's hand flapped once, like an air-logged gill. Dying in a hostile element. Like Derry Wilson.

Derry.

It is all suffocation. We die where we drink. We die where we breathe. We die where we warm ourselves. We die on the food-giving ground. We love in all the same places. It's our chance to hold off the enclosing airless place. Marian's heart pounded. Curling her hand around Clayton Girard's fingers, she felt a light squeeze. They sat companionably for a moment. Then she

242

watched his face soften, troubled. He struggled for sound, frustrated at the inability to shape a word. "Ch." He tried again to sharpen the word. It still came out "Ch." His eyes were questioning.

"Jack?" In return, a light squeeze. The man was asking about his son. The son who pays the bills, filled with revulsion. The son, lost. It was the toughest part of the story. Hanging on to the cool, curling fingers, she told him about Jack and Bella. Describing his son's life—his trailer haven—and his half-life on Providence with Bella Murphy. The relationship approaching him, where he was sleeping senseless in the sand of his own grief, like tide.

She looked at Clayton Girard, her story done.

He can read.

He can read Conrad.

He can turn pages.

And now I know, despite what you say, Jack, he can cry. Very slowly, Marian picked up the tray from the floor and set it back in place. He didn't seem to notice. She replaced the Conrad. "I'll go to him with the truth," she told him, "when I have it all." With the back of her hand, she touched his cheek. Thought of Jack, years ago, setting aside Bella to embrace his father, removing her hands from his neck. A simple act, then. To do the same thing now is impossible. To set aside Bella, to embrace his father—it won't be in a spirit of laughing banter. Assuming, Warner, he even tries. She felt sick to her stomach. Either way.

Back in the Volvo, she closed the door, kicked off her boots, and pulled out her phone. Then she called the Carthage Development Corporation, grateful for a private place where she was still safe in what she knew were the final moments of ignorance, where no one could find her. Not Charlie, not Girard, not Khartoukian, not Bella.

No one except the dead.

Derry.

And Hughes.

At the other end of the line a cheery temp was saying good afternoon for the third time. While Marian stared. Past the Sanitex walls where Clayton Girard had spent the last two years. She saw it, then, complete. How Jesse

Connor Hughes had died.

And why.

Chapter Fifty-Three

As the cement mixer approached her on the narrow road leading down to the trailer, Marian pulled over and flagged it down. The day was becoming a sullen gray. The driver rolled down the frosty window. "Where's Girard?" she called.

Wearing a Cincinnati Reds baseball cap with the peak turned to the back, he shook his head, pointing straight ahead. "Worksite west of town. Stay on River Street, not even ten miles. On the left. You'll see the sign."

Damn. Another drive. Yelling thanks, she pulled the Volvo around, passed the cement mixer, and headed into Carthage. The wind picked up, blowing big wet flakes onto the windshield. The kid in the cement mixer was right: nearly ten miles west of town, she saw a clearing on the left. Beyond it, a long, dense woods stretching to the horizon. Future Home of something for the Department of the Interior. MCG Construction.

She turned down a crudely plowed dirt road—crusty from cold, hard to follow in the gathering snow—marked for construction vehicles only. Serviceable four-by-fours were angled over the site, parked just short of where the heavy equipment was doing the work of redefining the landscape. Pulling to a stop near a leaning, blue Port-o-Let, Marian looked around the clearing for Jack Girard. A burly worker in a hard hat and unzipped down vest came over to the Ram Charger near her.

"Girard?" She walked toward him. The man raised his eyebrows, cupped a massive hand over his eyes, and looked over the site.

"Far side," he pointed. "Blue hood."

Marian saw. She walked briskly around the perimeter of the site, her boots slipping on rocky shards of ice, down to the place where three men were working on a disabled bulldozer. From where he was working on the engine, in hardy coveralls, Girard looked up, saw her, and pushed back the blue hood of his sweatshirt. Wiping his hands on a rag, he came over. She couldn't read him yet, but whatever he felt didn't seem as hard as last night at Mazeppa's Ride. Her meeting, her speech. Unlike Khartoukian, he wasn't co-opting her. "I have to talk to you."

"Can it wait?"

"No."

He looked away. "Is it personal?"

"Yes." Her heart pounded. She felt miserable at what she was about to do to him.

Then Jack Girard tilted his head toward a path going into the woods. "This all right?" She nodded. As all right as anything could be. "Rodie, catch," he called to the lanky young man near the bulldozer, tossing him the rag. As Marian stuffed her gloved hands into her pockets, they started down the path. Since he said nothing, neither did she. "Here?" he said, shrugging.

"Farther." Never in her life had she felt so clear.

She simply wanted to keep walking. To forget why she'd come. To play in the snow. To walk until spring and then find forsythia. Her eyes stung. Not possible. At a bend in the path, she stopped, looking hard at the trees. Shaggy-bark hickory, walnut—no, black walnut—it all mattered. They made it dense and private. She faced him, his hand scraping through his hair. He was waiting. She wanted a good look at him, at the innocent misery she was about to undo. Only to replace it with a different kind of misery.

She spoke it. "Bella killed Derry Wilson."

Some part of him retreated. "No—" He started to walk away.

"She killed Jesse Hughes."

Jack Girard stopped, his hand rubbing the back of his neck. "Jesus, Marian—"

And then the last. The molten center. "She lied to you about your father. The sexual abuse never happened." He turned, his face awful. Gently: "It never happened."

"Tell me you're lying."

"No."

He lost control. "Tell me you're lying," he cried, grabbing her collar, rushing them both up against the tree.

"No," she shouted. "I wouldn't do that to you." She stood half-pinned, pressed against the tree, his arms braced on the tree trunk. Crushing her words with his weight. Scattering them outside her remembered arms. His chest heaving, Girard rolled his head, shaking the burden. She couldn't touch him, couldn't lean into him, couldn't make it less. He had to feel it all himself. The range and size of it. Feel Bella's abuse of him. Feel the deceit. Feel the loss of his father. Feel the murder. And the crime of his own ignorance—offering shelter to a thing impervious to the elements, laying waste his tenderness in a toxic place where nothing grows.

He shuddered.

Bliss and grief.

I can no longer tell them apart.

She cried. Only one thing was left. A last line. "'Though I sang in my chains like the sea.'" He moved his head slightly, hearing her. "Jack." An affirmation. To herself. An intimacy of name. Bringing it out of her heart, giving it to the air, sending it earthward with the snow. This thing has a name, that roiling part of her that jokes, writes, sips, chews, and practices passion in lesser arms. These earthbound things. Have a single name.

Now she knew.

Girard touched her shoulder, dazed, then moved beside her. "Christ, I'm sorry." Unsteady, he felt for the tree trunk, slipping down to a crouch. "I guess I'd better hear it, Marian," he said, blinking away the snow. "All of it." He couldn't look at her.

Crouching beside him, she began with the field trial—Girard frowned—and sketched in Barb Hauser's history of his relationship with Bella. Pulling off his thick gloves, he amended nothing. Marian went on to describe Bella's career at Kittatinny College for Women. The paper brokering. The extortion. The death of Tai-Jue Su. And the dean's conviction that any tale Bella told of sexual abuse was false.

Girard was watching the snow fall, his jaw set.

Marian glanced at him. "I needed the information."

He nodded, pressing his hands into the snow.

She looked down. "I went back to your father. To ask him."

"And?"

She described Clayton's response. His anger at the accusation. Old anger, accustomed anger. Bella's lie wasn't news. What Marian couldn't figure was how he had known about it.

"From me."

She sat back.

He scanned her face. "Two years ago. When Bella first told me. I confronted him." Girard opened his hands. "He's my father." In it was a child's definition of fishing trips, endless games of catch, enforced chores, starry talks. "I had to know. Only I guess I wasn't asking." He looked down. "He was in pretty bad shape. And he wasn't happy to see me. Not just from pain. Something else. I thought later he knew what was coming, somehow. When I told him I knew all about Bella—what he'd done to her—he looked wild. Cornered." His shoulders hunched. "It was awful."

"You took it for guilt."

"What else could it be?"

"Horror at the lie."

Bella had run a paper brokering scam. She had run a dog scam. But the Girards. The Girards were her masterpiece. To secure Jack, she was taking no chances: two years ago she engineered an irreparable break between the father and son, she bound Jack to her in shame, and four nights ago she killed Derry Wilson to secure the lie for all time.

Oh, God, it was thorough.

And evil.

Marian narrowed her eyes against the snow. "Did you ever tell Bella you confronted him?"

"No. It would have seemed —"

"Like you doubted her."

He looked away. "Like I doubted her," he said. "Jesus."

248

CHAPTER FIFTY-THREE

"When you went to your father—"

"He saw right away what she'd done."

They sat quietly, like arctic explorers, feeling the elements encroach. Regarding the white and silent death with a patient longing. Marian looked up. *There is nothing celestial except what we find in this earthy place, our feet bare in the good grass.* She has stood there, that much she knew, she and Jack Girard. Through the years of dark yearning, it would have to be enough.

"What about Derry?" His voice low.

Chapter Fifty-Four

The death of Derry Wilson.

Began, in some ways, the summer Bella was thirteen.

Marian described the calls she'd made before leaving Sparta Vale. Barb Hauser recalled meeting Bella and Derry outside the ice cream parlor the summer Bella was thirteen. It was a blistering day late in August, and the Hausers had just returned from France, where Cy had led his French majors on a six-week tour of cathedral country. Bella, who seemed florid with good health, was complaining about what a bad letter writer Jack was.

Polly Gundersen went through some old snapshots of Derry and herself. One was taken the weekend mid-July—just a couple of months before Derry went on the road—when they blew off Carthage for a long weekend and splurged at King's Island. With them in the photo—in a tank top with a small floral print, the skin of her young arms flawless—was Bella Murphy.

Cindy Wilson recalled the summer she herself was in County Londonderry was profitable for her daughter. Derry ran the coffee shop and worked for Clayton Girard—who paid her good money to stay with the Murphy girl and paint the interior of the ranch since he was away a lot. Derry and the girl—no, she had no idea how old the child was at the time—stayed at the bungalow.

Bill Cain was apoplectic that Great Seal Power & Light just withdrew its interest in the Mission House property because the goddamn deal was taking too long—add to that the fact that city council was alerted to some new evidence on the premises of the Mission House that could authenticate it and make that dilapidated piece of shit a National Historic Landmark.

He barked that yes, the summer before Derry left Carthage, she quit him to work for bigger bucks for Clayton, doing odd jobs and babysitting. And yes, that was the same summer MCG put in the extension to Highway 433 north of Dayton. Big commute to Carthage. Big motel bills. Testy: Is that all, for God's sake?

Clayton had a paralyzing stroke.

Polly Gundersen, whose information was only partial, hardly knew Jack.

Derry Wilson, the babysitter, left town ten years ago.

Barb Hauser was in France during the period in question. Which probably spared her life.

And between Bill Cain and Jack Girard, family secrets went undisclosed.

The people in the strongest position to refute Bella's claim of abuse were one way or another, out of the way. Clayton couldn't deny it. Barb wasn't around to account for the actions of Clayton and Bella. And only Derry—who shepherded Bella during a busy, out-of-town construction season—could attest to Clayton's lack of opportunity. The fearful summer nights Bella had described, impressed into a kind of sexual servitude, were actually spent in safety either at the Wilson bungalow or the ranch on the hill—in the company of Derry.

Who came back to Carthage unexpectedly. And for good.

Imagine Bella's alarm.

Bella was watchful, waiting until it seemed Derry and Jack would resume contact. Last Friday night, at the dinner party on Providence, it was Charlie who gave Girard a message from Derry. That she wanted to see him. The two who overhead it—and heard Girard's interest, too—were Cy Hauser and Bella. She was swift, then, and bold. To pull it off, she needed two things: an opportunity to snag Derry and an alibi for Jack. The next night, as far as she could tell, presented both. Derry sang at Mazeppa's Ride until just after ten-thirty—Bella sat parked in the Bronco on a side street with a clear view of the saloon—and Jack was supposed to be holed up in Zanesville on business. When Derry came out, alone, and started up the empty street, Bella pulled alongside. *Hi! Need a lift?* And Derry, seeing it was an old friend, accepted.

Catch-up chatter.

Laughs about old times.

It was Bella's idea to swing by Jack's—*he's just doing paperwork, he'll be happy for the rescue,* she lied, *we can have a few drinks and a real reunion, how's that?* Derry more than agreeable. Driving out Highway Eight, arriving disappointed, the jeep gone. *It doesn't necessarily mean anything,* Bella improvised, *sometimes he leaves it up the hill if the weather's going to be bad,* and Derry, unquestioning. The trailer was dark. *What do you say we wake him up?* said Bella. And as they got out of the Bronco, she pulled Norton's stick from the back and came up behind Derry. Who never got to the trailer, never got the drink, never got the reunion.

"I know the rest." He stared at nothing.

"I'm sorry."

"So am I."

"About all of it."

Jack Girard turned to look at Marian. "So am I." Included in their global regret was something, she could tell, about each other.

They got to their feet. There was nothing more to tell.

"What happened to the stick?" he said finally.

"My guess is she burned it," Marian said. "It's not in the bin in the back of the Bronco. The frisbees and dummies are there. But not Norton's stick. Khartoukian can check the fireplace on Providence." She suddenly felt wearier than she could ever remember. "And the Bronco for trace evidence."

"What are you going to do?"

It was a question she expected. "Nothing."

He gave her a long look. "What are you saying?"

She exhaled, and the cold surrounded her. "It's your story." It was all she could say. "It's your story. I'm giving it to you." She crossed her arms tight around her chest. "I just don't have the heart for it anymore, Jack."

"What do you mean you're giving it to me?"

"It's yours to tell Khartoukian." She started to back away.

His face was unreadable. "How do you know I will?"

She nearly smiled. Only she couldn't control the hurt. "I've got faith."

CHAPTER FIFTY-FOUR

He heard it. "Where are you going?"

Suddenly Marian needed to put 500 miles between her and this job and these woods. "Home. I have to go home."

"Why?"

"I leave. It's what I do. Ask Charlie."

His eyes widened. "I don't have to ask Charlie."

She felt awful. "The other night," she blurted.

"I'm listening."

"I was scared." She made a futile gesture.

"Of what?"

"Of you."

He looked down. "Because of Derry Wilson."

"No."

"Then why?"

She shouldn't have brought it up. "You figure it out."

"Don't play games with me. If I could figure it out, we wouldn't be standing here in the—"

"I was scared of what you could mean to me," she came in, fierce. Her cheeks burned. Or froze. She couldn't tell.

"Well," he said, finally, pulling on his work gloves, "I guess you turned on the light and the shadows went away."

Let him think it.

He needs a clear head.

So she said nothing.

Girard looked at her. "If you're leaving, you'd better get going." Not angry. Just plain. "The roads could be bad."

Marian felt uneasy. "Be careful."

His voice was quiet. "Bella wouldn't hurt me."

Ah, honey. She already has. She left him, then, on the whitening path.

"Marian," he called after her. She turned. "Why Hughes? What did she have against him?"

"Nothing."

"Then why —?" He couldn't even finish it.

In some ways, it was the worst.

"Bella didn't even know who it was."

He was speechless.

"Lowther saw somebody there that night. I think it was Bella," Marian said. "She turned the lock on a stranger to put the screws to Alice Lowther, her only competition in town." Her legs shaky, she continued up the path. When she reached the clearing where the rumbling steam shovel gabbled at the rocky soil, she turned and saw Jack Girard still standing in the woods. Indistinct. Snow falling on his hair and across his shoulders. As she watched him slowly pull up his blue hood, his head down, the snow seemed to collect in the air between them. Without moving, he receded. Without looking away, she hardly saw.

She trotted to the Volvo with a resolve even a brandy couldn't warm.

Chapter Fifty-Five

Back at The Briars, Marian flung clothes—clean, dirty, and anyone's guess—into the one suitcase she had brought. She swept her few toiletries into a ditty bag she tied and tossed on top of the heaped clothes. Then she slung her backpack over her shoulder and hurried downstairs.

While Cy put the room charges on her Visa and Barb fussed over the cream and sugar set, she shrugged into her long dress coat and stuffed the jacket into the suitcase she could now barely zip. Then she called Charlie's office. To the pert voice who was taking his calls, explaining that Mr. Levitan was in a meeting, Marian left her name and a simple message. "Tell him to call Jack Girard about Derry. That's all." Some day she'd tell him the truth about Paul Seeks. But not now. Not yet.

Two rounds of hugs, and she was gone. 3:05. At this rate, she'd be back at the cabin in time for the eleven o'clock news she never watched. Still. Right about now, the prospect seemed better than any amount of Mr. Bubble. Surely she had in her cupboard some Lemon Lift tea and a few stale Chips Ahoy. Whoever says life gets better than that, she'd put up against Bella Murphy any day. As she zipped past the Mission House, she saluted. It had, for the present at least, outlasted Bill Cain. Back where it belonged, the fireplace facing would guarantee the Mission House some federal protection—whether the committee will decide the first Jesuit mission in the Northwest Territories has historic significance for the entire nation, Marian and Joan and Alice Lowther and Jack Girard would have to wait and see. Even if it just gets listed along with the 90,000 other places on the National Register, a notch below Historic Landmark status, the Mission House in Carthage, Ohio, will be preserved.

Marian turned the heat to full blast and clattered around in the box of CDs on the passenger seat. What was called for—she glanced through them without going into a skid—was something sixties with lots of instruments and a pounding beat. She picked up Highway 53 East and drove through the outskirts of Carthage. Passing the strip of every fast-food joint known to man. Passing the hospital, the Days Inn, the billboard paid for by the Chamber of Commerce: *Come Back to Carthage—Don't Leave Your History Behind!* Who writes their copy? Marian wondered as the town changed into wintry fields, fallow in the snow. Stumpy stalks poked up like the earth's bristles. It was beautiful. For a moment, she felt herself settling down.

Don't Leave Your History Behind!

From the glove compartment, she pulled a battered bottle of generic aspirin. With her elbows doing the steering, Marian roughed up her fingertips, trying to line up arrows and lift off the cap. She shook three pills into her hand and downed them without water.

Don't Leave.

Your History.

Behind.

Ahead of her by something like seven-plus hours was the cabin where she'd lived alone for the last year. Wasn't that her history? It was her center of operations. Her base. From there, she went into the city to meet the occasional friend for dinner. Or the occasional man for something more. From there, she called Charlie, hundreds of miles away.

Such was her life. And, she supposed, her history. It was a place she visited since childhood. Years. Years are what count. What matters. History is a thing of many years. Ask Alice Lowther, who robs it. Ask Bill Cain, who destroys it. Ask Jack Girard, who pays for it all.

Ask yourself, Warner.

Ask yourself.

Who leaves it behind.

The history of a week and a half. In a place that contains Charlie and

Derry. Khartoukian. Jack Girard. *I leave. It's what I do. Ask Charlie.* As if it's a life's work. Poke around, write some reports, then leave. Just one of her many services. Truth be told, she realized as she switched off the music, maybe it was. Remembering Girard, slowly covering his head, standing alone like wreckage in the snow. Maybe leaving is a kindness. A goddamn public service. Ahead of her, the fields extended barren and colorless all the way to the horizon. The Volvo seemed to lose speed, confronted with a level landscape unrelieved by anything, even a sign for Goat Milk Fudge.

Then she thought of Paul. The first Paul. The dead Paul. The Paul who had shelled out her heart all those years ago when he had died in a shower of shrapnel and body parts. And because she had cared, she had somehow felt responsible. Caring, it seemed, had something to do with precipice. That much she had learned from Paul Seeks. Although he never knew it. Caring meant letting him walk the precipice. But it also meant calling him back. Ever since that afternoon when broken, bloodied glass on a Manhattan street just meant overtime for the Department of Sanitation, she had the sense that she forgot to call him back.

The sense that she had let him die.

She had cared. But she hadn't loved.

She hadn't loved.

With Paul, with Charlie, with others, she had indeed turned on the light. Dispelling fear. But dispelling hope, as well. Suddenly she minded the trade. She jerked the Volvo over to the berm, idling. A quick look in the rearview mirror. Carthage was gone.

Marian, the back stops here.

Pulling out her phone, she tapped the number for MCG Construction. "Come on, come on, pick up." She was wrong. Twelve miles out of Carthage, and she knew she was wrong. It was his story, all right, but he shouldn't have to tell it alone. Finally, someone answered.

"MCG." A voice high and good-natured. "Prescott speaking." Rodie. Back from the DOI site. She asked for the boss. "Not here, sorry."

She felt deflated. "Can you tell me where he is?"

"He stopped by to clean up. Then said he was going into town."

"Did he say where?" She glanced at her watch. She could get to Khartoukian in fifteen minutes.

"The house."

The house.

He went to Bella's.

Chapter Fifty-Six

Making a noisy U-turn, Marian headed back to Carthage, doing nearly fifteen over the speed limit. If she hadn't been in such a damn hurry to leave her history behind, she could have made it to Providence right about the time Jack Girard did. Which, for reasons she couldn't articulate, would have made her feel a whole lot better. Relieved to see the intersection of Main and Mission Streets, Marian quickly circled the block around the county courthouse, where the sheriff's department was annexed, in search of the Jeep.

Nowhere.

So be it. Taking a deep breath, Marian drove slowly down Main Street, turning into the alley she had walked to Bella's house the night of the dinner party. What she wanted was the lay of the land. She eased down another alley running parallel to Providence, behind the houses across the street from Bella's. Parking the Volvo at the entrance to someone's new two-car garage, Marian pocketed the keys.

Then, with a strange detachment, she pulled the Chief's Special from her backpack and loaded a couple of rounds. She left the car, cutting across snowy lawns. On the street was Girard's jeep. She cursed herself for not going to Khartoukian in the first damn place. At the corner, she leaned into the alley for a quick look at the back of the house. Bella's Bronco. On the other side of the chain link fence, the dogs were darting around, pumped up from the afternoon's shoot, their tongues still flapping. Bella and the dogs were back—but only just.

Girard had gone in the front.

But he hadn't quite closed the door.

Marian was up the steps in a flash. Where she listened unseen. The Chief's Special, tucked into the waistband of her jeans, was the single most comforting thing she had experienced since spending the night in Girard's trailer. Only, where in the house were they? "Bella," she heard him say, "where's Norton's stick?"

The hall. They were in the hall.

"What?" Bella's voice was light. She was stalling.

"Norton's stick. Where is it?"

There was a sound of gunmetal on wood. The twelve-gauge. Bella was rattled, couldn't he see? Oh, honey, Marian bit her lip, forcing herself into Girard's brain, she's got what you might call superior firepower, and you, sweet honey, have none at all. "I don't know," Bella said, concerned. "Have you checked the back of the jeep?"

Bella wouldn't hurt me, he had said. Maybe not, but if she decided to, Marian could picture her wailing to a grim Khartoukian something about a terrible, terrible accident while a couple of deputies swept into a single pile what was left of the fine chest of Jack Girard. Uh-uh. Girard was right, after all: she had no faith.

"It's not there."

"Then I don't know." Their voices sounded peculiar, slow, and Marian knew they were standing still. She felt sick. Ten seconds more, Jack, ten seconds more to handle it your way, and that's all. Trembling slightly, Marian flexed her hand three times fast and pulled out the Chief's Special. "If it's gone," Bella said, "we'll get another."

"I don't think so."

"What's the matter with you?"

He was silent for only a moment. "What did you do with it," he said, "after you killed Derry?"

Jesus.

"Talk sense." Bella's voice was sharp.

"Marian's right, isn't she?" he said softly.

"What does Marian have to do with it?"

"Did you burn it?" he said. "That's what she thinks."

"Fuck what she thinks," she struggled. Then: "You're hurting my arm."

"Your arm," he said, "will heal. Only not as fast as it did ten years ago. Will it?"

There was silence.

"Will it?"

"No." Her voice was strange.

"What the hell have you done?" Revulsion.

"I brought you home," she said fiercely. "I kept you home."

There was a sudden sound of a swinging hinge—the dog door in the kitchen—and into the entrance hall came the darting, snuffling sounds of the Labs. How many of them? Two? Three? How soon before the others would come in, too? Damn. Too many variables, Jack. Time's up. Her gun held low, behind the folds of her open coat, Marian stepped inside. As Jack Girard turned, surprised, Bella pulled free from him, stepping backwards against the table. Norton came wagging over. "Good boy, Norton," Marian whispered, her eyes on Bella's, "now go on." With her right leg, she tried to push him aside.

A sharp whistle from Girard—his face awful—"Norton, Trixie, let's go," he reached for a collar, turning away. Every part of Bella's unsmiling face seemed attentive to some point on Marian's cheek. Her skin felt necrotic. Then the other woman's eyes slanted around toward the table. And the twelve-gauge.

Jesus, Marian breathed.

Oh, Bella, don't do it.

Don't give me a reason.

She saw Jack look back just as Bella grabbed and cocked the shotgun at her—a deafening *No!*— not hers, not Bella's—a gale in the great, empty hall—and Marian brought up her arms and fired, just as he lunged. A single shot, center mass. As Bella fell back, the twelve-gauge exploded, and he fell with her. There were screaming dogs. Gunpowder like brimstone. And a rosy nebula on the perfect white chest of Bella Murphy. Marian let her gun fall—"Don't touch the guns," she choked, "don't touch anything," and coughing, stumbled outside. She got as far as the front yard before she fell to her knees and started retching into the gathering snow.

Chapter Fifty-Seven

Y ou mind telling me what the hell happened here?" Khartoukian asked, not unkind, helping her into the cruiser. And she did, for the next three hours, peeling crescents of Styrofoam from the one useless cup of coffee they'd given her when she arrived at the station, her head and arm sprawled out finally on Khartoukian's desk. Someone took a statement. Someone else typed. For a brief while, there, she smelled pizza, which she declined, and while she was counting the spaces in the wire mesh of Khartoukian's In/Out baskets, she saw Jack Girard through the half-glass walls, standing in another room, head down, his hands on his hips.

Marian groaned and rotated her head. Time to cool the other cheek on the metal desk that smelled like pencil erasers. Marian heard the deputy talking to Khartoukian just outside the door. *Blast took one of the dogs.* She bit her lip, frowning. *Pretty chocolate bitch,* he added. Trixie. Marian started sobbing. *...got a hell of a cleanup job back there.*

She covered her head and ears with her arms, remembering suddenly his hand on her head while she braced herself feebly in the snow, unable to control her stomach. "Go away," she had said, pulling a shaky hand across her mouth. "Go away." He left her then, without a word, and went back inside to death and confusion.

"Well, Marian, Girard's story confirms yours," Khartoukian was saying, sliding her PI license to her across the table. Just then, she heard Charlie's voice, eastern and wired, out in the hall. "We'll investigate," Khartoukian added, "but for now, we're calling it a justified. The county prosecutor will show some interest, but it won't amount to anything."

And in another moment, Charlie was grabbing her out of her chair, going on to the others about counsel, unorthodox methods, dinner, and humanity. Even before Khartoukian muttered she was free to go, Charlie was walking her out. Past the deputies. Past the dispatcher on the radio about a 912 in progress. Past the room where Girard was still being questioned, his back to her, one hand rubbing his eyes. She let herself be walked.

Soon she was pulling on Charlie's pajama top. Please let this be the head hole, she thought, because she didn't have the strength to fight. In the kitchen Hannah and her father were talking quietly. Marian turned out the living room light and crawled into the sleeping bag Hannah had put out for her. Body bag by L.L. Bean. A nice bag, Hannah was right. Marian had dug down as close to the bottom as possible and lay on her back, feeling a rift of air at the top of her head. If only the zipper went clear around, this would be a damn near perfect bag. Open up whole new markets for catalog sales—Tijuana, Cape Town, St. Louis.

She floated, her mind emptied of every blessed thing. Loft. Quallofil. These words were safe. Her mind, a waving, watery thing, took them in like plankton. Stitches per square inch. Also good. Cadet blue. *O camerado close! O you and me at last, and us two only.* A darkened mind. In a darkened bag. In a darkened world: the layered look. And still too much light.

For a while, she drifted, heard Charlie nearby, telling her to sit up and have this homemade kreplach soup his mother packs frozen in a Styrofoam chest, ships to Columbus by air and then to Carthage by bus. So she did, steam rising from the broth in the mug. Charlie sat on the edge of a chair next to the sleeping bag, his hands clasped between his knees. "Crackers?" he said.

She shook her head. "I should go help him, Charlie."

"No, you shouldn't."

"But Trixie," she whispered, her throat closing. When she imagined Jack Girard alone, spading the hard ground into some kind of grave, the lantern bleak, the dogs with their heads on their paws, her ribs felt as rickety as bamboo. "Shit, what a mess."

"It's his mess. Let him deal with it."

"It isn't his mess."

"Let him deal with it anyway." He took the half-empty mug she held out to him. "Marian, the other night I couldn't sleep," he told her. "So I drove over to the gravel pit to stare at the place where they found Derry. I thought it might help." He stopped.

Marian understood. "You saw the Volvo."

He nodded. "I saw the Volvo. And the jeep. From the top of the hill," he said. "And there weren't any lights on in the trailer."

Her hand seemed small on his knee. "I guess we keep missing each other, don't we, Charlie?"

He scanned her face. "So far."

"I'm tired," she said, lying back down.

"So, sleep," he said. "But don't help Jack Girard. It gives him something to do. For days." Charlie stood. "Maybe weeks." Crouching beside her, he pushed the bag in around her sides. "One more thing," he said. "What do you want me to tell him when he calls?"

"Tell him I'm gone."

"But you're not."

"I will be."

"You know what I mean."

Marian dug down deeper until the bag covered her face. Her hands across her chest, she levitated, her mind slipping into all the warm unseen places her body alone didn't fill. She was damaged. That much she knew. And there was no difference, really, between all those places he had touched—places, even, that had nothing to do with skin—and those that now felt nicked and dented. "Tell him," she said to Charlie, "tell him about the salamander"—and she turned on her side, already asleep.

The night of the blast, Marian walked back from Battery Park. She didn't know how long it took, but she found Charlie waiting for her, crouched, in front of her building. He was rubbing his eyes. "Come on up," she said. Upstairs it was all she could do to stow the uneaten takeout in the refrigerator. Charlie stretched out on the couch and stared at the ceiling, one arm curled under his head. She pushed aside his legs and sat down at the other end.

"Maybe he wasn't there," Charlie said quietly.

"What do you mean?"

"Maybe Paul wasn't there. Maybe he'd gone out for a paper. Or some cigarettes." She was weary. "Or to walk the dog."

"Don't be funny."

"Then don't be a jackass," she said, angry. "He was there, Charlie. All right? He was there. And he blew himself up."

"All right," he sat up fast, squeezing her arm. "Then try this. The dumb fuck could have killed you." He pushed her away and lay back down, but not before she saw the tears in his eyes, and she realized they had been crying about different things, after all.

Acknowledgements

Thanks always to our long-standing Brainstorming group, Casey Daniels, Emilie Richards, and Serena B. Miller. Who would think annual observations like "It's too complicated," "I don't like it," and "Well, that's all right, but what if…" and "Is it time to go eat?" would lead to dozens of murder plots and years of friendship?

About the Author

Shelley Costa's work has been nominated for both the Edgar and Agatha Awards and has received a Special Mention for The Pushcart Prize. In addition to several mystery novels, she is the author of short stories in *The Georgia Review*, *North American Review*, *The World's Finest Mystery and Crime Stories*, *Alfred Hitchcock Mystery Magazine*, *Blood on Their Hands*, and *Odd Partners*. With a Ph.D. in English, Shelley was on the Liberal Arts faculty at the Cleveland Institute of Art for nearly twenty years.

SOCIAL MEDIA HANDLES:
  Facebook: shelleycostamysteryauthor

AUTHOR WEBSITE:
  www.shelleycosta.com

Also by Shelley Costa

Evil Under the Tuscan Sun (Penguin Random House, 2022)

Crime of the Ancient Marinara (Penguin Random House, 2021)

Al Dente's Inferno (Penguin Random House, 2020)

A Killer's Guide to Good Works (Henery Press, 2016)

Practical Sins for Cold Climates (Henery Press, 2016)

Basil Instinct (Simon & Schuster, 2014)

You Cannoli Die Once (Simon & Schuster, 2013)

Alfred Hitchcock's Mystery Magazine (April 2010): "As the Screw Turns" (fiction)

Alfred Hitchcock's Mystery Magazine (November 2011): "The Burning Grounds" (fiction)

Alfred Hitchcock's Mystery Magazine (November 2012): "Strangle Vine" (fiction)

Alfred Hitchcock's Mystery Magazine (June 2014): "The Specific Gravity of Blood in Sunlight" (fiction)

The Everything Guide to Edgar Allan Poe (Adams Media, 2007)

Crimewave (UK), Fall 2006: "Blue Morpho" (fiction)

The Georgia Review, Fall 2004: "From the Personal Record Collection of Beniamino Gigli" (fiction)

The World's Finest Mystery and Crime Stories, Ed Gorman, ed. (Forge, 2004): "Black Heart and Cabin Girl" (reprint)

Blood on Their Hands, Lawrence Block, ed. (Berkley, 2003): "Black Heart and Cabin Girl" (fiction)

Crimewave (UK), Spring 2002: "The Generator" (fiction)

The Georgia Review, Fall 2001: "Getting the Story" (fiction)

Crimewave (UK), Spring 2001: "Face Value" (fiction)

The Georgia Review, Winter 2000: "The Chief Creatures of God" (fiction)

Crimewave (UK), Fall 2000: "Double Fault" (fiction)

The North American Review, March 1987: "The Passion of Marisol" (fiction)

The North American Review, June 1980: "A Woman of Quality" (fiction)

Cleveland Magazine, December 1978: "The Great Wings Beating Still"

www.ingramcontent.com/pod-product-compliance
Lightning Source LLC
Chambersburg PA
CBHW032002130726
47903CB00012B/579